Anmol Arora was born in
journalism, climate change
He is a recipient of the British Council GREAT scholarship
and is currently pursuing an MSc degree in climate change and
international development at the University of East Anglia in
England. *The Last Dance* is his first novel.

The Last Dance

A Novel

ANMOL ARORA

SPEAKING
TIGER

SPEAKING TIGER PUBLISHING PVT. LTD
4381/4, Ansari Road, Daryaganj
New Delhi 110002

First published in paperback by Speaking Tiger 2019

Copyright © Anmol Arora 2019

ISBN: 978-93-89231-03-8
eISBN: 978-93-89231-02-1

10 9 8 7 6 5 4 3 2 1

To my mother

Kurds have no friends, but the mountains.

—Anonymous

CONTENTS

Prologue

'Let me go,' I screamed.

He punched me hard in the gut. Held me by my hair and dragged me away from the exit, back to the stage. I tried to grab hold of the chairs, the drapes, anything to resist him, but he was too strong, too evil.

'The session is not over, Ayla, where do you think you are going?' he asked.

'Don't do this,' I pleaded. 'You are my Guru.'

'Consider this a lesson in humility, your Gurudakshina.'

I cried from anger, from pain, and from helplessness. I was locked up with an animal.

He pinned me to the floor and tore off my blouse. He bit into my nipples like he would rip them off. The pain was unimaginable. I sank my nails into his face and scratched the skin beneath his left eye. That didn't stop him either. I tried to shout for help. His elbow pressed against my face to silence me. I had no strength to either retaliate or endure. Giddiness took over me.

I couldn't breathe. My body was smeared with his saliva—thick, sticky and disgusting. His tongue and teeth ran through every inch of my body, lustily. He had complete control over my body.

My repeated pleas of mercy had no effect on him. His hand slid inside my underwear. Found its way to my vagina and entered with full force. It was the first time I was penetrated. The pain was unbearable.

'It's hurting. Please don't do this.'

But he wouldn't listen. He took his pants off. I shouted my lungs out.

'I beg you. I won't be able to dance tomorrow.'

He didn't listen. Bit me on the navel and between my thighs. When his hunger was satisfied, he lay down next to me breathing heavily. He was not human; he was a monster.

'Don't mention this to anyone,' he commanded. 'Remember, you have a dance performance tomorrow. We don't want to ruin that, do we?'

When I didn't respond, he grabbed me by the neck with both hands and told me to repeat after him, 'This will be our little secret.'

'This will be our little secret,' I mumbled.

I was suffocating. My vision became hazy. I was going to die. He let go of my neck and gently stroked my hair. I coughed my guts out.

He threw my clothes back at me and left. I remained motionless. I lay there for a long time staring at the ceiling, not knowing what to do. The stage for my first performance had become the stage of my shame. It took all my strength to get up and step out of the auditorium. The road was deserted. It had begun to rain.

It was neither a downpour nor a drizzle. Tears trickled down my cheeks like raindrops falling from the sky. I was drenched in anger and shame.

My chappals got stuck in the mud. The straps came off. I couldn't pull them out. *To hell with it*, I thought and began walking barefoot. Sharp pebbles pierced my feet but I didn't feel any pain now; I was numb.

No autorickshaw or taxi stopped to give me a ride. I knew I would have to walk the twelve kilometres back home. My fate.

People looked at me with suspicion. They stared at my torn clothes, ruffled hair and bleeding feet. When their eyes met mine, they hastily looked away. They didn't want anything to do with me. The world can be a cruel, cruel place.

May Allah never make another woman suffer like me, but was He listening?

I

1

A Murder in Mardin

Ayla

I still remember sneaking behind *Bapîr,* my grandfather, and pulling his beard in the middle of his sermon at the Ulu Camii mosque in Mardin, Turkey. When he could no longer ignore my mischiefs, he would open his eyes and chase after me, threatening me with punishment. I would scream my lungs out and run for my life. When he finally caught me, he would throw me up in the air and both of us would burst into laughter. After the prayers, we would sit together and have *tirsik*, vegetables, and *mehîr*, a yogurt wheat drink, which *Dayê* had sent. My mother always made sure we didn't go hungry.

Bapîr was the mullah of the Kurdish community in Mardin province. People came to seek his counsel on religious and personal matters.

However, all that changed in the mid-1990s. My family was torn apart by a bloody political conflict between the Turkish government and the Kurdish community in Turkey. The Partiya Karkeren Kurdistane (PKK)—the Kurdistan Workers Party—refused to follow the decree of the Turkish state. They demanded a separate state of Kurdistan, in addition to greater political and economic rights for Kurds in Turkey.

Military leaders blatantly refused to comply. Instead, they took every oppressive measure to deny us our identity. They destroyed over 3,000 villages and razed down forests to drive away the rebels. Words like 'Kurds', 'Kurdish' and 'Kurdistan' were banned by the Turkish government in the garb of modernisation. Kurds were imprisoned for using their native language, dress, folklore, and even Kurdish names.

I was named Leyla, but the authorities refused to register me as a citizen. Instead, they imposed a Turkish name, Ayla. All these seemingly trivial impositions triggered mass protests across southeast Turkey.

Violence reached its peak in 1994; Mardin became the heart of conflicts. All suspected sympathisers of the 'Kurdish cause' were put in jail. Thousands were killed. The *gendarmerie,* the Turkish Army, declared martial law.

'Shoot at sight,' came the order from them.

There were high-ranking officials in the establishment who detested the goodwill and influence Bapîr enjoyed within the Kurdish community. They were apprehensive of the mullahs and *agha*s, influential landowners, and considered them a threat to the state.

The officials tried to coax and bribe him into joining their cause. Bapîr stood firm. He believed religion was a deeply personal conversation between Allah and his followers. Politics had no place in it. He shielded the mosque from turning into a political playground.

'Mullah Defies Allah's Will' read the headline in the

gendarmerie-funded local newspaper. It accused him of embezzling mosque funds. An absurd figure of 50,000 liras was linked to an offshore bank account in his name.

Bapîr was shocked. He quietly retired to his room and wrote his resignation letter to the agha. The agha dismissed the salacious allegations.

'You are our conscience-keeper. Gendarmerie cannot fool us,' he said and asked Bapîr to perform the evening prayer. There was respect and admiration in their warm embrace.

~

'Your *Bavo* has changed,' Dayê had once confessed to me about my father. 'I can see defeat and bitterness in his eyes.'

She revealed no more, but I remember that incident like it happened yesterday.

The silence of the night was broken by the blare of sirens and vehicles. There was an insistent knock at the front door. Dayê hurriedly took me to the bathroom, switched off the lights and latched the door from outside.

'Don't make any noise,' she had said and left me in the dark.

I peeped through the tiny hole in the door. There were fifteen uniformed men inside my house wielding guns. When Bapîr asked them for an identification, their leader hit him with the butt of his gun.

'This is my identification,' he said.

One of the soldiers moved towards Dayê but Bavo blocked his path. The soldier kicked him in one quick motion and elbowed him to the ground. They gathered around Bavo and began to kick him mercilessly.

Dayê screamed and rushed forward to protect Bavo. One soldier slapped her hard and she fell to the ground. Bavo managed to punch him in the face and he started to bleed from the lip.

'Is that the best you can do, you dirty terrorist?' the soldier roared and spat on the floor.

Four of them handcuffed Bavo and took him away. 'Leave no trace,' one soldier said, before leaving.

They set the house on fire before they left. Bapîr and Dayê tried to break open the door, but it was locked from outside. We were going to burn to death. It was only because of the agha's intervention that we escaped in the nick of time.

~

Bavo was taken to an undisclosed location by JİTEM, the Turkish intelligence agency. There was no official record of any such military agency, but everyone knew they existed and that their sole purpose was to kill and torture Kurds. They hung Bavo upside down and tortured him with hot iron rods till he passed out, and then they rubbed chilli on his wounds. His flesh felt as though it was on fire. One nasty blow dislocated his left shoulder. Even after all these years, he is unable to raise his hand above his shoulder.

The police wouldn't tell us where he had been incarcerated or what his condition was. In fact, they denied any knowledge of the arrest.

By next morning, the whole village community had gathered in front of the charred remains of our house.

'Blood for blood,' some young men shouted.

Words and assurances didn't comfort Dayê. She marched

all by herself to the military base, sat on the floor outside the entrance, and wept. She refused to move, eat or drink. Many women from our neighbourhood joined her in solidarity. They were in turn joined by friends, relatives and their social circle.

Soon, the number of protestors swelled to 2,000. It was a movement started and sustained by women. No one was able to enter or exit the base. The soldiers knew that if they touched these women, they would invite trouble for themselves. Kurdish men could bear many insults, but would not tolerate any form of assault on their women. In a week's time, there were 7,000 women protestors on the ground from nearby areas like Diyarbakır. The entire Kurdish tribe had united to support my family.

A few local journalists covered the protest on the local radio. It piqued the interest of the international community. Two reporters from the British Broadcasting Corporation came to shoot the protest. The gendarmerie turned them away. The subsequent morning, journalists from *Der Spiegel*, *The Guardian* and *The New York Times* arrived with their questions and there were broadcasting vans everywhere. Reports of human rights violation were beginning to be heard across Europe and America.

Those in the corridors of power had to field many uncomfortable questions. The situation turned delicate. If they tried to kill Bavo, the entire local community would be antagonised and if they released him, the establishment's lies would be revealed. The JİTEM approached Bapîr with an ultimatum. They would release Bavo only if Dayê returned home and withdrew the agitation. They gave us twenty-four hours to decide.

Next morning, Bavo was found bruised and beaten to a pulp outside the mosque. He was in deep shock and doctors weren't sure whether he would survive the assault. It took three weeks of intensive care before he regained consciousness.

~

The harassment didn't stop. They cut off the electricity and water supply to our house during peak winter. Despite his dislocated shoulder, Bavo would collect wood to keep the home fires burning, every day. When the wood ran out in the wee hours of the morning, the cold became unbearable.

The municipal authority refused to take any action. One of the officers informed that the orders to cut off the supplies came 'right from the top.'

A friend of Bapîr with connections in the home ministry warned us to leave Turkey immediately. 'They are soon going to slap charges of treason against your son. It is a non-bailable offence. He will be taken to an undisclosed military prison and you will never see him again. Get him out before it is too late.'

'But, where will he go?' Bapîr said.

'A cargo plane from Istanbul is leaving for India, tomorrow morning. I will arrange for your family's safe passage, but you have to reach Istanbul by 7 am tomorrow.'

'I owe you, my friend. He will be in Istanbul.'

Dayê packed a few clothes, some jewellery and the three of us left Mardin in the middle of the night. Bapîr wasn't ready to leave yet, but he promised to join us soon. The next morning, we were on that plane to India.

We spent a whole week inside the Delhi airport. The

authorities wouldn't let us step into the country until the Supreme Court granted us political asylum. Fortunately, the court ruled in our favour. So, we became refugees.

Bapîr raised his voice against the injustice and harassment of the Turkish State. On Friday evenings, the entire town would gather at the mosque to hear his sermon. The mosque became a place for Kurdish people to express their anger and frustration at the state that brutally suppressed every expression of our identity and forced us to wear clothes, use a language and follow traditions that were foreign to us. PKK sympathisers found their way into these meetings and started recruiting young members for the armed struggle, others offered sanctuary and information.

Two days after we fled Turkey, the army charged Bapîr with treason. They coerced the agha to testify against him. They even accused my family of planning a coup to overthrow the government.

Bapîr didn't waste time and appealed to the local authorities. He petitioned against the indictment in the Supreme Court. He accused JITEM of torture and subverting the law of the state. It pitted my family directly against the most powerful institution in the country, the gendarmerie.

On the morning of the final hearing, just as he was about to enter the court chambers, Bapîr was shot dead by two masked gunmen on a bike. The first bullet hit him square in the shoulder and knocked him over. One assailant got off the bike and riddled his body with bullets.

The scene of the crime was watered within a few minutes, wiping away any forensic evidence that could have led to the perpetrators. Bavo went to the Turkish embassy in Delhi and applied for permission to return home. He was the only son and needed to perform the last rites. The government was afraid of the pandemonium his return could cause. The foreign office rejected his application; his passport was declared null and void.

His heart turned bitter from the pain of losing the man he idolised. He became withdrawn and silent, gave into smoking. Dayê would urge him to stop, but all in vain.

We waited for a change of guard in the Turkish political regime. Many years passed, the conflict had its peaks and troughs, but the breakthrough that we were looking for, never came. Memories of the past became hazy as the door of our motherland was shut on us. India became our adopted nation.

2

Pride of Thanjavur

Guru Chandrashekhar

My father was the finest *nattuvanar* (guru) in India. Aspiring dancers left their home and came all the way to Thanjavur to seek his blessings. Two months of training with father was worth a year of practice with anyone else in India. He was revered among his trainees as well as peers.

He taught one hundred students daily. In fact, he trained more students in one day than any other guru could train in a week. Often, he would come home past midnight only to leave before sunrise the following day.

Some of the dancers who came to train with my father didn't even have enough money to pay the fees, but that never prevented father from mentoring them.

Mother would have to cook and clean for all of us, including the students. She would perform all the household chores and take care of six children. There was no rest or respite for her either.

The workload got the better of her, sometimes. She let her displeasure be known to father by observing a stoic silence at dinner.

Father would understand her silence and sympathise with her. He accepted her authority in the house as long as it didn't encroach on his dance principles.

When everyone retired to their rooms, he would calmly assuage her saying, 'They are part of our family. Please accept them as our children too.'

His message was polite but clear: no one was to ever be turned away from our house.

~

I had never shown any inclination towards dance during my childhood; I used to while away days playing cricket with neighbourhood friends. It was on 20 October 1979, that I decided to become a dance teacher—the commemoration day at the Brihadeshwara Temple in Thanjavur. The celebration left an indelible mark on me.

Father choreographed the biggest dance show of the century with the largest ensemble of dancers from all across India. It took almost three years to bring all the elements together. More than 200 dancers were handpicked by my father. For one month, prior to the performance, he didn't come home from the natyalaya. The tiffin box that mother sent with me in the morning came back unopened in the evening.

That evening, Thanjavur resembled a decked-up bride. Lights added a majestic glow to the streets and people danced with joy. Women and children wore their best attire and enjoyed the local fare.

At sunset, the massive granite structure of the temple was illuminated by hundreds of bulbs and a night sky of stars. Even the gods must have been envious looking at the spectacle.

The Brihadeshwara Temple is a symbol of everything Thanjavur takes pride in—be it culture, dance, music or the drive for perfection. The performance was Thanjavur's expression of gratitude to God Dakshinamurthy for the many gifts He had bestowed on us.

Inside the temple, there was chatter, discussions and last-minute preparations. The chief minister of Tamil Nadu, M.G. Ramachandran, and the who's who of the country graced the occasion.

Dancers entered in groups like ocean waves. Standing tall with their heads held high, they smiled a smile of confidence and reverence. As the first notes of music wafted through the air, there was hushed silence in the audience.

Two hundred dancers tapped the ground in unison. The reverberating sounds engulfed Thanjavur, touching countless hearts and minds. Father was at the forefront of it all, guiding his students with subtle hand gestures and expressions.

His calmness soothed nerves.

His choreography struck the right balance of music, rhythmic patterns and dance repertoire. It demanded flawless delivery and coordination from the performers. After an hour of feverish activity, the dancers were exhausted. He softened the tempo, seamlessly. And picked it up once again, just when the audience thought the best was behind them.

There was no hesitation in their motion. No one tried to follow or look at one another. They were one with the beat. And the beat was one with them. There was a mystical energy in the air.

I saw him up close. He had a look of intense focus and determination throughout the performance. He was one with the moment.

For those 150 magical minutes, the audience was transported to another time, another realm; far away from the grim realities of life. Everything was good and just in the world.

By the end of it all, when the dancers took a bow, the audience rose from their seats and applauded. It was an applause that seemed endless. Some, including the composed chief minister, were teary-eyed.

Mother looked up at the sky and thanked the gods. She understood why father treated the dancers with love and affection. When the moment of reckoning came, they responded to his call and gave their best on the dance stage.

That evening, everyone returned home a better human being. The spectacle had a profound impact on me. I had found my calling.

~

Next morning, I joined father for breakfast. As he sipped on his filter coffee, father's face looked serene. 'Appa, I want to become a dance teacher like you,' I said.

He was overcome with joy and hugged me. It was a priceless moment.

The next nine years of my life were devoted to learning the nuances of Bharatanatyam under his tutelage. Father was particularly tough on me. I had to dance better than everyone else, all the time. It was pressure—intense and relentless.

It drove me to work hard and at another level, it bogged me down too. I had to meet impossible standards. Rarely, when I did manage to do so, it wasn't a big deal. My father and his father before him had already done it. I fought a battle which I couldn't win.

Food, comforts and education were all forgotten at the pedestal of this sacred art. I didn't have a life outside the natyalaya and it wasn't long before I left formal education altogether. Father decided to hold my arangetram at Natyanjali Dance Festival in the town of Chidambram in Tamil Nadu on March 6, 1988. The arangetram is one of the most important moments in a dancer's life—the first solo public performance. Though dancers start performing in public within three or four years of training, they dance with seniors and teachers. It is only when a teacher trusts a student with literally every aspect of the dance—when the Guru is confident that his student can perform a complete margam—the traditional seven-part Bharatnatyam performance—that he or she is allowed to perform alone on stage. That is the arangetram. It was the moment I had dreamed about since I had begun practise nine years ago.

There were a hundred members in the audience, including my parents. I had been waiting for this moment, my first public performance, all my life.

When it arrived, the announcer introduced me as the son of the great Bharatanatyam exponent, Dharmesh. The audience gave a thunderous applause, but I was crestfallen.

From that moment on it didn't matter how I danced. I knew I would never be judged on my merit. It was harsh; it was unfair, but it was my reality.

My surname was a burden I couldn't wish away. They called me the scion of the Balasubramaniam family. I was lost in the admiration that inevitably followed. I wanted nothing to do with that tag attached to my surname. I felt uncomfortable with the notion of reflected glory.

I was aware the privileges offered to me were not of my own doing. What I didn't deserve I didn't want to claim. I wanted to practise my art and teach young dancers far away from the shadow of my family. Somewhere, I wanted to make a name for myself and for my dance institution.

~

As time passed, I became determined and turned desperate. Every male member in my family had been a dance guru. There was no big deal in my choice of profession and I wanted to be a big, *big* deal.

It took me a while to figure it out. I packed my bags and bought a train ticket to the capital. I had decided to go to Delhi and start my own dance school. Suddenly, for the first time in my life, my parents looked at me with a sense of surprise. This was indeed a big deal. At least, I had captured their attention for something that I, Chandrashekhar, had done.

Delhi, 2,600 kilometres away from home, was a good place to begin afresh. I would get a chance to build my reputation from scratch, without fear or favour. I wanted to identify young students and help them evolve into great dancers. That was my destiny.

The decision didn't go down well with father.

'What is wrong with Thanjavur?' he asked, 'The best dancers come here. Why do you want to move to Delhi of all places?'

'Because your shadow will not reach there,' I replied.

Father urged me to reconsider, 'They are loud, brutish, lack etiquette, and have no sense of culture. Go to Kolkata if you must. At least, they appreciate art and culture.'

'I have made up my mind,' I said.

'I will not help you in this foolish endeavour,' he replied and left the meal half-finished.

Late at night, mother came to my room. She handed me ten thousand rupees. 'I will send more money next month,' she said. 'I have one request.'

'Anything,' I said to her with gratitude.

'Don't ever besmirch the pride of our family.' I took her hands in mine and promised I wouldn't.

At that precise moment, I decided to name my dance school—Pratishtha.

3

An Evil Spirit

Ayla

Dayê deposited her gold chain and jewels as collateral to the bank, so Bavo could borrow money and rent a small shop in Connaught Place to start his business. My uncle, Mustafa Boran, had a thriving carpet export business in Istanbul and he gave Bavo an opportunity to sell merchandise in India.

Bavo thought that he could find potential buyers amongst the small but well-to-do Muslim families in Delhi. The primary motifs seen on these rugs were *harshang* (crab), *raqa* (pond turtle), *kisal* (land turtle) and *gul* (latch-hooked diamonds).Their composition, colour palette and fabric were unmistakably Kurdish. Handcrafted by Kurds in the mountains of Turkey, no two pieces were alike. The simplicity in the designs and richness in colours pleased buyers who had grown bored of machine-manufactured rugs.

Bavo, single-handedly, managed the business of rugs. Corruption and delays were endemic in this line of work. Indian custom officials were notorious for red tapism and Bavo loathed them. The officials would keep the goods in their custody until satiated by a fat bribe, they would make him wait for no reason.

Soon, we fit into the lifestyle of a quintessentially lower middle-class family in Delhi. Bavo rented a two-bedroom flat in Vasant Kunj. Our house was surrounded by thick foliage and the constant chirp of birds was music to our ears. It felt like we were living at the edge of a forest, but it was the only place we could afford.

During weekends, on my insistence, we would dine out at a restaurant. We would jump to the main course because appetisers and desserts left too big a hole in the pocket. Dayê almost always gave her share of the food to me and Bavo restricted himself to minimal helpings. Until I grew up, I didn't understand that the reason behind their loss of appetite when we went out to eat was financial constraints.

With great difficulty, Bavo enrolled me in one of South Delhi's private schools. He didn't trust the autorickshaw drivers or anyone else to take me to school, so he bought a Chetak scooter so he could drop me every morning.

Girls who arrived in their Ambassador cars had many friends. Even our teachers were partial towards them. They belonged to families of politicians and bureaucrats. Next in hierarchy were those students who came by Maruti, a car mostly used by the business class. Girls who came by a Luna or scooter were ridiculed.

Delhi was a city of the rich and the powerful. Survival depended on who you knew. Name-dropping was the favourite pastime the locals indulged in. It didn't matter how distant these connections were. Delhiites harboured mistrust as far as migrants were concerned and treated them with suspicion and hostility. However, if you met the same people after citing an important connection, they would not hesitate to welcome you to their homes and offer you their hospitality.

While our hopes of returning to Turkey faded into oblivion, we got immersed in our daily struggles. Bavo spent all his energy in building and consolidating his business of exporting Kurdish rugs. He worked fifteen hours a day so he could put some money aside for my education and marriage. I was his only priority.

~

I wasn't meant to live an ordinary life; I was destined for greatness—neither in a remote branch of science where I would be praised by a handful of bespectacled and unshaven men, nor in a small town with limited career opportunities. No. My talent would draw applause from all over the world. Young and old, rich and poor, men and women; they would all queue up just for a fleeting glance of me. I was certain.

You don't believe me, do you? You think that's a tall claim for anyone to make, let alone a young and naïve girl from Turkey. That's okay. I shall prove myself.

I, Ayla Erol, was ten years old when my Dayê took me grocery shopping to Vasant Vihar. The high and the mighty of Delhi lived in this part of the city. I remember seeing the most luxurious cars, with engines roaring like lions, lined up on the road. Those who stepped out of these cars made headlines and appeared on television as well. Spotting a celebrity was nothing out of the ordinary; only the super successful were crowd-pullers.

That Sunday afternoon, the marketplace was teeming with

people. College boys and girls queued outside the cinema halls and chatted excitedly. Grown-ups were on their weekly shopping tours and foreigners could be seen crowding the multi-storeyed grocery stores for imported spices and frozen food.

In a dark corner of the plaza, under the shade of an old peepal tree, sat a fortune-teller. He was an odd-looking man flaunting an unruly white beard that sprung from different parts on his face, like mushrooms sprouting in a forest. As if in deep contemplation, he kept straightening his stubborn beard. He was dressed in a bright orange robe with *Om* inscribed across the length of his attire, and a loose sacred thread hung around his neck.

He called out to my mother, 'Slow down, please. There is a murderer on the run. He will stab you with a screwdriver. The same tool he used to escape from the prison, and then he will run away with your purse. The vision makes me shudder; the pool of blood. Har har Mahadev.'

Dayê froze. 'What do we do?' she said, looking around in panic.

'If you pause for five minutes, your paths will never cross. Use this time, instead, to find what fate has in store for your daughter. Show me her hand and I will give you a peek into her future.'

The fortune-teller's left eye was shut and dangerously swollen. 'What happened to your eye?' I asked.

'Three-eyed Lord Shiva demanded this sacrifice of me. When I acceded, not only did he restore my vision, but also rewarded me with the gift to look into the future. Now I can see beyond this world, into the next realm, by simply looking at the lines on your palm.'

He held my hand, took a magnifying glass, and scrutinised the web of lines. He turned my hand over to the left and then to the right. Then he looked at my face with a strange expression. Tight lines formed on his forehead. 'Your daughter,' he said to Dayê, 'is meant for great things. The moon turned crimson at her birth to create a force so strong that it could unleash a tsunami. She is on a stage, one leg folded over the other. Her head is tilted at an angle of mockery and arrogance. She is above all mortals. A princess who needs no crown or tiara.'

Dayê held on to every word this fortune-teller uttered. In her mind, the more unconventional a cult, the more authentic its findings. She wanted to know more.

'You may ask me two questions for five hundred rupees. This token sum is a small tribute to Lord Shiva for warning you of the impending crisis,' the fortune-teller said.

Dayê thought for some time and then said, 'First, what profession will she choose and second, who will she marry?'

'I sense a dormant energy in your daughter, she derives her strength from the power of silence. She is like a volcano waiting to erupt. There is a possibility of fame and success, but her path will be paved with thorns,' the fortune-teller spoke.

Dayê was puzzled. What sort of a profession could that be? On the second question, he went silent. His hands trembled and his lips quivered. He couldn't understand the meaning of what he saw. After a long pause, he said, 'There is not one, but two men in her life.'

'What rubbish!' Dayê exclaimed, dismissing his prediction, 'That cannot be.'

'She will indeed look up to a man, but she won't marry

him. She will surrender her body to one and soul to another. The choice she makes will define her fate. This relationship can either be her death or her salvation.'

We were leaving when he added, 'An evil eye is staring down at your daughter with greed and thirst. It is salacious; a ball of fire threatens to consume her. Be warned, the devil will try to snatch her away. Keep her close and protect her. It is your responsibility.'

The last words scared the daylights out of my mother. She was a simple woman, a homemaker, who stitched her life around mundane routines. She kept reciting verses from the Quran on our way back home.

~

Dayê didn't know whether to be worried or happy about the prophecy. She went to Bavo to quell her restlessness.

'I want her to become a lawyer so she can fight for the political and civil rights of our people at the European Court of Human Rights,' he said. 'It is the only way Turkey can be brought to justice for what they have done to our family and community.'

'Haven't we seen and suffered enough? She should become an artist, travel the world and enjoy a life of freedom and safety,' Dayê countered.

There was a pause. Bavo switched on the television. Doordarshan was broadcasting a young girl's dance performance in Chennai. Dressed in a colourful outfit, she personified dignity and grace. Looking at her, something stirred in Dayê's soul.

'Dancer. Ayla could become a dancer,' Dayê blurted out.

Bavo was silent.

If there was one contribution Kurdish people could claim as their own, that would certainly be in the area of dance and music.

The performing arts were an inseparable part of our culture. They weren't merely a source of entertainment for us. These were powerful tools to challenge the dictates of an oppressive rule and assert our Kurdishness. Even our guerrilla fighters, *peshmergas*, danced in uniform at celebrations. Our dance was accompanied by the sounds of drums and *oboe* (surnâ/zurnâ). Musicians doubled up as singers. Men and women would hold hands and participate in group dances during social celebrations. Such customs were not prevalent in other more conservative Islamic sects. In Dayê's favourite dance forms, the dancing girl refused the love of the dancing man who offered her money, jewellery and a sword. But she would accept him when offered the stem of a flower. It was Dayê's sense of nostalgia that made her single out this profession for me.

Dayê insisted, 'She doesn't have any friends in school. Her class teacher told me she eats her lunch alone. Maybe, she will make friends at the dance centre. She doesn't have to pursue dance professionally. She can go out and meet a few people and get invited to birthday parties, if nothing else.'

Bavo still remained silent and switched off the television.

Dayê didn't openly protest against Bavo, but she didn't need to do so. She had subtle ways of letting her displeasure be known, and her silence would echo in the house.

Next morning, there was neither mutton nor a sweet dish in Bavo's lunchbox. She served him leafy vegetables and black lentils for two consecutive weeks. These were Bavo's least favourite dishes. He preferred to go hungry than to eat only vegetables and lentils.

He protested against this inhuman treatment, 'I am tired. You have packed black lentils for lunch, again,' Bavo said, exasperated.

'It is no mistake. The doctor has advised you to cut down on non-vegetarian food as well as sweets. Leafy vegetables are good for your heart. I am going to be very particular about that from now on,' she said with a wry smile.

'My heart is perfectly fine,' Bavo asserted, slowly understanding Dayê's ploy. 'You are doing this because I forbade Ayla to dance, aren't you?'

'They are two completely independent matters,' Dayê replied with all the sincerity she could muster. 'I am your wife and it is my duty to make sure you are healthy. By the way, I found a pack of cigarettes in your trouser pocket. I have flushed it down the pot.'

Bavo was aghast. One of his guilty pleasures was to step out of the house at night on the pretext of dumping the trash to enjoy a smoke.

She threw a glare at Bavo, who looked like a convict. Bavo had to accept defeat. 'Fine, take Ayla for dance classes.'

'Thank you. I am lucky to have a *shohar* like you,' she said and winked at me.

The decision was made. People choose their profession on the basis of passion, curiosity and future prospects. Not me. My fate was sealed with the words of a supposed oracle and a quasi-compromise reached between a non-believer husband and his superstitious wife.

~

Dayê waved at an autorickshaw and asked the driver, 'How much for Gautam Nagar?'

'One hundred rupees,' the driver replied, adjusting his hair.

'Do you think it's my first day in Delhi? Go away. We will take another auto,' Dayê retorted.

Chastened by her prompt dismissal, the driver moved the auto ahead to keep pace with us and asked, 'How much will you give?' This time, with more respect.

'Not a penny more than forty rupees,' she said.

'That is too little. I will take eighty.'

'Not a penny more than forty.'

As the negotiations continued, an empty autorickshaw slowed down and veered towards us. The first auto driver knew his time was up, so he made his final pitch.

'Madam, it is far off,' he said, making a dramatic gesture with his hand. 'Besides, there is a traffic jam at Ber Sarai.'

'You know it doesn't cost more than forty rupees. The most I can give you is fifty.'

'Okay, okay. I will take you for sixty.'

Dayê asked me to sit in the autorickshaw. She had sealed the deal.

Indians weren't very different from the Kurds in that regard, especially at the bazaars. The local vendors quoted twice, sometimes, three times the actual market price of the product. A seasoned negotiator like Dayê would completely disregard or even mock the quoted price. She would then quote an equally outrageous number on the lower side. Both sides would then respect each other and settle on an acceptable sum of money, somewhere close to the median.

This negotiation was not a hassle but considered an art. Dayê enjoyed it. Not so much for the savings, but because it gave her a semblance of home.

We were on our way to Pratishtha Natyalaya where a new batch of Bharatanatyam dancers was set to begin training.

~

The bustle of Gautam Nagar market, the constant blare of horns gave way to the thumping of feet and the sound of ankle bells. We crossed a small waiting area that led to Pratishtha's dance floor.

The room was small and strangely warm. It was full of saree-clad young girls. Their movements were uninhibited and in perfect sync. Their costumes were not as colourful or elaborate as Kurdish dancers, but the similarity was unmistakable. Dayê and I looked at each other in recognition of something that seemed familiar to home. The wooden floor creaked each time I took a step. The front wall was covered with an eight-foot-long mirror. The back wall had mirrors and so did the side walls. It was a room of mirrors.

Every movement, turn and expression, was reflected in these mirrors. They exposed the flaws and strengths, smiles and tears. Nothing could be hidden here.

In the extreme left corner of the floor stood Nataraja—a black sculpture of Lord Shiva—Lord of Dance.

There were ten or twelve young girls inside, but only one person spoke. It was easy to spot the teacher, Guru Chandrashekhar. He stood right in front of the dancers, mouthing instructions and pointing out errors.

His frantic hand gestures made me feel as if he would hit

one of them any moment. The dancers had their hands behind their backs and they nodded vigorously in acquiescence to whatever he said.

He would be livid one moment, curse a dancer for getting the steps wrong and the next instance, he would smile at another in approval. The rest of the world was dead to him. He barely noticed me. He didn't care or worry about another soul, but the ones that danced in front of him.

He sat down once the dance sequence concluded. To his left was the shruti, an accordion-like musical instrument box, the tattukazhi, a musical instrument, was in the front and to his right was a pile of books about dance. These formed an impregnable fortress around him. He opened the briefcase-shaped wooden instrument with his left hand. It revealed a beautiful harmonium.

He played it with his left hand, used the right hand to signal instructions to his trainees, and began to sing—all at once. With every movement, his chest swelled with pride. The tempo of the dance changed with his cues. He was in complete control. It was no less than a miraculous spectacle.

Chandrashekhar was dressed in a red kurta and white pyjamas. A small streak of ash was drawn in a straight line on his forehead. It was warm inside, but he wore a brown shawl over the kurta.

Guruji, as everyone called him, looked tall from afar. He had salt-and-pepper hair which gave him an aura of wisdom and sophistication. If it wasn't for his frantic movements, one could easily mistake him for a grumpy university professor. This was *his* territory. He oozed the confidence reserved only for the masters of their domain.

The dancers seemed to understand each other's intentions. They were here for the same cause and that united them in an invisible bond. The room had a positive energy about it.

The musician and the guru communicated without saying a word. The music began to play and the dancers took their positions, instantly. They moved together, each and every step was immaculately timed.

He watched the dancers like a hawk. His eyes shifted from one dancer to another. He didn't utter a word but corrected the erring dancers using hand gestures. The dancers too, quickly rectified their mistakes. He nodded his head either in approval or shook it in anger. He would correct the hand gestures of one dancer and point out an incorrect leg movement to another. None of the dancers escaped his attention. Allah was looking at the performance through his eyes.

Sudha Shukla, the mridangam player, was the first to notice us. She greeted Dayê with folded hands and said, 'Namaste.'

'Namaste,' Dayê replied. 'I am here to enrol my daughter.'

'What's your name?' Sudha bent down and asked me with a smile.

'Ayla.'

'What does it mean?'

'It is the halo around the moon.'

'That's wonderful! She can start training from tomorrow. Remember to wear a saree.'

'May we stay back and watch the rest of the dance session?' Dayê asked.

'I am sorry but that wouldn't be possible,' Sudha said.

The smile was almost fixed on her face and no matter what she said, she did it with kindness. That softened the blow of rejection.

'Guru Chandrashekhar doesn't allow any outsider to watch the dance session or even enter the dance floor.'

From anyone else, this sort of stricture could have come across as rude, however, Sudha was cut from a different cloth. She wore aromatic jasmine flowers in her hair. Her persona was gentle and pleasant.

Before exiting the centre, I took one last look at the dancers. When they formed particular postures like aramandi (half-squat) or muzhu mandi (full-squat), the pleats of their sarees unfurled beautifully below the waist. It fascinated me. There was magic in this dance form and I knew I wanted to master it.

4

Delusional in Delhi

Guru Chandrashekhar

The scorching sun was merciless on that noisy May afternooon of 1988. At the crowded New Delhi railway station, the coolie mumbled something in Hindi and plonked my luggage on his head without my consent. Before I realised what was happening, he was rushing towards the exit. I pushed and elbowed people to not lose sight of him. Within five minutes of my arrival, I had become as uncouth and abrasive as any northerner. God save me.

I headed straight to my school friend, Arun's house. He had married into a wealthy family and settled down in a luxurious house in Central Delhi. He was kind enough to host me and I was happy to save every penny I possibly could. He held a small get-together at his house that evening and invited some high-flying Delhiites.

It was one of those high-society events where name-dropping, showing off, and crass music were common. I was beginning to think of an appropriate excuse to go to bed when I saw her—Sudha. She looked different. There was a certain grace in her demeanour that was alien to this gathering. She wore a beautiful green saree and the smile on her face felt authentic. She actually took time to listen to the guests and not waltz her way from one group to another.

'Who is she?' I asked Arun.

'She is a classical singer and she is way out of your league,' he said.

'What's a classical singer doing at your party?' I said.

He didn't take the bait. 'Recently, she turned down an IAS officer. His disinterest in music and culture irked her. She is too headstrong.'

'Let me be the judge of that. You said, she is a classical singer, right?

'Yes.'

'Can we get her to sing?'

'We can try.'

Arun asked his wife to request Sudha. She hesitantly agreed.

I recognised the raagam the moment she parted her lips. She sang one of my favourite Carnatic renditions of 'Nagumomu Ganaleni'. Her voice rose from a whisper to a high pitch without any jerks. I moved closer to her. She paused for a second, but a few people encouraged her to continue. She had tremendous voice modulation. She could be such an asset at Pratishtha. I could see her teaching alongside me. Our eyes met and I acknowledged her beautiful voice with a smile.

Later that evening, I introduced myself to Sudha and told her all about my dream to start Pratishtha. She was encouraging and gave many useful suggestions to improve the quality of the dance school. I didn't have to mention my surname for her to take me seriously. She seemed better than these petty, worldly things. That was comforting. Over the next few weeks, we spoke often. My passion seemed to have made a few cracks on the wall of her scepticism. It still took three months to persuade her to join my natyalaya.

~

Renting a place to stay in Delhi was difficult. Soon, I had my first dealing with the tribe of brokers and landlords. All I wanted was a simple one-bedroom accommodation. Alas, nothing was simple in Delhi.

'Are you in love with a *flexible* dancer?' asked a middle-aged Punjabi landlady with a booming laugh when I told her I was a dance teacher. 'What are your plans for marriage?' I didn't miss her emphasis on the word *flexible* or marriage. Her house in Punjabi Bagh was clean and ideal, but her propensity to gossip wasn't.

'I am not interested in starting a family. I want to focus on building my dance school first.'

'Nonsense! Are you a homo?' she said with another explosive bout of laughter. I didn't know whether she was serious or joking. 'There are many fair and cultured girls in Delhi. I can introduce you to them, but you really should put haldi on your face. It is good for the complexion.'

North Indians had an inexplicable obsession with white skin. The newspapers were replete with matrimonial advertisements—grooms in search of fair-skinned brides. It was a curse to be dark-skinned. They treated my lot as inferior.

'There is no need to get angry,' she said, reading my

expression. 'We are an educated and well-travelled lot. I just want to make sure that no woman of dubious character enters my house,' she explained, offering me samosas dripping with oil. Neither her mind nor her food was healthy.

I thanked her for the hospitality and walked out as soon as possible. She wasn't an exception. Another wealthy lady, whose husband had been a senior government official, offered to lend her attic in Panchsheel Vihar as long as three of her servants shared the same space. It almost seemed like I was the fourth in the distinguished list.

When I finally found a decent enough place with an affordable rent, I was turned away because I was a bachelor. Single men like me were considered miscreants and notorious. We were treated with more suspicion and hostility than, perhaps, terrorists.

Interestingly, the same lot, in the company of women, were welcomed graciously. Marriage seemed to credit men with respectability and acceptance in society. Did women turn wild carnivorous men into herbivorous pets?

After a two-month hunt, I found a place in Nizamuddin. It was a small room with bare necessities. It wasn't much to boast of, but with some effort, it could pass off as a comfortable space.

I had to admit, although grudgingly, that my father was right about Delhi. Delhiites did reek of arrogance. People had little to show by way of achievements, and this they compensated for by dropping names of VIPs and other influential beings at the slightest convenience or pretext. Cultural nuances were barely understood, but tickets to the latest art show caused pandemonium.

Delhi dealt in extremes—the weather was either too hot or too cold. People were either too forthcoming or blatantly racist. The less said about their way of treating women, the better. The city truly belonged to only those who had power and position. And those who let this power slip away, met tragic ends.

~

The plan was to start a natyalaya immediately but the plan couldn't be materialised. Before dance came into the picture, there was this small matter of permissions, paperwork and procedures. I couldn't start something as simple as a dance school without taking multiple rounds of the court, seeking permission from lawyers and government officials for a lease agreement, and so on.

The government officials in Thanjavur rose up to greet me and uttered my name with respect. But here, even a clerk spoke indifferently, with gutka in his mouth.

One babu from the Ministry of Culture even asked why anyone would keep such a surname as mine. Much as I was riled, I sat in front of him with my hands folded. And then I had to bribe him too. I had always been critical of the special treatment I received in Thanjavur, but I wasn't enjoying this apathy, either.

After three months of running from pillar to post, I was able to secure all the permissions and rent a space. Carpenters, electricians and technicians made modifications, and a whole lot of noise. A big mirror was placed on the front wall for dancers to study their movements, a ceiling fan was installed and pink drapes were used to cover the windows and lend some colour to the otherwise Spartan space.

After inordinate delays, Pratishtha was ready to welcome dancers. It was my refuge from the chaos of the city. Delhi's rules didn't apply to my school of dance.

II

5

A Pariah

Ayla

On the first day of my dance training, I learned the difference between prophecy and practice. Pratishtha offered no flattery. Only the thundering voice of our Guruji echoed and the dancers' meek obedience mattered.

I entered Pratishtha and saw all the dancers touching Guruji's feet. Going by the norm, I too approached him and touched his feet. He wasn't even looking in my direction. With an angry glare, he suddenly said, 'What is your name?'

'Ayla Erol,' I replied, wondering what I could have possibly done wrong; I had barely taken two steps in the natyalaya.

'Is this your aharya—your costume and make-up? Why are you dressed in jeans and shirt?' he asked. His forehead had worry lines all over; I came to learn that was the sign of impending danger. That day on, it never ceased to instil fear in my bones.

'If you can't get this right, you are useless. Wear a saree at all times at Pratishtha.'

'Dayê was busy all of yesterday. She will buy me a saree tomorrow. It's no big deal.'

Silence descended. There was shock and disapproval on the face of many dancers, all of whom were dressed in sarees. Everyone was startled by my response; some looked at me with the same pity with which goats are looked upon before Bakra Eid.

He didn't cancel my admission perhaps because I was new or because Sudha had just entered the natyalaya. Her presence infused some moderation in his behaviour.

'I must have forgotten to mention the rule about wearing a saree,' Sudha said. She hadn't. She was lying for my sake. I knew that she was a well-wisher and I could always count on her.

'I cannot allow you to dance in this attire. You can sit on the floor and watch the session. Pay careful attention to what I say and observe how different mudras are performed.'

There was nothing to be gained from arguing further. Thus, my first dance session ended even before it had begun. Sir, I mean, Guruji was a teacher, tormentor and sergeant major all rolled into one.

~

Finding a saree was not the end of my problems; it was only the beginning. Wearing it was tougher than acquiring a PhD in astrophysics. The dancers wrapped the saree around their waists with the fall draped over their shoulders.

Believe me, it is trickier than it sounds in theory. Most of the girls sought help from their mothers and grandmothers, but Dayê had no experience in wearing one. The next morning, I rolled myself round the cloth several times over that I almost fell from giddiness. Allah only knew how I would survive the dance session.

'Gulum, what is taking you so long?' Dayê enquired, knocking on the bathroom door twice, 'You will get late for your class and that teacher will find another reason to stop you from dancing.'

'I will be out in a minute.'

There was no time to get everything in order. I wrapped the saree the best I could and rushed for my class, fingers crossed.

'You look like a princess,' Dayê said and kissed me on the forehead. I had goosebumps entering Pratishtha. What if he scolded me in front of everyone else again? I waited in a corner till he finished his conversation with one of the students. Then I hurried towards him to touch his feet, hoping I would go unnoticed.

'New saree?' Guruji asked, looking impressed. Not much escaped his attention.

'Where did you buy it from?'

'Nalli in Connaught Place,' I replied, relieved to see a faint smile appear on his face.

'Join the girls for namaskaram.'

I breathed a sigh of relief.

Forgive me; I need to tell you about the significance of namaskaram first. It's performed at the beginning and at the end of every dance session. The dancer prays to Mother Earth, the supporter of life.

Through this movement, the dancer attempts to sanitise the surroundings. She submits herself to nature and brings positive energy to the space.

I joined the dancers for namaskaram. Soon, I felt everyone's gaze on me. Was I doing something wrong, I wondered? I followed the steps exactly as the girl next to me.

'Ayla.'

'Yes, Guruji,' I replied, dreading a reprimand.

He burst out laughing. It was the first time I had seen him laugh; I too gave an awkward smile in return. Everybody joined him after a few seconds. They were stifling their giggles and as soon as Guruji laughed, there was permission for the outburst. Two girls pointed at me and exchanged high-fives.

I examined myself. My saree had come off. It must have happened when I bent. I was left standing in my petticoat and blouse. I was shaking from embarrassment and I froze.

'Go, fix your saree,' Guruji commanded.

I hurriedly disappeared. The saree left a trail and one of the students, Sara, stomped her feet on the loose end of the cloth. The sudden halt made me lose balance. I went crashing to the ground, just when I thought things couldn't get worse.

The room echoed with resounding laughter. I swear, Sara did it on purpose; I could make out the smirk on her face when she apologised. Not one student came forward to help me. They hated me. All of them. Even at school, they made fun of my skin colour and my accent. Humiliated and embarrassed, I shut myself in the changing room and started crying. They would continue to laugh at me for the rest of my life. I would never be accepted at Pratishtha. I just wanted to go back home.

Suddenly, I heard footsteps outside the changing room.

'Can you help me tie the saree, please?' I said from behind the door, hoping it was Sudha.

'Yes. Open the door.'

The voice on the other side was shrill. It wasn't Sudha, but I didn't care. I just wanted someone to help me out. I opened the door and found Kartik looking at me. He was the only boy in Guruji's class. I was embarrassed that he saw me in such a state and angry that he didn't reveal his identity before. Otherwise, I would never have opened the door.

Surely, he had come here to mock me. He was going to go back and tell others about me sobbing inside the changing room.

What would he know about tying a saree? He was a boy; he had never worn one. For a moment, I thought of shouting at him and then I thought of asking him to leave, but I couldn't do either. He was the only help available.

I continued to cry. He looked at me awkwardly and mumbled something. He put his hand on my shoulder, and I shrugged it off.

'How will you tie a saree if you keep crying,' he said. It was a valid a point. 'But I don't...don't know how to tie a saree.'

'Stop crying,' he sounded more embarrassed than me.

'I will help you. Take one end of the saree and tuck it inside, now wrap the cloth around. Take the other end and drape it over your shoulder. It is done, as simple as that,' he demonstrated.

He nudged me to follow his instructions, step by step. By the time he finished, I had managed to drape the saree well, and for the first time I felt comfortable wearing it.

'How do you know all this?'

'My father owns a saree store in Connaught Place. I actually know how to tie a saree in fifteen different styles. It is the first thing he taught me. The cotton saree you are wearing is from my shop.'

I suddenly felt awkward in his presence and proximity.

I hurried back to the class to more guffaws over my technique, but at least my saree didn't come off.

~

My dance training didn't begin with dance. According to the tradition, I performed namaskaram on the dance floor and stepped aside. Guruji ordered me to observe the senior dancers and study the Tamil poet Kambar's book, *Kamba Ramayanam*, every day.

For three insufferable months, I came to the natyalaya, sat on the floor and simply watched the other dancers. The girls who had joined with me were making inroads, while I merely sat and observed.

'Why don't you allow me to dance like the other girls? I can dance better than them,' I said.

'If you were from India and trained in Sanskrit or Hindi, I wouldn't ask you to do this homework. Now, are you from India and trained in our languages and music?'

'No, I am not.'

'Exactly. So, do as I say and don't question my judgement and authority.'

I knew the real reason behind his coldness. I wasn't one of them. I was less capable. I was an outsider and I didn't belong.

I was sick of reading scriptures and books on dance. I had never bothered reading the Quran despite repeated attempts by Dayê, why should I have cared about the Hindu texts such as the *Ramayana* or the *Bhagavad Gita*?

To hell with Bharatanatyam, I thought to myself on many occasions and decided to skip the next class altogether. I even came up with many excuses I would tell Dayê for my inability to attend. However, when the time came for the next session, I would attend it without protest. *Why did I persist?* I asked myself the question repeatedly. No one enjoyed Guruji's scoldings. I know I didn't.

I knew the answer each time I saw Guruji's students performing Bharatanatyam. I knew it was my true calling. It became an addiction of sorts—vivid expressions, soulful rhythm, sharpness of hand movements, refined footwork, colourful clothes and make-up. It had all the elements of a spectacle and the dancer occupied centre-stage. Everything else faded in comparison.

~

'Ayla.'

'Yes, Guruji.'

'Is this a modelling centre? Tie your hair in a braid. How will you see your own abhinaya, your expressions, in the mirror when your hair is falling all over your eyes and face? It's distracting.'

'Sorry, Guruji,' I said and promptly tied my hair with a rubber band.

I hated this rule above all others. I loved the feeling when my hair bounced on my face while I danced. It made me feel free and in control as if I had all the power in the world. But Guruji, the stickler that he was, would have none of it. Anything that made me happy made him miserable.

The first dance move he taught me was the tap of the feet on the ground. It was as personal and distinct as a fingerprint. There was no right or wrong sound. I had to work hard to discover and understand the sound which felt right to me and didn't damage my feet. Not even Guruji could teach me that. It depended on one's own instinct.

'It's with the triangle-like portion under the toe from where the proper sound is generated,' Guruji explained. 'The foot is folded behind, with the ankle touching the hip, before it rests on the ground with full velocity. This continuous and rhythmic movement of the feet is the base of many Bharatanatyam acts. Every dancer's tap is unique.'

After an hour of dance, I felt the first sign of exhaustion. A tiny drop of sweat trickled from my forehead into my right eye. It burned. I desperately waited for a signal from Guruji that it was time for a pause, water break, anything at all to catch my breath, but it never came. He kept egging us on, pushing us further. Believe it or not, even my jaw began to hurt.

The air was thick from the sweat and toil of ten dancers in the room. I looked at the wall clock. There was one more hour to survive.

After my first dance class, I couldn't even climb the stairs to reach my home on the second floor. I sat on the stairs for a few minutes and I realised that the only way to get to my bed was to crawl. I used my hands and climbed the stairs like a dog. Once inside, I immediately went to sleep and I was dead to the world for the next twelve hours.

Dayê allowed me to skip school that morning and sleep till afternoon. It didn't count for much though. My hips and thighs felt like they were made of stone. I had to drag myself from one corner of the house to another. Every time I bent down, my lower back cursed me. The recovery would easily take a week, if not more.

There was no question of taking the day off. Apparently, exhaustion and stiffness were part of the training. If anyone so much as much as made a face, Guruji made them do extra practice as punishment. If you missed more than three dance sessions in a month, you were asked to leave Pratishtha and your money was returned. Those were the rules. Sometimes, it felt more like an army school than a dance centre.

~

It took me an entire year, may be two, to find my feet at Pratishtha. There came a point when I got past my insecurities and even learnt how to tie a saree properly. I began to enjoy dancing. It was demanding and fulfilling at the same time. Everything that was uncomfortable and impossible earlier now became routine. There was freedom in dance that I had never experienced before.

Dayê and Bavo made all my decisions for me: how I could dress, what I could eat, where I would study and how much time I would spend in front of the television. Everything was decided by them except what I did on the dance floor. At Pratishtha, I disconnected from the rest of the world. There was no homework, household chores or family duties to take care of. I did only what Guruji asked of me. There were certain days, some moments, when my body moved just as I wanted it to, in perfect harmony. These moments were fleeting, but they left me craving for more.

While dancing, I could feel something come over me, a greater power of some sort. The common term for such moments is 'being in the zone,' but there is only one word that can describe what I felt in those moments: divinity.

I felt like I belonged. Like I was part of something incredible.

For the first time in my life, I was doing something that mattered. It felt right.

With the passage of time, Guruji became more patient with me. Sometimes, he praised my energy in front of the entire class. Even the girls at the natyalaya accepted me albeit grudgingly. Most importantly, Kartik and I became good friends. He was always silly and I laughed at all his terrible jokes. Pratishtha became my second home.

My dance became a source of pride in the family. Bavo, who had initially been reluctant about sending me to dance classes, now spoke like it was his idea in the first place.

He invited clients to our house on Newroz every year. It didn't matter what time they came and for how long they stayed. The kitchen was open, promising a gastronomical fare of biryani, korma and kheer.

These were important occasions both on personal as well as business levels. In India, professional relationships often spilled into personal lives. Religious festivals, be it Diwali, Holi or Newroz, served a more indirect purpose. They were opportunities to build trust among people. Eid was typically the day Bavo received most guests.

Dayê's kebabs and koftas, served with black tea, went a long way in making sure that clients continued to do business with Bavo instead of his competitors. Dayê was an excellent cook and every client of Bavo swore by the taste of the delicacies. They fished for dinner invitations to our house.

On one such occasion, Bavo asked me to show his guests what I had learned at my dance school. I performed a short dance piece. Everyone cheered me on.

They complimented Bavo and Dayê for my talent. Bavo's face gleamed with pride.

~

Evenings were reserved for the five best dancers at Pratishtha. They were a special lot and Guruji took singular interest in their training.

The chosen few made dance look so graceful and easy. They were anything but ordinary. These girls spoke and walked with an air of confidence; I was in awe of them. Even Sudha spoke to them as an equal. I watched their routine every day.

The energy and intensity with which they performed was something else. Guruji had a different, much tougher warm-up routine for them. He made them do exercises that we wouldn't dare to attempt. They danced at a high tempo without so much as a pause. Guruji had to only name the sequence and they would perform to near perfection. He only made subtle modifications to their dance routines.

They were all young, between the ages of eighteen and twenty-two. I wondered if I would ever be able to dance as well as them. Not only were they famous in the natyalaya but outside as well. They performed at different dance festivals. Connoisseurs came to watch them. What a charmed life they lived!

Guruji treated them like family. They joked around with him. Sometimes audacious enough to make fun of him. We couldn't even imagine talking to Guruji in that casual tone. Oh! How I would do anything to be part of the group.

With time, I realised there was a hierarchy even within that closed group of top five dancers. The best dancer always took the lead spot. She was always at the forefront. The second and third best dancers secured the place to her left and right. The rest formed the invisible group behind them.

All dancers coveted the lead spot, nursed ambitions to replace those who stood in their way. It didn't matter whether they were at the beginner, intermediate or the advance stages of learning. Everyone wanted to hog the spotlight. All of us felt it was our destiny. If that meant someone had to be uprooted, then so be it. Secretly, we all saw ourselves as the lead dancer. It was a struggle invisible to an outsider, hidden behind a generous smile and a friendly hug.

No one remembered the girl who occupied the right-hand corner or stood second from left. The praise and recognition were earned by the lead dancer. She was the queen bee.

At the end of each session, Guruji asked his favourite student, Ratna, to wash his teacup and keep the musical instruments inside the locker. She also cleaned the floor before and after the session. It was the simplest way to determine who was Guruji's favourite shishya, and the best dancer at Pratishtha.

To an outsider, mopping the floor and washing utensils could have been perceived as a sign of shame or even punishment. At Pratishtha, it was considered the highest honour. I, too, desired Guruji's respect, singular attention and the keys to the natyalaya.

6

Baptism by Fire

Guru Chandrashekhar

The first year of building Pratishtha felt like pushing a rock up a mountain. It was financially and emotionally draining. I couldn't count on anyone for support. The money that mother had given me was exhausted. I had sleepless nights wondering where the rent for the next month was going to come from. I thought twice about every rupee I spent. It was painful.

There were days when I survived on just water and slept without eating a morsel. It made me furious at my father. The one time I needed his support and guidance, he had washed his hands off me. I was plagued by self-doubts. Somehow, I willed myself to go on.

The first batch had only three girls, all of whom came because of Sudha's goodwill and connections. Two of those girls left the next month and joined another better-known natyalaya.

Delhi was no place for the underdogs. People had enough money to splurge, but little patience for an upstart.

The fourth girl to join the natyalaya, Madhavi, was the

daughter of an influential politician. One of his staff members
came to enquire about the classes and then enrolled her. I
later found out that the politician was Tamil Nadu's revenue
minister. That was just the break we needed. I hoped that
more and more ambitious dancers would follow her.

Madhavi was a sweet girl with varied interests. She was
only in the sixth standard but her calendar was more packed
than her father's. She took piano lessons, badminton classes
and math tuitions daily. Dance was squeezed into the one
free hour that she had in the evenings.

She often came late. I didn't say anything during the first
week, but then it became a recurring feature. She would show
up 10-15 minutes late every day. I pointed my watch towards
the politician's minion who accompanied her to each class,
but he didn't show any sign of remorse.

I gave her a stern warning and she was apologetic. The
indiscipline continued for three more days.

'Return the fees. Ask her to find another dance centre,'
I told Sudha.

'But we need the money. How are we going to pay the
studio rent?'

'The rent won't come at the cost of our principles. I don't
want to see her at the dance school from tomorrow.'

Madhavi was shocked. She cried and pleaded with me to
take her back, but my decision was final. I could not tolerate
such blatant indiscipline.

The subsequent afternoon, the minion came to the
natyalaya. He carried a personal message from the revenue
minister.

'Bitiya is minister sahib's only child. He was very upset

to see her cry yesterday. Anyway, these things happen in the heat of the moment. He is willing to forgive you. We will pay twice the fees so that her punctuality issues do not create a problem.'

I listened to him intently and with every word that he spoke, my resolve became stronger. It reaffirmed the kind of dance centre I wanted to run. Indiscipline and favouritism had no place in it. I would have taken her back had Madhavi apologised earnestly and promised to be punctual. The offer of money only made me more determined not to allow her back.

'Tell minister sahib I gave her three chances. She faltered thrice. No one gets a fourth chance at Pratishtha,' I said.

'Sahib wasn't requesting. He was ordering,' the man said in a menacing voice. 'If bitiya doesn't dance in the natyalaya then no one else will.'

'She will never dance at Pratishtha. Close the door behind you. My students are waiting.'

He left without another word.

~

If you want to experience how drunk Delhi really is on power and privilege, then you should puncture a politician's ego. The next morning, six officials from the Ministry of Urban Development stormed inside the natyalaya. They demanded to see the permission for playing background music and holding dance sessions. Their questions weren't followed by a pause delegated for response. It was an unequivocal indictment by judge, jury and executioner. They didn't even make eye contact with me while we spoke. It was beneath their dignity. It seemed as though they had a score to settle.

I showed them all the relevant documents. They invented additional permissions that were missing, scrutinised every scrap and picked faults. I refused to vacate the premises without an official order.

Five policemen arrived at the scene within minutes. They brandished batons at me and asked us to vacate Pratishtha immediately. When I resisted, one of them pushed me out and locked the gate. All of this happened in front of Sudha and my students. I was furious at the policemen and the man on whose behest they were doing this.

I went to the nearest police station to file a complaint against the minister, but they refused to lodge an FIR.

For the next six weeks, the natyalaya remained shut. The students were gone. Sudha and I went from pillar to post filling up forms and talking to lawyers.

'There comes a time in every man's life when he has to bow down to circumstances,' Sudha said. 'If you don't allow Madhavi back, there will be no natyalaya.'

I was reminded of the promise I had made to my mother.

'I won't compromise on my principles, not even for myself.'

News spread fast in Delhi, gossip faster. Pratishtha's closure became common knowledge in dance circles. My father in Thanjavur got a whiff of it. He hadn't spoken to me since I left Thanjavur, but he called me one evening. 'I heard you are facing trouble. Do you want to come back?'

'It's nothing serious. I can take care of it. I don't intend to return anytime soon.'

There was a dramatic pause. 'For how long has the natyalaya been shut?'

'Six weeks.'

'Six weeks. You are so stubborn.'

'Thanks!' I said, sardonically.

'Let me see what I can do,' he said and left it at that.

The next morning, I got a call confirming that all the resubmitted forms and documents had been checked and verified. The locks were removed, and I could resume my coaching. Behind the scenes, Father had spoken to the chief minister of Tamil Nadu. He was the chief guest at the celebration held in Brihadeshwara Temple, and had immense respect for my father. The CM had called up the revenue minister and asked him to put an end to the harassment. My father would train the minister's daughter in my stead.

This ugly spat turned out to be a blessing in disguise. Pratishtha's esteem grew amongst the dance community. They recognised it as the natyalaya that refused the daughter of a powerful minister. People began to take us seriously. Many dancers, tired of commercial studios that were more talk than action, gravitated towards us.

~

The first six months of training was akin to punishment. The programme was physically daunting and mentally taxing. We practised adavus (basic dance steps) that would make the trainees hold aramandi (the half-sitting position) and natyarambham (wide-shoulder position) for long durations and put intense stress on their shoulders and quad muscles. I wanted to test their will and readiness to suffer. Skills could be taught later.

Two dancers, Mukti and Shefali, complained about the lack of air conditioning at Pratishtha.

'The humidity is unbearable, Guruji. We get a migraine after the dance class. Can you please get an air conditioner installed?'

'Then leave and don't bother to come back,' I said, calmly. 'Those who baulk at sweat or heat have no place in my school.'

It was only after repeated pleas for forgiveness and Sudha's intervention that the pair was allowed back into the school. Nothing about dance was going to be easy—striving for perfection, overcoming personal insecurities and contesting against the best in the country—absolutely nothing. I wanted that hammered in their heads. I had to train them with a certain element of ruthlessness, so they wouldn't be vulnerable the rest of their lives.

They didn't realise that the window of opportunity was closing on them with each passing day. Dancers had at best ten or fifteen years to accomplish their dreams, before reality forced its way into their lives. Time was their enemy.

A dancer's body is at its physical prime between eighteen and twenty-five. It is within this age bracket that a dancer can undergo strenuous physical labour. Beyond this range, the body stops responding. It takes longer to recover from gruelling dance sessions; muscles become stiff and the list of injuries only grows longer.

The dancer has to reach a degree of perfection as early as their adolescence. They can either strive for greatness or lead an average life. No great dancer I knew had both.

Most of my students would not become world-renowned dancers. Forget the world, they wouldn't even be known in India. Their sizeable investment in this craft wouldn't lead to an equal return. These were the odds that every dancer had to negotiate and contend with.

Many students left within a few weeks, even fewer survived for months. Those who managed to continue for a year were the ones I was interested in. They were the future of dance.

Bharatanatyam isn't a hobby; it's not even a dance, it's a calling. A form of art that requires absolute and unwavering devotion.

Only with such tapasya, devotion to their art, do they receive the blessing of perfection, or something close to it. Sometimes, it takes a lifetime; sometimes, even a lifetime isn't enough.

~

The Tamil community celebrates the end of harvest season with the festival of Pongal. Since the largest numbers of students at Pratishtha were Tamil girls, I announced a holiday on the first of the four-day festival. However, the natyalaya was open for anyone who wanted to come for extra practice.

Ayla was the only student who came for training that day.

'You didn't want a break?' I asked her.

'I wanted to dance.'

'Okay. What would you like to learn today?'

'Tillana.'

'Tillana,' I replied in a doubtful tone. 'That is for the senior batch, Ayla. You will learn it in two years' time. Let's practise something less difficult.'

'But I can do it as well as any of the seniors. I have been observing them daily. Please give me a chance.'

'You really think you can do that,' I said.

'Yes.'

I had serious doubts. Tillana is a brisk dance sequence with formidable poses. It made for a grand finale act. I was hesitant to teach her because she would get disheartened and go into a sulk if she failed. However, I also realised that she wouldn't be easily deterred. I would have to dissuade her indirectly.

'I will teach you Tillana on one condition. You have to prove that you are worthy of this lesson.'

'How do I do that?'

'You have to finish a hundred squats in one minute. However, if you are unable to do it, you will come to Pratishtha an hour before every other student for one month and read *Kamba Ramayanam*.'

'I will do it,' she said promptly, her sense of optimism intact.

There was no way she would complete one hundred squats within a minute. Girls much stronger and older than Ayla weren't able to manage that number. However, Ayla didn't know that. It is when we don't set limitations on our abilities that we outperform ourselves.

'Are you ready?' I asked.

'Yes,' she replied and bent down for the first squat.

She was fresh and began confidently. I counted each squat to make sure she didn't fudge numbers. She finished thirty-five squats in fifteen seconds. If she could continue at this pace, she would win the challenge—easier said than done.

As she progressed, she would have to match strength with stamina. At fifty-five squats, her speed slowed down considerably. Rising up from a knee-bent position took a lot of energy and effort. She was panting.

'Are we done already?' I taunted.

It provoked her. She gained momentum and increased her speed once again. Fifteen squats later, she slowed down. It was a struggle all over again. She was all out of physical energy now; every squat came from her willpower to continue.

Eighty-seven. Eighty-eight. Eighty-nine. Ninety.

She was close. *She would actually pull it off*, I thought to myself. There was still five seconds left on the clock and only ten more squats to go. Ayla continued until she had reached ninety-three. When she bent down for the ninety-fourth, her body refused to rise up again. She could do no more and collapsed. It was an applause-worthy valiant effort.

She looked at me disconsolately. She thought she had failed. She was too young to realise that failure was an inseparable part of success. I wasn't testing her strength; I was testing her grit. She had to fail once, and then a second time and continue failing just a little better every time. And one day, all those accumulated failures would add up to one spectacular success.

'Get up,' I said. 'Let's begin Tillana.'

~

Countless dance sessions began with the sound of ankle bells in my ears and ended with chants of *Om*. Over time, the stature of Pratishtha and the number of students grew. Mornings turned to evenings, weeks to months, and just like that ten years passed. Sudha and I managed to keep our heads above water. So much had happened and changed—I was living a dream.

Ayla turned twenty-two. At five-feet-six-inches, she was

one of the tallest and most seasoned dancers at Pratishtha. Her radiance and talent were difficult to miss. Her unruly hair had to be reined in with clips during dance sessions and performances, and her spirit was indomitable. She brought a sense of freedom and flourish to the dance floor. That time when she couldn't tie a saree was a thing of the past. She dressed modestly, yet elegantly. She smiled at people but from a distance and left people asking for more. It was part of her charm. Ayla had matured into a young woman.

She was not Indian, it was quite apparent. But in her Bharatanatyam costume, accessorised with her long, braided hair, she looked as Indian as any foreigner could.

She had taken the numero uno position in the intermediate batch.

Her promotion to the senior group along with the top five dancers at Pratishtha was overdue. I had been waiting for the right moment. That opportunity presented itself when four dance troupes from across India were chosen for a special performance on the occasion of the Delhi International Dance Festival at the India Habitat Centre.

My father's protégé was the head organiser of the event. He asked me to choreograph a dance sequence and even invited my parents to Delhi to attend the festival. This would be the first time my father would see my choreography since I had left home and come to Delhi.

I decided to hold a three-act recital with a grand finale by Ayla. This was going to be our baptism by fire.

7

The Red Line

Ayla

The entrance to the India Habitat Centre was lined with bright, fragrant yellow roses, tulips and sunflowers.

After a short walk, crossing the fountains and the bushes, I reached the plaza steps—the makeshift stage for the performance.

A flight of stairs led to the rectangular floor where we were supposed to perform. There was a makeshift backstage with only a maze-like wall whose exit was blocked from one side. The other side opened on to the main stage.

The plaza steps faced the buildings, trees and shrubs, all else that was part of this huge edifice. And all of them looked at the dancers with great expectation.

'Do you feel the pressure?' Guruji said to me moments before the festival was about to begin.

'Yes.'

He looked at the stage and said to me with pride, 'Remember, Ayla, pressure is a privilege.'

There was something comforting about his statement.

By the time the clock struck seven, the place was packed to the brim.

The backstage was a jungle full of wild and unruly dancers. Costumes, shoes and bags lay scattered on the floor. There were forty manic dancers running helter-skelter.

Some stretched, some jogged, some drowned themselves in loud music and others flashed smiles at everyone. But these weren't uninhibited smiles; there was a hint of nervousness too. It was a way to reassure ourselves that everything was under control when nothing was under our control.

There were hundreds of spectators, waiting for the show to begin. I could hear their chatter. When the first act was announced, a loud hoot went up in the air.

~

The first in line was a six-member group of contemporary dancers, three boys and three girls. They entered the backstage, just ten minutes before the show.

The boys wore a red bow tie over a plain white shirt and the girls were dressed in black tights and red tops.

The head of the crew, Sam, walked in with both his collar and chin up. When one of the organisers told the crew to hurry up, they hardly paid heed. But the moment Sam asked them to warm up, they started to stretch.

Sam had spent two years learning contemporary dance at the Pineapple Dance Studio in London and another year on a dance scholarship in Japan. On his return to India, he opened a studio and took four young dancers under his wing.

They called themselves—Free to Move.

Sam's choreography was a fusion of ballet, jazz and

Japanese butoh. He had borrowed the most distinct elements of different dance forms, used his personal dislike for conventions and created an extraordinary dance fusion. Five years ago, his group had first performed at this very show. Their confidence and enthusiasm were daunting.

His two favourite trainees, Suday and Aishwarya, were the X-factor. Suday was known for his strength, while Aishwarya epitomised grace. They were a pair on and off the stage.

As soon as they stepped onto the stage, the audience was overcome with rapture. A group of girls screamed Suday's name. He looked in their direction for an extra second. One of them nearly fainted.

Aishwarya ruled the stage with splits and arches. She was so graceful that I wondered if she was putting any effort at all.

Free to Move owned the stage. They checked all the boxes. A thunderous applause awaited them at the end of their act.

You don't just walk in and execute near-perfect choreography like this. No, they had spent weeks, possibly months, preparing for this act. Even if they pretended to be cool and unaffected, they meant business.

The organisers were smart to begin the show with Free to Move.

~

Six exceptionally tall and slim ballerinas walked onto the stage, in tow with their Russian teacher, Nicolas Keifer. He was unusually graceful for a man his size. His black V-neck t-shirt accentuated his broad chest and a black blazer lent elegance to his appearance.

He waved to the crowd and bowed his head in

acknowledgement of the large contingent from the Russian embassy seated in the front row.

The ballerinas looked immaculate in their tutus and shoes. They were as tall as the men and their bodies were chiselled as if carved by a sculptor. If the audience was mesmerised with the contemporary dancers, they were fascinated by the ballerinas.

They started a romantic ballet. The girl who played Giselle was exceptional. She played the part of a village girl to perfection. Her movements were captivating. Even Aishwarya paled in comparison.

The other ballerinas added to the visual narrative. They did everything on the stage: twirl and leap, bend and glide. Before the audience could marvel at one bend, they were already executing another gravity-defying move. They drew the audience into their magical story.

~

As soon as the anchor announced that a belly dance sequence was next, a section of the crowd, mostly young boys and girls, began to hoot. Six dancers walked onto the stage with flair and attitude.

They wore scarlet tribal dresses and flaunted their navels and bare arms. Their pink skirts had ruffles attached over the slits and belts. They would have been welcomed in palaces with honours and gifts. I wished our dance had some of their flashiness.

The lead performer was as presumptuous as she was beautiful. She had an inflated sense of self-importance and had walked past me ignoring my greeting earlier in the day.

She stepped onto the stage and flashed an infectious smile. She had arrested everyone's attention even before the dance began.

The lights went out; there was complete darkness, but for the glow of the moon. They sat on the floor and covered themselves with a glittery golden cloth. A sense of mystery and anticipation built up.

Red lights came on in a flash. Strong musical beats began to play. The dancers removed the glittery golden cloth, smiled at the audience and were rewarded with another thunderous applause. The place came to life. It felt like there were a few thousand people watching, not a few hundred.

They stopped at all the right places and looked at the audience, almost demanding appreciation. The spectators were only too happy to oblige.

Their dance was full of energy. Their sparkling smiles never once dimmed. They didn't want to be anywhere in the world, but on this stage. The audience felt special. They were good when they were fast but they were spectacular when they went slow.

'Encore.'

'Encore.'

'Encore.'

The crowd blew kisses, screamed and cheered. They had won the hearts of the audience and exited the stage as conquerors.

~

Had we performed prior to the belly dancers, we could have made an impact, but now the audience was too overwhelmed to even notice us. To be honest, Bharatanatyam lacked the flair to woo an audience like this one.

Meenakshi, to my right, was supposed to follow my lead but she started a second too late. It was an uncharacteristic mistake from her considering she had five years of stage experience. It created confusion in the ranks.

We were coming across as two disparate groups dancing to our own pace and rhythm instead of one synchronised team.

The audience was unforgiving. The noise levels dropped, threatening to be replaced by sounds of boos. Their attention wavered. Now, only a small, more patient number of spectators still continued to cheer.

The mixed response spread panic among the dance groups. The first casualty was loss of composure. Every dance step seemed hurried and devoid of grace. Big, big mistake. My dance lacked expressions and emotions. I was too conscious of the audience's reaction.

The other girls left the stage after the first two acts. From the corner of my eye, I saw Guruji's blank expression. I could imagine his disappointment. I had to salvage Guruji's reputation at any cost. I remembered what he had told me earlier. Pressure is a privilege.

There was an energy about the place. It took complete control of me. I could distinctly hear every scream, every shout and every hoot.

I stood tall, roving my eyes over the audience. I performed big jumps and low bends. And then I went sideways, my body resting on one leg. I increased the pace of the movements to strike a chord with the audience and improvised my expressions to fit the tempo. The tap of the feet became faster and faster and faster.

The audience was hooked and it encouraged me to improvise further. I continued beyond the time allotted to us despite the exhaustion and the giddiness. When the music finally slowed down, the audience gave a resounding applause. It was the first real applause for our performance; it was the first real applause of my dance career. I felt so grateful to Guruji for giving me this opportunity. I turned towards him and took a bow.

No one remembered the lack of coordination or anything else, not even the belly dancers. My solo feat was a runaway success.

~

Guruji walked towards me after the performance. I stayed silent, continued mingling with the crowd, waiting for his word of praise. Maybe, even a pat on the back.

His appreciation, even gratitude would mean everything. I turned towards him in anticipation, but he said nothing. His hand moved towards me. Not to pat my back, but to slap my cheek. Silence descended.

'Who gave you the permission for cheap gimmicks on stage?' Guruji thundered. 'This was supposed to be a classical dance performance, not a *vulgar* act.'

'But the audience liked it,' I said.

'My reputation is in tatters, all because of you. I should never have trusted you.'

His words hurt me more than his slap. Not all the praise from the audience could erase the sting of those words.

I had to get out of that place. I rushed to the washroom to get a hold of myself. I still couldn't believe Guruji had hit me; I couldn't stifle my tears. My eyes had turned red. The eye-liner was smudged. I kept splashing water on my face as if it would help get rid of the anger I was feeling. I didn't deserve such ignominy.

When I stepped out of the washroom, a number of people came forward and complimented me for the courage and composure I showed on the stage. A dance blogger approached me with praise and many questions.

When I mentioned I was a political exile, he asked me about my family. It was going to be the story peg for the next day's article. He wanted to feature me on his website. I invited him over to my house for coffee, the following evening.

Somewhere in his incessant questions and curiosity, I forgot about the slap. I felt redeemed. He understood I had talent even if my Guruji was blind to it. I was the one to 'watch out for', he said.

8

I Choose Drishti

Guru Chandrashekhar

Would you believe her audacity? She had no authority to break the choreography and flaunt her acrobatic skills. This wasn't supposed to be a circus and I don't care what her reasons were or what the outcome was. She disobeyed me.

My father walked away after the performance without saying a word. Disappointment was written all over his face. Even my mother didn't approve. Ayla was drawn to cheap applause. She betrayed my trust.

The organisers were glad that I had added *flair* to the traditional recital. They were all praises for Ayla and invited her to perform at four subsequent events scheduled across India. I felt like a total sell-out.

I couldn't admit the truth, that the improvisation was not of my doing. It would only undermine my credibility further and reduce me to a laughing stock. I had no choice but to accept the offer.

In the next performance, another trainee could go by her whims and justify it saying she followed her gut. I might as well hang my boots and watch my students run riot on stage. No. This was unacceptable, and I had to act.

My intention was not to hit her. I went backstage to confront her. I thought she would be contrite. But she was standing there basking in the glory of her foolishness. That made me even more furious and I slapped her on an impulse.

Later, I realised how wrong I was. I should have controlled my temper. Gone about things differently. I regretted hitting her. That was unbecoming of a guru. It was the first and last time I had raised my hand on a student.

~

A frivolous ten-minute act was all that it took to generate frenzy about her. Many people asked when I would hold her arangetram. It was ridiculous and premature to put her on a pedestal.

This was a crucial time in her career. It was important for her to focus on her dance. Constant hunger for improvement was the only way she would fulfil her ambitions.

Ayla disappeared after the dance festival. She neither came to the natyalaya nor informed anyone about her absence. I assumed she had taken the scolding to heart and needed some time to cool down. I didn't make an issue out of it but after a week's absence, I finally called to ask her whereabouts.

'She has gone to Mumbai with her father,' her mother said. I later found out that during this absence, she worked with a few choreographers as a freelance dancer. They asked her to participate in a dance reality show and she accepted without even seeking my permission.

Ayla didn't once think about all the classes she was going

to miss or that she needed to consult me. I had seen this happen to dancers before her. They started to believe they were special and they alone deserved the applause. Their art took a backseat. The focus shifted to what others thought of them and what was being written about them. That was the beginning of the end.

~

I didn't see much of Ayla in the next one year. She travelled to different parts of the country for dance festivals and events. She had to adjust to different stages, cities and audiences among other things. Ayla gained confidence and stature through consistent performance and execution. There was a certain disobedience in her dance, a streak of rebellion in her ways that caught everyone's attention.

She was no longer a pariah trying to make her way to the mainstream. Whether she went to Mumbai, Hyderabad, Bangalore or Chennai, people recognised her and they came in large numbers to watch her—Ayla of Delhi International Dance Festival fame.

In the brief spells when she did return to Pratishtha, I saw a change in her attitude that was unmistakable. Her chin was always an inch higher, her voice full of sarcasm. She had become complacent and distant. Worse, her attitude towards her juniors reeked of condescension. She had lost her hunger, her drive to listen and learn.

On more than one occasion, she arrived late for the classes. No one stopped her or pointed out these follies. I was about to say something, but my eyes met with Sudha's. Her gaze beseeched me to practise restraint.

This had an adverse effect on Pratishtha's environment. When I pointed out a mistake in her dance; she would retort, 'But I am dancing exactly as I did earlier.'

'I don't care how you danced earlier,' I said in a fit of anger. 'But it isn't good enough now.'

She did rectify her movements, but not before contorting her face. She was irritated at something or someone. I couldn't understand what and she never bothered to explain.

~

Her footwork lost its sharpness. Even some of the mudras needed improvement. These glitches were like open wounds. They were harmless when corrected in the nick of time, but if left to fester they would turn into serious infections.

In ordinary circumstances, I would have corrected them within days. But I was teaching a famous dancer with an inflated ego. She was too proud to admit her faults and amend.

Everybody maintained a safe distance from her. She was cold to her contemporaries and patronising to her juniors, particularly Drishti. It was the friction between the pair that brought about Ayla's downfall.

Seventeen-year-old Drishti was a remarkable dancer. She was the fastest to be promoted to the advance group. What took dancers months to learn, she managed within days. In some ways, she was almost the antithesis of Ayla.

Drishti came from a South Indian Iyer family of high-ranking government officers. Her knowledge of Carnatic music played a vital role in her rise as a dancer. She picked up nuances of music and dance that others remained oblivious to.

We were preparing for a prestigious dance performance when their tussle turned into a showdown. Drishti and Ayla were standing parallel to each other for this sequence. According to the choreography, Ayla was supposed to be slightly ahead of the others. However, when the dance sequence began, Drishti overtook Ayla.

'What is wrong with you?' Ayla snapped. 'You are supposed to stay behind me. Put that in your thick head.'

'Enough!' I said. 'Everyone, take a break. Drishti and Ayla, step forward.'

I was furious at Ayla's crass language and not unaware of Drishti's fault in the matter.

'Drishti, try and maintain your position. Your first two steps were too long, which is why you came in front of Ayla. I don't want to see that happen again.'

'I am sorry, Guruji. I didn't realise it,' Drishti said.

'Shut it, will you,' Ayla spoke out of turn once again. 'This is not the first time you have broken ranks. You have been trying to hog the lead for months now. I know what you are up to and it's not going to work.'

'You are mistaken,' Drishti said.

'You are fighting like children. Drishti, go, join the practice.'

'Yes, Guruji.'

'Wait a minute, Ayla,' I said. 'If I hear you speak like that to any of my students again, that will be your last day at Pratishtha. You are a senior. Try to behave like one.'

'But, Guruji, she is trying to poach my position. I don't even understand why she is part of the advance batch.'

'I will not tolerate another word from you. You stink of arrogance.'

'Fine. I would like to take the day off. I don't think I can dance anymore,' she said coldly, turned around and stormed out of the class. She knew very well that the practice would have to be cancelled. Her ego was more important than the dance performance. This was not the Ayla I knew.

'Let's just stop here today,' I said to the students once Ayla left. 'We will resume tomorrow.'

I was tired of dealing with all this teenage bickering; I needed a change of air.

~

Later that evening, I went to visit Nizamuddin dargah. I had discovered the dargah, quite by accident, in the winter of 1988. I was running all over Delhi in search of a space for my dance school. After another energy-sapping day of hunting, I was walking on the streets when I heard strains of music emanating from the dargah and I entered the gates out of curiosity.

The full moon was half hidden behind a cover of clouds. A sea of worshippers in embroidered white caps sat on their knees in prayer, beggars fanned the visitors in hope of alms, and a host of other people were occupied by chores. Everyone was gathered to experience the magic of the place. I was the only one lost.

The tombstone of the Sufi saint Nizamuddin looked mesmerising in the night's glow. The crystal chandeliers added to the grandeur and the Farsi inscriptions embellished the ornate walls. However, it was the scent of rose petals that spoke to me. In a place filled with human stench, it provided a sense of relief.

It was impossible to make sense of all that was taking place in front of my eyes. I sat on the cold marble floor and watched chaos reign.

From a dark corner of the dargah, I heard gut-wrenching screams. Someone was being mercilessly beaten up. I wondered if it was the shriek of a woman. But it turned out to be a young boy.

Every time he broke from the circle around him, people pulled him back and the punishment continued. I asked them why the boy was being punished.

'It is not him we are beating, but the jinn inside.'

'What are jinns?'

'You don't know jinns? They are supernatural creatures made of fire. We can't see them, but they are here, even at this moment, right in front of our eyes. Some of them are evil. The boy's body has been overtaken by one. Only when they beat him to the very limit of his life, will the jinn release him.'

I couldn't take it. Just as I was about to leave, seven men wearing shimmering bronze and golden caps took centre-stage.

The performance began with a series of claps. They sat in front of the sanctum and the crowd gathered around them. The lead vocalist was a short and plump man dressed in an immaculate white kurta-pyjama. The harmonium player sat on his right and the percussionist to his left.

They clapped and clapped until the music lent them voice. From a soft chant to all-out crooning, the music permeated through every corner of the shrine and touched every soul. All the whispers, shouts and arguments drowned under its weight; even the boy was released.

The music praised the Lord. A beautiful woman in a blue salwar kameez and green dupatta followed the tune while swaying her head, as if she was in a trance. A wealthy-looking man walked towards the procession, currency notes clutched in his fist, and with one flick threw them in the air, as if they were worthless. He then took the ringside view close to the musicians, as if by right.

'*There is nothing more valuable than wealth.*

My God says life has no meaning without respect,' followed the next verse.

They sang with a passion and fervour that turned me into a believer (albeit for a few minutes). I had not stepped inside the tomb until now, but now I wanted to seek blessings for my dance school.

I entered the rectangular chamber embellished by a pool of rose petals. *Ahhh.* The fragrance. I prayed to the saint to fill my school with the same scent in which his chamber was bathed.

Within a week of my visit to the dargah, I found a space for my dance school. I returned to offer my gratitude to the dargah. The visits to the dargah became a ritual of sorts. I came here in search of answers.

I reminisced and felt the same sense of peace I had felt the first time I came here. My thoughts went back to Pratishtha. Ayla and Drishti were both important to me. I needed to do more to nurture their talent. I sat on the floor and prayed for their success.

~

I presented ankle bells to Drishti.

'You are ready for your arangetram,' I announced. 'You have worked hard in the previous five years and it shows. Go home and give your parents the good news. We will finalise a date within the next three months and begin preparations.'

'Thank you, Guruji! This is a great honour,' she replied and touched my feet.

Ayla was sweeping the dance floor. I had almost forgotten her presence until she made a disapproving sound.

'How can Drishti hold her arangetram before me? I am the lead dancer; I have spent twice as much time at Pratishtha.'

'Because she is ready. Your time will also come. You just need to be a little patient.'

'Little more patient. Are you serious, Guruji? I have been working hard for the past ten years and you couldn't spare a word of praise for me. But when I made a single mistake, you slapped me. I have corrected my technique and practised my movements several times over, and I did all this without a word of complaint. *Little more patience*, you say.'

There were tears in her eyes. She had lost control of herself. I had never seen her break down like this before.

'Drishti, we will continue this discussion tomorrow. I want to have a private word with Ayla,' I said.

'Yes, Guruji,' she said and left the natyalaya.

'No one is denying the effort you have put in, Ayla. That's why you are part of the advance group. Drishti has proved herself and this is her reward.'

'Say that to others, but we both know what the truth is.'

'What's the truth?'

'You prefer her because she is South Indian and her father is a senior government official.'

'What rubbish! She has earned her chance fair and square. If you had not lost your head with all the media hype, your arangetram would have happened a long time ago.'

'So that is why you have been punishing me. You are jealous that all the attention is directed at me and not your school,' she said. 'People warned me earlier, but I didn't believe them. They told me I had to let you go in order to move ahead in my career. They told me you would hold me back.'

'Ayla, I just want you to focus on dance and let go of these distractions. You no longer want to be a great dancer. Instead, you are worried about what happens to Drishti and Maitreyi about who writes about you and who doesn't. That's a recipe for disaster.

'Truth be told, you have stagnated, while youngsters such as Drishti have grown in ability and skill. Get all this poison out of your head. Go home. Start afresh tomorrow. There is still time,' I exhorted her.

'I am not naïve. You can't command me according to your whim and fancy, anymore. It feels disgusting to be treated like this over and over again. I won't let this happen to me. You will have to choose between Drishti and me,' Ayla said.

'Fine. I choose Drishti,' I said.

9

One Stage, Two Masters

Ayla

I know I said some terrible things. They were spoken out of anger, especially the personal bit. I didn't mean any of it. But words once spoken cannot be taken back.

I hoped Guruji would put our differences aside and allow me to join the classes once again. All said and done, I was still his favourite student and the most experienced trainee at Pratishtha. He couldn't just disown me.

I tried to make amends. Called him many times to apologise, but he wouldn't take my calls. I went to the natyalaya, but the guard had orders not to let me in.

A month passed. I didn't hear from him. I was worried sick about my future. I sought Sudha's help; if anyone could persuade Guruji to take me back, it was her.

'I have called him several times, but he won't answer my calls,' I said over the phone, 'I know I was out of line and I feel terrible about it.'

'He is furious, Ayla. He has forbidden the very mention of your name.'

'You have to persuade him,' I said, 'There is a performance, three weeks from now. He will have to cancel the show without me.'

There was silence. Sudha was scrambling for the right words that would cause the least hurt. 'Forget about the performance. Just give him some time to cool down.'

'What do you mean, forget about the performance?'

'He has already asked Drishti to be the lead,' she said in a low voice, 'I have to go now. I will talk to you later.'

I threw the phone away. I didn't realise I could be dispensed with so easily. Drishti was clearly more important to him. I couldn't go back to Pratishtha now, even if he forgave me. My place was already taken, and I was not going to beg and crawl for a spot behind her.

'Go to Turkey and study law,' Bavo said.

I was outraged at the suggestion and he hastily retreated.

'I am not asking you to give up on your dance. You can continue it as a hobby, but it's time to secure your career.'

I was not in the least interested in law; I couldn't imagine life without dance.

I went to various dance teachers offering to lead their dance ensemble. They knew of me and praised my passion and skill, however that was not enough to secure a place in their dance schools.

The first question everyone asked was why I left Pratishtha after so many years. It was difficult to answer truthfully. I couldn't reveal my frustration at not being allowed to perform my arangetram. These people wouldn't understand. So, I told them politely that Guru Chandrashekhar and I had creative differences.

They shifted uncomfortably. Some even tried to put on a show of being open-minded and flexible, but I could see them judging me. My skin colour and reasons for departure were too peculiar for their liking.

~

There was only one door left and I was hesitant to knock on it. I had avoided reaching out to Guru Ranmohan, owner of Studio Anubhooti, because my Guruji couldn't stand him. I knew if I went to Guru Ranmohan, I would cross the Lakshman Rekha with Guru Chandrashekhar—there would be no chance of returning to Pratishtha after that.

I made the call. Any further delay would have given Bavo an excuse to send me off to Turkey.

Ranmohan lived in a mansion in Safdarjung Enclave. It was a sprawling two-storey building made of grey marble and glass walls. I had never imagined that a dance professional could live a life of such luxury. On the marble surface of the entrance was inscribed in bold letters—STUDIO ANUBHOOTI.

The drawing room wall was adorned by certificates and pictures of Ranmohan with the 'who's who' of the country. A separate wall was decorated by a huge framed photograph—Ranmohan receiving the Guru Dronacharya Award from the former President of India, Dr APJ Abdul Kalam.

Within a few years of his arrival in Delhi, he had established himself as one of the best dance teachers in the country.

It was his choreography for Queen Elizabeth II's reception in India in 1997 that sealed his popularity and earned him rewards. The Queen had remarked that it was one of the finest performances she had seen in decades.

Indian media and British tabloids went to town with the story. Ranmohan's name and interviews were everywhere. He had made the country proud. Everyone got carried away in a surge of patriotism. Soon, his success stories led him to be awarded with one of India's highest honours.

My thoughts were interrupted as Ranmohan walked in. He was short and stocky with a parrot-like nose. He also had a potbelly. The sight didn't inspire confidence until he spoke. That's when I understood what made him so special.

'Good afternoon, Ayla,' he welcomed me in his unique baritone. There was an ease about his demeanour and confidence in his stance. 'There is no need to touch my feet.'

'Okay, Sir.'

'No need to call me "Sir" either,' he said, smiling.

'Okay, Ranmohan ji.'

Guru Chandrashekhar had never invited me to his house. He was brusque and aloof. In comparison, Ranmohan was warm and polite.

'I have heard good things about your dance, Ayla. I even saw your performance at the dance festival last year. You saved your dance crew and teacher lot of embarrassment.'

'How do you know I had improvised?'

'Chandrashekhar would rather eat rat poison than add flair to his choreography. His blood pressure must have gone through the roof,' he said, smiling.

'Unfortunately, I also saw him slap you backstage.'

The sting of that slap felt fresh again.

'Do you think I was wrong?'

'Of course, you were wrong. You went against his wishes,' he said, much to my chagrin. 'Having said that, if I were your Guru, I would have understood. Sometimes, the circumstances demand us to do the wrong thing for the right reasons.'

Finally, I was speaking to someone who understood my point of view. It was such a relief.

'I am guessing that is why you are here. Because Chandrashekhar sees things *differently*.'

'Yes. I am looking to join a new, different dance school. Please give me a chance to prove my skills at Anubhooti. I won't let you down.'

'Had it been anger, you should have left his school right after the event. A year has already passed. What took you so long?'

I hesitated to broach the subject.

'I can't trust you, if you won't trust me,' Ranmohan said.

'I worked extremely hard for eleven years and yet Guruji didn't give me blessings for my arangetram. He wouldn't have allowed my arangetram for the next twenty years.'

'Seriously? You haven't had your arangetram yet? The problem with our dance gurus is that they don't think big. With talent like yours, Ayla, you should be performing at international events. Take my trainee, Nirupama, for instance—she recently represented India at the classical dance festival in Vienna.'

'Am I good enough to perform abroad?' I asked.

'Of course. You are not the first student who has come to me, disillusioned. Some of them are too late. I can't do anything for them. However, there might still be a chance for you.'

'I will work hard and prove myself,' I tried to reassure him.

'I will accept you in my dance school on one condition. You will have to cut all ties with Chandrashekhar. I don't want you to speak to him ever again. There cannot be two masters on one stage.'

'But, he has mentored me since I was a young girl. It would be disrespectful,' I argued.

'Was he showing you respect when he slapped you in front of everyone? You are a young girl. If you don't stand up for yourself, people will walk all over you. Let that be your first lesson under my tutelage.'

~

'Sudha called an hour ago,' Dayê said. 'She has convinced Chandrashekhar to take you back. He wants you to join the dance session from three o' clock, tomorrow.'

I couldn't stop laughing. Dayê looked at me in puzzlement. From having no guru for more than three months, I now had two. I told Dayê about my meeting with Ranmohan.

'What are you going to do?'

'I have no idea. Where do you think I should go?'

'Go to the teacher who respects and values you.'

'I will think about it tomorrow.'

~

'Where do you want to go, madam?' the autorickshaw driver asked. I was still uncertain. I knew too little about Anubhooti, and too much about Pratishtha.

They say that when in doubt, flip a coin. Once it goes up, we realise what we really want. Thinking wasn't getting me anywhere. I decided to try this technique.

I took a five-rupee coin out of my purse. Tails, I return to Pratishtha; heads, I try my luck at Anubhooti.

I tossed it with a flick of my thumb. It went up, flipping from one side to another, pausing mid-air for a fleeting moment. I caught it in my palm and looked at it for the great revelation.

Fate had chosen Pratishtha for me.

'Madam, where?' the driver asked again.

'Safdarjung Enclave. Take me to Studio Anubhooti,' I said. I had made my decision.

~

The spiral staircase led me to the dance school located at the basement of Ranmohan's palatial mansion. I had finally found a studio that befitted a dancer of my stature. The floor was made of special wood to ease pressure on the knees. There were huge spotless mirrors for a better evaluation of postures and expressions.

Ranmohan was teaching a beginners' batch. He winked at me. I smiled back, but his gaze had already shifted to a student. He sat on his leather chair, a glass of iced tea resting in his hand.

There were beam-lights and a crystal chandelier on the ceiling, which emanated orange rays on the floor. The setting lent an aura to the otherwise-average dancers' performance.

Every now and then, Ranmohan would crack a joke or say something witty. The trainees would laugh and somewhere between the laughter and merry-making, he would insert suggestions on ways they could improve their dance. He pushed them without being aggressive and taught without being preachy.

One of the walls was embellished with framed posters of Ranmohan's most successful trainees including Henna Mukherjee, the famed Bollywood actor, who had trained with Ranmohan for three years.

She was a typical Indian beauty—dusky with delicate skin, expressive eyes and lustrous hair. At twenty-one, Henna had made a successful transition from dance to Bollywood. Her impassioned dance moves in her debut movie *Rasleela* had catapulted her to the status of a diva. All the young dancers were awed by her. However, I didn't find either her or her dance that appealing. To be honest, I fancied myself as Henna's equal, maybe, even superior.

~

Senior dancers began to trickle in. Ranmohan was busy talking to them.

Thirty-seven girls filled the space and their laughter echoed. Many of them looked younger than me. I recognised a few from some of the dance performances in the past. Fifteen minutes later, Ranmohan signalled with a clap and we took our respective positions.

'Before we begin today's class, I would like all of you to welcome Ayla. Some of you may already know her from her past performances. She is a new trainee at our dance studio, so please help her in every way possible,' Ranmohan said and everyone's attention shifted to me. The girls introduced themselves and I shook hands with them. There were a few friendly faces in the group.

'Is it okay if I leave my hair open?' I asked, hesitantly.

Ranmohan gave me a benign smile and said, 'It's your hair, do whatever you want.'

The class began, abruptly. I was shaken initially and struggled to keep pace with the group. By the time my body warmed up, the class was about to finish.

Guru Chandrashekhar's technique was to go slow, and ensure that the dancers mastered the lesson at the same time. We started with stretches, moved to slokas and subsequently hand movements. Gradually, we would begin dancing. The intensity picked up slowly and steadily.

Only when everyone had got the steps right did the whole class move forward to the next routine. The class went on for three hours, sometimes even longer.

At Studio Anubhooti too, the mistakes were pointed out immediately, but the class didn't stop for anyone to take corrective measures. The trainees picked up the sequences within a few attempts. They found their own way of dance instead of relying on Ranmohan. It was left to the pupils to practise and fine-tune their ways. I sat down on the floor trying to take it all in.

'How was the first session?' Ranmohan asked.

'It was very different from my earlier training,' I said.

'You mean *good* different or *bad* different.'

'Just different,' I said, apprehensively. But Ramohan was not offended.

'Don't worry about it,' he said with a smile. 'It's only your first day. It will take you some time to get used to our style of dance, but once you get the hang of it, there will be no stopping you.'

~

Dreams come true, but they take their own sweet time. I chased mine day after day, month after month for many years. It evaded me. I felt like I was chasing a shadow, always out of reach.

When I finally came face to face with it, I was no longer the person I once was at the beginning of the journey. The reflection staring at me in the mirror changed. That is the beauty of dreams. They transform us.

'I have good news for you, Ayla,' Ranmohan said, 'you are ready for your arangetram.'

I had always wondered how I would react to this announcement. As it turned out, my reaction was no reaction at all. There was a blackout.

'Are you all right?' he said and clicked his fingers in front of my eyes. My thoughts returned to the studio.

'YESSSSSSS!'

A wide smile appeared on my face. There was a rush of blood in my head. I hugged Ranmohan in front of all the students and kissed him on the cheek.

In that moment, I felt infinite hope. I had wanted this for so long and I had achieved it. I would prove that I was as good as any of them. My world would never be the same again.

Ranmohan was startled by my reaction. He was used to students touching his feet and asking for blessings. He went red in the face and looked around the room as though wondering how anyone would take his lectures on discipline and grace seriously after this.

Leave quickly, Ayla, before he changes his mind, I thought to myself and hurried to the exit.

I couldn't wait to share the news with Dayê and Bavo.

'Ask your father to come and meet me tomorrow. We

will begin the preparations right away,' Ranmohan shouted as I made my way out.

~

I gave Dayê a bear hug and blurted out, 'It's happening.'

'What is happening?' she said, putting away the frying pan. The aroma of homemade mutton korma reached every corner of the house. She had prepared my favourite dish. All the signs were pointing towards the right direction.

'Ranmohan gave his blessings for my arangetram. He said, I am ready,' I announced, excitedly.

'*Alhamdulillah,* praise the Lord. This is great news. Your Bavo is going to be ecstatic. When is the performance?'

'He didn't mention any date, but he asked Bavo to come to the studio tomorrow.'

'Your new teacher is a good man. May Allah bless him. You made the right decision. I am so proud of you.

'How about I make Tahin halva for dinner. My Gulum is going to be the best Bharatanatyam dancer this country has ever seen. Insha'Allah.'

All her love came pouring in through spoonfuls of sugar.

Tahin halva was Dayê's answer to everything good or bad; it oozed of sugar, milk and pistachios. Whether Bavo's export business faced any problems, I had trouble at school, or there was a cause for celebration; halva was the go-to recipe. It gave her a sense of empowerment. If all else failed, her food provided solace.

I was not very fond of the halva. It was too sweet for my palate, but that didn't matter. It was the one thing that made Dayê feel good. I relished it as if it were my favourite dessert in the world.

10

The Art of Deceit

Guru Ranmohan

Ayla came to the studio with her father. He gawked at every artefact as if strolling in a museum of exhibits. It was evident he had never seen a dance studio like this before.

'Welcome to my modest dance school,' I said and shook his hand firmly.

'You have a nice setup. No wonder Ayla likes it so much here,' he replied.

'I try to provide the best facilities for my students. Halim ji, your daughter is supremely talented and well-behaved. You have done a great job in her upbringing. I wish more of my trainees were like her,' I said. His face turned into a mix of embarrassment and delight.

The easiest way to curry the favour of a parent was to praise their children.

I continued, 'Ayla can go places. Unfortunately, she is already late for her arangetram. I can't imagine what her previous guru was thinking. Your daughter is so talented, the sky's the limit for her. He should have held it four years ago. We are running out of time.'

This was the second step and it worked like magic. It established how the child had wasted precious time with other teachers. I was doing everything in my power to right the wrong. Thus, I was elevated to the position of a saviour.

'I don't want to waste your money or time. The sooner she gets this done, the faster she can embark on her dance career. We have a saying that the dancer only begins to come into her own after the arangetram.'

This was the last piece of the straw; the possibility of a successful career. Parents worried about the viability of dance as a profession. By assuring them of a bright future, I assuaged their worries. More importantly, it relaxed them enough to loosen their purse strings.

There was nothing more to say. Parents would themselves ask me to take all their money and do whatever was needed for the future of their child. I waited for a minute, so Halim could process all the information.

'I am obliged for everything you have done,' he said in a voice dripping with gratitude. 'She is my only child. Her happiness is paramount. She is very excited about her debut performance. We all are. You will have to guide me through the whole process.'

'Ayla is like a daughter to me too,' I said, 'I will definitely help out with the arrangements. Let me be upfront with you, it requires a lot of effort and money. And it should. It's the single most important performance of Ayla's career. How she does at her arangetram may very well impact her future prospects. I will make sure that some of the most influential names from the city come to watch her show.'

'I couldn't agree more. How do we get started?' Halim ji asked.

'The three most important elements are—choreography, venue and live orchestra. I will begin the choreography from today itself. That is entirely my responsibility, but I will need your money for venue booking and live orchestra.

'Then there are secondary requirements like decorations, lights and sound professionals, make-up crew and videographers. Getting the right chief guest too is another tricky matter but that can wait; costumes, jewellery and catering services are also important. You see, many things have to be looked into,' I explained.

'I thought this was going to be a simple affair. This sounds like a lot of work and expenditure. I don't want to compromise on the quality. Having said that, we come from a middle-class family. Try to remove anything that could be done without,' he said.

'I completely understand your point. You will not pay an extra penny under my watch. I give you my word,' I assured him.

'Now some of these vendors are crooks. They will charge you a ransom especially because you are a foreigner.'

'I experience it all the time. If you can share a ballpark figure, I will negotiate with them accordingly,' Halim ji said.

'There are no ballpark figures. They go by their whims, especially with outsiders,' I explained.

I hesitated for a second, 'Maybe, I should do the talking and get you the best rates. Just make sure that funds are available at short notice.'

'That would be really helpful. Please don't mind me asking, but I would like to know your fees as well. It's because of you that this performance is taking place.'

'You are embarrassing me, Halim ji. I am just trying to make sure that Ayla gets the right platform. This is a centuries-old tradition. Devotees like me try to stay true to its rules as well as spirit. I will charge a fee of 100,000 rupees only. Along with that, the student is supposed to present the teacher three kilograms of gold, fifteen silver coins and a gift on the day of the show.

'This is what the tradition dictates. But all of that is for later. For now, you just have to deposit 75,000 rupees.'

'What's the advance for?' Halim ji asked.

'For the preparations. It's a standard practice.'

'Okay. Sure. Give me a few days to put the money together.'

'Take all the time you need. We can schedule the performance four months from now. All the preparations will be done by that time. I will also be free from other engagements,' I said.

~

Many in the dance community were envious of my position. They accused me of using my family's connections to become rich and famous. These morons knew nothing about building a brand.

My father was one of the finest painters in India. He introduced me to the right people. In fact, he set up my appointment with the minister of culture when the Queen of England announced her trip to India. But who do you think sensed that opportunity?

The Queen loved my choreography because it was flawless. I received the Guru Dronacharya Award because the President found me worthy. The best dancers came to Anubhooti because they received the best training here. I made all that happen.

I refused to run my family's art gallery in Kolkata. I wasn't interested in drinking fine wine, or understanding the varying connotations of abstract art and all its hidden meanings. I wanted to be a man who creates the art and pushes the boundaries. The talking could be left to other Bengalis.

Bharatanatyam was free of such compulsion and it was an untapped market for an enterprising man like me. The purists were holding on way too strong. In the process, they were distancing the youth. I saw it from miles apart. I was going to be the change-maker; I would be the reformist. It was the demand of the time and there was a lot of money to be made here. *Screw* Kolkata, I moved to the capital.

It took me twenty-seven years of sweat and toil to build my reputation. I deserved to be adequately rewarded for my efforts. Dance is not charity. Artists don't survive on air and water, nor do teachers.

Ayla was lost and abandoned when she came to me. I gave her direction. An opportunity to move ahead in the dance world. In return, I wanted a good return on my investment.

11

Kneel Before Your Guru

Ayla

My life, my dreams would all come down to those crucial ninety minutes on stage tomorrow. Twenty-four hours remained before I stepped onto the stage for my arangetram. I couldn't eat anything. Sleep deserted me. Sitting still was impossible. The previous four months felt like a blur. The incessant phone calls from well-wishers only added to my nervousness.

There was a flurry of activities in my house. Preparations were far from complete. Bavo and Dayê went searching for a food caterer in the afternoon. The first vendor had backed out at the last minute. Floral arrangements needed to be changed. Guruji had ordered jasmine flowers to be flown in from Chennai, but the flight had been rescheduled due to inclement weather.

I couldn't concern myself with these issues anymore. I left them to my parents' discretion. I wanted to get away from the noise and only focus on the performance. I insisted that Ranmohan and I schedule another dry-run that evening. I had already done a mock performance at the Antralaya auditorium the day before, but I wanted to go through the whole routine once again, just to soothe my frayed nerves.

Ranmohan used his influence to arrange a late-night practice session.

This was strictly off the books, so the manager asked us to report at nine, when all the staff left and the place was locked down. He provided Ranmohan his personal access key.

'Henna Mukherjee will be the chief guest at your show, tomorrow,' Ranmohan said as I entered the auditorium.

'Are you serious? That's amazing,' I replied.

'I told Henna that the most beautiful and talented trainee of mine has her debut show. You must come and support her. Her manager confirmed this morning.'

'Ahh...Now I get it. That is why you were so secretive about the chief guest. So, you were waiting for her to confirm. What if she had declined?' I asked.

'Of course, she was going to come,' he dismissed my query. 'She knows better than to refuse the man who made her famous.'

'This calls for a celebration, so I brought a bottle of Scotch. Go ahead, take a swig,' he said and poured me a drink.

'I am sorry, I can't. It's a religious thing.'

'Oh, come on. Don't give me that nonsense. You think I don't know what you young girls do behind your parents' back? My dear, one glass of Scotch hardly qualifies as drinking,' he said and pushed the glass in my hand.

'I really can't, but I am very happy with this news,' I replied, as curtly as possible.

'Never mind, I will drink on your behalf,' he said and downed both the glasses in quick succession.

'Give your Guru a hug at least, and thank him for making all this happen. Chandrashekhar couldn't have managed to get Henna's clerk as chief guest,' he said and embraced me.

He reeked of alcohol. I moved away quickly. It wasn't just a glass of Scotch for celebration's sake, he had been drinking for a while. The bottle of Glenfiddich was almost empty.

'Why did you cringe?' he said.

I didn't want to complain about the smell. It wasn't my place to speak. That would have just spoiled his mood, or worse, offended him. I quickly made up an excuse.

'It was your beard. It...um...tickled me.'

He put one hand around my waist and in a quick, jerky motion pulled me towards him. I lost my balance and my hands, involuntarily, rested on his shoulders. He started to rub his beard all over my face. He was completely inebriated; the booze had clearly taken its toll. I knew what he was doing was inappropriate, but I didn't want to make a scene. I tried to move away as politely as I could.

Moreover, I didn't want to offend him. Not after he had spoken to Henna Mukherjee for my sake. He was just an old man who had had one drink too many, nothing that I couldn't handle.

'Let's get back to the practice,' I reminded him.

'You are right,' he said and moved away quickly.

He took one big swig from the bottle and switched on the music for the first act of the arangetram.

I began to dance but Ranmohan stopped me within a few seconds. 'Ayla, you are late in following the beat. You need to listen carefully and tap your feet on the ground as soon as you hear the clap of my hands.'

'Go back to the half-squat position. I will help you out,' he said.

He stood right behind me as I continued to work on alarippu—the invocation piece where the dancer offers respect to God.

'Stop! Stop! Stop! You are doing it all wrong. Come back to aramandi. Now bend your feet lower and stretch your hands above your head,' he said. I could feel his warm breath on the nape of my neck.

'Rest your hands on my neck and let your body loose. Give me the perfect abhinaya.'

I shuddered from his touch. It wasn't just his heavy breath, but his erect penis touched my butt. He whispered into my ear and I felt a strange ticklish sensation as he planted a kiss below my right ear. I tried to move my body away. However, his right hand had a vice-like grip on my waist.

I was frozen to the spot, not knowing how to react. His left hand slid across my navel, inside my panties. I stopped him, but by that time his right hand had found its way up my blouse. He pinched my nipple hard.

'Stop it,' I shouted.

That's when I realised I was in trouble.

'What the hell are you doing? Are you out of your mind?'

He had crossed all limits of decency. His behaviour was disgusting, no matter how drunk he was. I didn't want to continue anymore. I decided to go home immediately.

'This is part of your preparation. My love and blessings will only help in your performance. Take off that blouse right now. You are wearing a pink demi-bra, aren't you?

'I have often noticed the wide straps go astray in dance

sessions. I have lain awake at night many a time, imagining your breasts cupped in my hands.'

I didn't know whether to reason with him, shout or just make a run for my life. We were alone. No one but my parents knew. My heart skipped a beat. I was going to pass out.

'Come back to your senses. I have a performance tomorrow.'

'Stop your act now. Don't pretend like you don't want this,' he said. 'You are the one who started all this. You were all over me the day I announced your arangetram. You hugged me in front of everyone and kissed me not once, but twice. You want this.

'I am only returning your affection. You can do this much for your teacher, can't you? I have done so much for you,' he said and moved forward to kiss me, but I pushed him away.

I took a few steps back, 'Bavo will be here any moment now.'

'No, he won't. I am supposed to drop you home tonight after the session. We have all night to finish what you started four months ago.'

There was no way to reason with him; I quietly turned around to leave.

'You dare turn your back on me,' he said. 'Come back right now.'

I didn't pay any attention and kept walking towards the exit. He came charging towards me, pulled my hair from behind and dug his teeth into my neck. I screamed in pain and tried to free myself. He pinned me to the ground. I dug my nails into his face and scratched as hard as I could.

'Arghhhhh...fucking bitch,' he shouted as three red marks appeared below his left eye.

I ran from the stage, jumped a few stairs so I could get away from him. I had no control on the landing. My right ankle twisted and I crashed to the floor, hitting my head against the chair in front.

There was a throbbing pain in my ankle. I was in tears. My head was going to burst. I was disoriented. He was bleeding from his left eye. I hid under the chairs, waiting for an opportunity to dash towards the exit.

'You think you are a great dancer? I have trained a thousand better than you. The only reason I showed any interest in you is because you are an *outsider*. You are the goose that will lay golden eggs. Now come out before I lose my temper,' he shouted out of anger and pain. I was afraid he was going to kill me or do something even worse.

'You are not the first to kneel before me and you won't be the last. You hear me?'

He was too close. I had to move now. When I got up and dashed towards the exit, I felt excruciating pain in my right ankle. I lost my balance. I could barely hop on one leg. He saw me and turned around. I had to reach the exit door at any cost. This was my only chance.

The exit was two steps away; I was almost there. I could shout for help, someone would surely hear me. I put my hand on the doorknob and was about to shout for help when he grabbed me by my neck and dragged me back to the stage.

III

12

The Ankle Bells Fall

Guru Chandrashekhar

I wasn't invited to Ayla's arangetram. The man who taught her the fundamentals of dance wasn't extended an invitation, not even out of courtesy. But I still went.

Why?

I couldn't help myself.

She had grown up in front of my eyes. How could I miss one of the most important performances of her life? I worked hard to make her dreams come true and they took her away from me. This was not a moment to feel bitter, I had to remind myself.

I sneaked inside the auditorium from the back entrance. I didn't want to be recognised. What good would that do?

It had only been one-and-a-half years since we parted ways. I wondered if she had even completed a margam, the framework to approach Bharatanatyam recital, under Ranmohan. I suspect he was looking for a quick buck as usual. Men like him made me cynical about the world.

Out of all the amazing auditoriums available in the

capital, he chose Antralaya. The lighting was terrible and the sound quality was poor. Why would anyone in their sane mind perform here?

~

The stairway leading up to the hall was decorated with flowers and rangoli. At the reception desk, three girls welcomed the spectators with a bright smile and put tikas on their foreheads.

The photographer stood on the other side of the welcome area and took candid pictures of the guests entering the auditorium.

'Move out of the way,' he said to a group of giggling girls as they blocked his vision. They continued to giggle and disappeared.

The hall was packed with at least two hundred spectators. Dancers, teachers, journalists, celebrities and many connoisseurs graced the occasion. They greeted each other with warmth and ease. Words, praises, and glances were exchanged freely.

Women wore bright sarees and smiled at one another with familiarity. Their sparkling jewels drew much attention and they revelled in their finery. I sat in one dark corner of the hall, trying to hide myself from the roving eyes. I always preferred being in the shadows, but Ayla threw me into darkness.

Many guests, especially the male ones, looked puzzled and indifferent. Their disinterest could be gauged from their bored expressions and yawns. There were a few notable exceptions who wore crisp silk kurtas and mingled with the crowd. This lot knew even less about dance for all their artistic pretension.

I only cared about the children in the room. The real

excitement and energy came from young boys and girls. They spoke about dance with visible delight on their faces. The future of Bharatanatyam was in their hands.

The chair in which I sat creaked when I tried to recline. A few heads turned in my direction. I quickly looked down and covered my face, but a few people recognised me.

Before they could confirm their suspicions, the curtain rose on the stage. Everyone's gaze shifted towards the stage.

~

The stage looked hideous in all its extravagance. Two massive Roman pillars at the forefront were crowned by dancing Ganeshas. To add to the overall obnoxiousness, there was a grand chandelier dangling from top—unnecessary and surely a huge financial investment.

This was a classic case of misplaced priorities. Ayla and Ranmohan had made great efforts to amaze the audience with grandeur. What they didn't understand was that if the performance wasn't topnotch, these embellishments would not help the cause one bit.

'Good evening, ladies and gentlemen. We have gathered here for the arangetram of Ayla Erol, an extremely talented student of Dronacharya Awardee Ranmohan Roy. I request Ranmohan ji to come on the stage and say a few words.'

He was on the stage even before his name was announced.

'Good evening. I take great pleasure in welcoming you all. The chief guest for tonight's performance is my former student and famous actor, Henna Mukherjee.

'I would also like to give a special vote of thanks to the guest of honour, the Turkish ambassador, His Excellency

Mr Berk Koru. I request His Excellency and Henna ji to come on the stage and light the ceremonial lamp.'

The moment Henna got up from her chair, all eyes shifted towards her. No one cared about the Turkish ambassador anymore. Ten or fifteen photographers came to the front and started clicking her. She obliged with a smile and then moved forward to seek Ranmohan's blessings.

Attired in a green Kanjivaram silk saree, teamed with matching emerald earrings, she bent to touch his feet when Ranmohan held her by her shoulders and gave his blessings. They laughed in unison like they were sharing a private joke. The whole scene seemed rehearsed and fake. The hall, however, resounded with applause.

~

Soon, the stage was vacated for the dancer. Music began to play and the audience went silent. She walked gingerly onto the stage, tapping her feet on the ground. I had taught her this move. It helped get the blood flowing in the legs. At least she remembered something.

She was bright and vivacious in the spotlight. Ayla looked tall, strong and in command just as I remembered her.

'Smile a little more, Ayla. You mustn't forget to smile,' I whispered as if she could hear me. With a pang of hurt, I realised she no longer took instructions from me.

She had a deadpan expression on her face which was very unusual. In ten years, I don't remember any performance of hers where she didn't light up the stage with her infectious smile. *Was she nervous*, I thought.

She walked to the centre of the stage, greeted the audience

with a namaskaram and moved towards the orchestra. She folded her hands once again and greeted each musician with a bow.

Standing straight in front of Ranmohan and after a moment's hesitation, she prostrated herself—bent on her knees and touched his feet with both her hands, like he was God. The hall resounded with another thunderous applause at the humility of the student and the greatness of her Guru.

'This is ridiculous!' I said, in utter disgust.

I understood the need to acknowledge the effort of the musicians, but this gesture of absolute surrender wasn't required. It only inflated Ranmohan's ego. He needed everyone to know that he was the creator of this performance. He couldn't let the spotlight shift towards Ayla so easily.

~

'Ayla will begin the performance with Pushpanjali—the offering of flowers to God,' said the announcer.

She came to the stage carrying flowers. Her hands were outstretched with rose and orchid petals placed carefully between her palms. As she moved to the centre of the stage, she began with some basic foot movements. This was tricky business as she had flower petals in her hands. She had to tap her feet but not with vehemence lest the petals dropped. These were an offering to God; not to be spilled carelessly on the floor.

Soon, she sat in muzhu mandi (full-squat) pose and gently placed the flowers on the floor. After paying her obeisance to the dance floor, Ayla began.

'The next act is the Nataraja Kautvam. These are hymns

in praise of Nataraja—Lord of Dance,' the announcer proclaimed.

With the first note of the flute, a flicker of light filled the stage. Ayla's silhouette became visible. She stood firm like a rock in the half-squat position. Her hands pointed downwards, resting on her knees. The pleats of her saree unfurled like a peacock dancing in the rain. It was a mesmerising sight.

Dark red beams seamlessly changed to yellow rays. Ayla looked strong and confident. She held still for almost half a minute. Then she arose and struck a dynamic pose. This time, she was standing on one leg, the other foot mid-air, on the side, reaching her torso. What a beautiful display of physical strength and balance!

The drive and aggression in her movements were unmistakable. I had never witnessed that zeal in her dance before. As the performance progressed, it began to veer towards recklessness. It had all her energy but none of her grace. Her mind was someplace else and the body was doing its bidding without thought or care.

I can't explain but Ayla's performance made me deeply uncomfortable. Even the audience appeared not too at ease, a sombre mood engulfed the auditorium. I had never seen a performance where the dancer refused to smile. Ayla's dance conveyed a strong sense of defiance, not devotion.

Her footwork was deft. She was hardly concerned about the music and the rhythm. In fact, Ranmohan had to increase the tempo in order to keep pace, she was clearly racing ahead.

It could only mean one thing—she didn't care about complementing her steps with the Guru's instructions.

But how could she not care? She wanted to be on stage so desperately that she even left Pratishtha. This wasn't the girl I knew; this wasnot what I had taught her. There was no balance in her dance.

A Bharatanatyam dancer always faces the audience. Her expression, movements and smile are reserved for them. However, what people don't realise is the dancer's focus is somewhere else, she lends her ears only to the Guru. He controls the tempo of the show through his nattuvangam (cymbals). The feet hit the ground to the sound of the instrument in the Guru's hand. They stop when the Guru wants. But Ayla was neither listening to the Guru nor responding to the audience. There was a quick break followed by the Varnam. In addition to her outfit, she wrapped a loincloth around her waist for the next sequence. It was most unusual even for an unusual performance like this.

She began with deft neck movements. She then jumped from one side to another. Her biggest test was underway. Hands, legs and expressions came together to showcase the story of Narasimha—half-man, half-lion avatar of Lord Vishnu.

The Rig Veda contains an epithet attributed to Narasimha. The half-man, half-lion avatāra is described as: *Like some wild beast, dread, prowling, mountain-roaming. With waters' foam you tore off, Indra, the head of Namuci, subduing all contending hosts.*

This reference is believed to have culminated in the Puranic story, with Lord Vishnu—as Lord Narasimha— slaying the demon king Hiranyakashipu at the behest of his son, Prahlāda.

Ayla expressed this powerful story through her movements and expressions. She walked towards the edge of the stage where coloured sand was placed. Instead of stopping close to the rangoli, she stepped on it. Was it a mockery of the arangetram? Such crass representations had nothing to do with Bharatanatyam. It was flashy and unsophisticated. I looked around and was surprised that the audience didn't react adversely.

Her dance had by now picked up tremendous pace and her footwork was geometrical. She was trying to create something unusual, something incredible and quite impossible. She was going to draw the sketch of a lion's silhouette using only her feet. The loincloth covering her waist was symbolic.

It was excessive but I must confess, it was courageous. To dance well was difficult enough, but to sketch a silhouette was ambitious.

Her feet were now a painter's brush, and the floor was the canvas. So began her masterpiece. She started with straight movements and then retreated. She now came back to the rangoli beneath her feet and this time, she moved in semi-circles. That was the eye of the predator.

Lights dimmed, the beats became faster. Ayla was in a trance; her movements were now bold and the display-screen behind her zoomed in on the rangoli. Cameras were fitted to the chandelier which made it easier for the audience to witness the making of a creation. On the screen, the silhouette of the half-lion was clearly visible. She had immaculately drawn the eyes with every bend and twist of her feet.

The masterpiece was nearing completion. A few more strokes and the Varnam act would be a resounding success. There were collective gasps from the audience.

I sensed a hint of discomfort as she landed on her right ankle after a jump. She lost her balance. She tried to recover but she was clearly struggling with every step she took. There were murmurs and sighs in the audience.

It was in the middle of a turn that she lost her balance and fell on the floor. The pain and shock were visible on her face. A few people from the audience stood and uttered sympathetic words. Tears rolled down her mother's face. Her father climbed onto the stage to help her but Ayla managed to gather herself. She tried to continue her dance between sobs. Her father froze on the steps, unsure. The music played once again.

Moments later, she slipped and fell again. The music stopped. Everyone was too stunned to respond.

Halim lifted Ayla and took her backstage, away from the roving eyes, curious stares, clicking cameras and questions. Her mother followed, while others stood up and discussed the turn of events. The media went hysterical. Some members of the audience had already started clearing out.

The lion's sketch remained unfinished. In my twenty-five years of teaching and learning dance, I had never witnessed such a disaster. Ayla's ankle bells fell as her father carried her off stage.

I went to the stage and picked up the ankle bells. I didn't care anymore if people recognised me. She was in distress and I wanted to support her. I was about to enter the green room, but right outside, I heard Ranmohan and Ayla's father arguing.

'She is in tears and doesn't want to speak to anyone. We are taking her to the hospital. Come with us. She needs your support,' Halim beseeched.

'I can't. Henna still wants a press conference to talk about her upcoming movie. The press is eager for sound bites. Can't Ayla answer a few questions until the ambulance arrives?' Ranmohan said.

'What is the matter with you? My daughter is in pain. She needs help,' Halim said.

'The thing is, I promised Henna a press conference. Her agent insists on having one right now. Besides, I need to clear the payments to all the vendors. They are worried, they won't receive the money. Can you give me 50,000 rupees right now?'

'They will be paid to the last penny, but first, I must take my daughter to the hospital. Tell them to wait.'

'You are being very unprofessional.'

'It's ridiculous,' Halim roared. 'You don't care about my daughter. All you want is money,' he said, and threw a bundle of 500-rupee notes on Ranmohan's face. 'Take this and get out.'

Ranmohan went on his knees and picked up each and every note from the ground. I didn't have the heart to talk to her father after that. I never got a chance to return the ankle bells either. Halim carried his daughter to the ambulance and left the venue, while Ranmohan held a press conference with the chief guest. After a question or two about Ayla's health, the conversation turned to Henna's upcoming film, and her personal life. The press and the audience were joking now as if nothing had happened.

Some of the audience members murmured about Ayla's fall. One lady in the audience remarked, 'What do these outsiders understand about our culture and traditions. They should stick to their own. It is a shame.'

This was all that was left of the rich heritage of classical dance. A bunch of suave and educated people, with no respect or compassion. It was time for me to leave; I had seen enough.

When the ankle bells fall
India News Network, April 5

R.K. Srikanth

In rare dance recitals, the script goes so horribly wrong that there is no scope for redemption.

That is precisely what happened at the much-hyped arangetram of twenty-five-year-old Ayla Erol. The Turkish dancer dramatically collapsed on stage from a mix of exhaustion and nerves on Sunday. The spectacle left her Guru as well as the audience at the Antralaya auditorium in a complete tizzy.

Ayla was widely acclaimed for being the first refugee to have successfully imbibed the ways of Indian classical dance. The dance community embraced her with open arms. The 'who's who' of the dance world arrived to witness her performance. There were 200-plus spectators in attendance. Ayla was clearly unprepared for the show and the signs of exhaustion were visible from the beginning—that she was battling hormonal issues only added to the woes.

She tried her best to hide the flaws, and to some extent succeeded in the task, but eventually it proved to be too daunting for the young girl. The lack of sharpness in her movements was visible. It didn't help matters that she forgot her smile at home—another sign of her inexperience.

A visibly upset Ayla had to be carried off the stage by her father. There was an overwhelming sense of pity for the dancer.

Henna Mukherjee, acclaimed actor and chief guest of the evening, was charitable towards the young artiste. 'She is still raw and edgy. Let's not forget, she is an *outsider*. She will get better with hard work.'

Meanwhile, Iliyas Burman, a member of the audience and Bharatanatyam connoisseur, expressed his disappointment, 'I could clearly see the limp in her right foot. She was protecting her ankle from any pressure. There was no sense to schedule a performance if she was less than hundred per cent ready.'

It was a case of too much too soon for Ayla. However, one could not but feel sorry for Guru Ranmohan Roy who worked tirelessly to see his student's dream come true.

'Like all young dancers, she was in a hurry to have her arangetram,' he said, disappointment written on his face. 'In retrospect, I should have been less indulgent. It is a painful lesson for me as well.'

DISCLAIMER: *Views expressed above are the writer's own.*

It was an unforgiving verdict based on a single faulty performance. A personal attack of this kind was uncalled for. Her dedication, training and origin were all questioned by various news reports in the entertainment and city events section of *The Hindu, The Times of India, Hindustan Times, The Indian Express, The Asian Age,* and others.

13

Nightmare at Dawn

Ayla

The hospital staff put me in a wheelchair and ushered me to the emergency room. I was so cold; I had goosebumps. Bavo covered me with a blanket and the doctor arrived within a few minutes.

'What's your name?' a middle-aged gynaecologist asked.

'Ayla Erol.'

'What exactly happened?'

'I was in the middle of a dance performance when I felt a sharp pain in my stomach. I lost my balance and fell. I tried to resume but I couldn't. The pain was excruciating; I couldn't breathe properly. I got my period.'

'Was it due?'

'No.'

'I will give you an injection. You will feel better in a few minutes.'

'When did you get your last period?'

'Ummm...I don't remember the exact date.'

'Give me an idea?'

There was a lot of background noise. People were rushing in and out of the room. I couldn't think clearly.

'About two weeks ago.'

'Have you been exerting a lot?'

'I have been dancing extensively for this performance, but I have always danced.'

'Have you used any medicines lately, like birth control?'

I was embarrassed at the mention of birth control. Dayê was standing right next to me. She was taken aback. I looked at the doctor wondering what to say.

'No, I haven't taken any pills.'

'It is possibly the exhaustion and stress that led to this untimely cycle. You will feel much better with rest,' she said, and gave me an injection.

~

When I woke up the next morning, the nightmare began. My body felt heavy and my head hurt. My right ankle had swollen to the size of a football. I couldn't place it on the ground without feeling a sharp, shooting pain. My left nipple was bruised and had turned black. The shame and embarrassment of the past two days caused more pain than my injuries. I wanted to go back to sleep and never wake up.

'Gulum, are you awake?' Dayê said, and knocked at the door.

I quickly covered myself with a shawl to hide the scars.

'Yes, Dayê.'

She entered the room carrying food and medicines. Bavo followed her, and placed a glass of orange juice on the table.

She sat beside me and stroked my hair. Bavo avoided any eye contact.

'How do you know?' I asked Dayê.

'The gynaecologist told us, yesterday. She saw injury marks on your body.'

I broke down. All my strength and fortitude dissipated in an instant.

'Why didn't you tell us?' Dayê said.

'I...I...So much money and effort had gone into the performance. I didn't want to let you down.'

'Who did this?' Bavo asked. There was hatred in his eyes, the kind I had never seen before. It was the first time he had looked at me since the conversation began.

'Ranmohan. He threatened to kill me if I told anyone.'

'What! It can't be him,' Dayê said. 'I don't believe it.'

'You're not telling us the truth. Who are you trying to protect?' Bavo said.

'It was him. We met for rehearsals at Antralaya the night before the performance. He was drunk and attacked me. I couldn't do anything; I was completely helpless. When I returned home, I lied to you that I fell on the road. I wanted to tell you everything, but you were occupied wrapping presents for the Turkish ambassador. You were so thrilled that he had accepted the invitation. You asked me to give the performance of a lifetime. Dayê, how could I cancel the performance after that.'

Bavo listened to the whole incident with his back turned towards me; Dayê held my hand tightly. Tears trickled down her face when I showed her the bruises and marks.

Bavo paced the room. There was a rage building inside him. He went to the glass window and punched it. The glass was shattered into smithereens. A piece of glass injured his hand and blood oozed.

'He will pay for his deeds,' Bavo said, and picked up the same piece of broken glass. Dayê looked at me with fear in her eyes. She tried to calm him down. Pleaded with him to think things through, but he wasn't listening. He had lost all sense or reason. He was going to kill Ranmohan; I could see it in his eyes. He got into the car and left in a huff.

~

Three hours later, we found out where Bavo had been and what he had done. It changed our lives forever. I learnt the account of three eyewitnesses.

His car came to a screeching halt in front of Ranmohan's mansion. The guard was alarmed. He stood in front of the entrance to block Bavo's path.

'You can't go inside right now. Maalik is taking a class,' he said.

'Get out of my way,' Bavo said and took out the bloodstained piece of broken glass from his pocket. The guard retreated without further protests. When Bavo was a safe distance away, the guard dialled the police.

'How dare you touch my daughter with your filthy hands?' Bavo said and grabbed Ranmohan by his collar.

The music came to an eerie halt. The dancers froze. The whole room became silent and there was nervousness in the air. All eyes were fixed on Ranmohan.

'I don't know what you are talking about? Don't create a scene at my centre. I have a class going on. Come back later,' Ranmohan said, betraying fear and anxiety in his voice.

'You know exactly what I am talking about, you pervert. Did you think you would assault my daughter and get away with it? You bastard! I am going to finish you right here,' Halim roared.

Ranmohan was about to utter something, but the only sound that came out of his mouth was a painful howl. Bavo clenched his fist and went hard and straight at Ranmohan's face.

It only took one punch to break his nose. His green silk kurta was now bloodstained. The dancers screamed at the sight and ran hither-thither.

'You have lost your mind. I swear to God, I didn't...'

This only provoked Bavo further. He wasted no time and showed no mercy. He punched Ranmohan hard and attacked him in a frenzy. There was a pool of blood on the floor.

Ranmohan's left eye was dangerously bruised. He was blinded from one side and could barely defend himself. The indiscriminate punches and kicks left him writhing in pain. There was a big gash on his right cheek. His lips were cut open and Bavo was nowhere near finished—he was thirsty for more.

The father of one of the dancers tried to rein in Bavo, but he couldn't restrain him for long. Bavo pushed him back and the man stumbled on a stack of chairs, hurting his knee.

Ranmohan used the momentary distraction to escape Bavo's fury. He went crawling and tumbling under the chairs. Bavo followed the trail of blood and found him cowering behind his leather chair. He took out the shred of glass from his pocket.

Ranmohan stammered, 'I am sorry, I made a mistake. I was drunk. Please, just let me go. I will return all the money I took from you.'

Bavo kicked him hard in the gut. Ranmohan convulsed and let go of the leather chair. Bavo brought down the piece of glass in a flash. He was aiming for Ranmohan's eye, but Ranmohan ducked in time. The glass missed his left eye narrowly but it left a scar on his nose, going all the way to the side of his ear. Ranmohan's screams echoed. Moments later, he passed out from pain and fear. Bavo continued to kick his inert body.

A bunch of khaki-clad men rushed inside, brandishing lathis.

Five policemen grabbed Bavo and pulled him away from the defenceless Guru. Bavo elbowed one of them. That enraged them and they started to beat Bavo. Two policemen pounced on Bavo to overpower him, while the other two handcuffed him.

~

The phone rang.

'Hello.'

'Ayla, this is Bavo.'

'Where are you? We are so worried. Please come back home.'

'I can't.'

'Why not?'

'I am at the Safdarjung police station. Listen to me carefully, tell Dayê to speak to Sabina Zaidi and come here with my bail application.'

'What! But, why are you in a police station and who is Sabina Zaidi?'

'I am fine, Gulum. Ranmohan is in hospital. Trust me, he will not bother you again,' Bavo said with a cold sense of pride.

'You killed him,' I shrieked with horror.

'I just taught him a lesson he will remember all his life.'

'I can't talk right now. Ask Vahide to speak to Sabina. She is a lawyer, she will know what to do.'

~

Safdarjung police station was a dilapidated yellow building teeming with activity. We joined a long queue of complainants who awaited their turn near the entrance. A bespectacled policeman, sitting behind a desk, summarily dismissed people to different corners.

He was an old man with a wrinkled face and acne marks all over his cheeks and forehead. It was difficult to look at him without feeling repulsed. His expression and voice were devoid of any trace of warmth.

After an hour-long wait, we reached the front of the queue. Dayê was trying to explain our situation, but he cut her off mid-sentence.

'Wait for the station house officer to return,' he said.

'But my husband is in the lock-up. I am here for his release.'

'Madam, no one comes here for a picnic. Go, wait outside,' he commanded.

~

All sorts of terrible thoughts came to my mind about Bavo's condition. We got no information on when the SHO would return. Not a single person was willing to help us. Their rudeness bordered on condescension.

Thankfully, Sabina reached the station within twenty minutes. I had never seen her before, but Dayê recognised her at once. She was wearing a black coat, typical of lawyers, and her cheeks were dry and hollow like that of a gypsy woman. They looked even more prominent because of her short hair.

She walked with a sense of purpose and hurried steps. The resolve on her face was unmistakable and everyone avoided her gaze. Even policemen stayed out of her way.

She was not the least bit bothered by the heat or overwhelmed by the place. If anything, she looked at ease.

Sabina gave Dayê a sympathetic smile and assured her, 'Give me ten minutes. We will get Halim out of here.'

She walked straight past the entrance and jumped the long queue. Everyone observed her going inside, but no one dared to stop her. Dayê and I followed her like a shadow. Sabina was our only hope.

We were treated differently in Sabina's presence. Now, the policeman offered us a seat in the waiting lounge and a cup of tea. Five minutes later, we were directed to the chamber of the personal assistant to the SHO. Half of his table was covered with white-and-green files that had loose papers sticking out of them.

He ushered the three of us into the SHO's office ahead of the waiting queue.

'Sabina ji, please have a seat. What can I do for you?' Vijay Lal said, carefully placing his hat on the desk.

'Good afternoon, Inspector. I am here on behalf of Halim Erol. I am afraid your juniors made a mistake. They have incarcerated an innocent man.'

'He elbowed and pushed one of my constables. Poor fellow is getting bandaged outside. He told me a different story.'

'Halim Erol threatened to kill the dance teacher in full public view. He would have succeeded if my officers hadn't reached the studio. The doctors are worried the dance teacher's vision will be impaired. His right shoulder is dislocated. Does that sound like an innocent man to you?'

I smiled to myself. Ranmohan was in pain. He was suffering at this very moment. The thought gave me cold comfort. I was proud of Bavo's action.

'That monster assaulted my daughter,' Dayê intervened. 'Does that count for nothing?'

'If that is true, why haven't you registered a complaint against him, yet? Look, ma'am, I am not taking anyone's side here. But if people go killing each other over true or fabricated grievances, then our job becomes redundant,' the SHO said.

'My husband was protecting my family. Would you wait for an FIR had your daughter been raped?'

The SHO got up from his chair, enraged. 'If your daughter was having an affair with her teacher, it is none of my concern. Get out of my office.'

'Ranmohan was her teacher. He broke our trust,' Dayê screamed. She stood up as well, about to do something she would regret later.

Sabina intervened to calm frayed tempers.

'Please, Vahide,' she said, putting herself between the Inspector and Dayê. 'Inspector Vijay is a man of highest integrity and character. I have full faith in him. He will investigate this matter and find out the truth. Please go outside while I discuss the legalities with him.'

'Don't take this, personally. As you can see, she is very disturbed,' Sabina said.

'Sabina ji, what are you doing with these people?'

'I have been managing the legal work for Halim's shop for the past fifteen years. They are simple middle-class people. Please try to downplay this case. I will owe you one.'

The SHO took a deep breath. 'It's a serious matter. This Ranmohan guy is well connected.'

'Have you filled up the memo of arrest?' Sabina enquired.

'No, we haven't arrested him yet. We have only detained him. I will let him go because you have taken the trouble to come all the way. I will conduct a thorough investigation and file the charge sheet in the session court within sixty days. Ask him to surrender his passport, and not to leave the city until I say otherwise...'

'Is that really necessary? There is no threat of fleeing in their case. I can give a personal guarantee.'

'It is the standard procedure, Sabina ji. It is a sensitive matter; I am going by the book.'

'I understand.'

The Inspector pressed the bell and an attendant came to the room immediately.

'Ji, Saab,' he said.

'Release Halim Erol in Ward 37 and return all his belongings. Seize his passport and get a signed undertaking that he will not leave the country.'

~

Bavo's white kurta was soiled with dirt and blood. There was a deep cut on his upper lip, quite possibly the work of the police. However, the expression on his face was serene. The rage had disappeared. He hugged Dayê and me, and thanked Sabina for her timely help.

'Are you all right?' Dayê said.

'Yes. I have seen worse,' he replied.

'Let's go home, please?' I said.

'There is one thing left to do before you leave,' Sabina said.

'What?'

'File a rape case against Ranmohan.'

'These policemen arrested my husband and passed snide remarks against my daughter's character. Why should I trust them?' Dayê said.

'Because we don't have any other option. Ranmohan is in hospital. An FIR has been lodged. The police is going to investigate this matter. They will construe your silence as an admission of guilt. No one is going to take your story seriously if you remain silent now. That's not the position you want to be in, trust me,' Sabina explained.

We were in trouble either way. The consequences of Bavo's action began to dawn on me. Dayê, Sabina and I looked at Bavo for an answer.

'Sabina is right,' he said. 'Let's file the complaint.'

Sabina led us to the FIR counter. The officer on duty was the same man who had brushed us aside earlier that day.

'Sir,' he said, looking at Bavo, 'why report this silly mistake? You know how it is. Men get carried away, sometimes. When the investigation takes place, it is only your name that will get spoiled.'

Bavo stiffened at the response. Before he could reply, Sabina cut the policeman to size, 'Thank you for your advice, officer. Please write the report.'

'Madam, you are getting angry, pointlessly. These cases go on for years. I was just speaking for your benefit.'

~

One week later, the Saket Session Court summoned Bavo. Ranmohan had accused Bavo of attempt to murder.

Bavo was asked to report at the court on Tuesday.

Meanwhile, Ranmohan sought police protection, citing threat to his life.

The summon was a serious matter even though Bavo scoffed at it. Dayê fixed an appointment with Sabina that very day.

She was a shrewd lawyer, a no-nonsense woman who had made a name for herself based on sheer hard work and a thick skin. She took cases that no other lawyer would touch, and she won them too.

We reached her office just before lunch-time. Sabina sat on a brown cushioned chair, behind a polished wooden desk. There was not a hint of worry or tiredness on her face. Her table was vacant except for a silver nameplate with her name engraved on it. A framed copy of the Indian Constitution hung on the wall behind her.

The big shelf of law books behind her seat added weight to her words. It carried infinite wisdom and answers to many twisted problems. There was no right or wrong in law, even the truth was up for debate. She revelled in this grey area.

'Please, come in,' she said and stood up to greet us. 'Vahide, you were distressed on the phone. What's the matter?'

'I have been charged with an attempt to murder by the session court,' Bavo said, and handed the letter to Sabina.

She went through the letter carefully. 'You haven't been charged, you have been accused. There is a big difference.'

'How do we respond?' Dayê asked.

'Such summons are a dime a dozen. It is a desperate move by Ranmohan's lawyers. They want to rattle you.'

'So, I will have to appear in front of the court and justify my action,' Bavo asked.

'Yes. The objective behind this case is not to put you

behind bars, but bulldoze you into submission. It distracts the attention from the sexual assault case and projects Ranmohan as a victim and not a sex offender.'

'What do we do now?'

'I checked the medical reports shared by Gangaram Hospital. Ranmohan required an emergency eye surgery. His vision is impaired for life and that puts us in a soup. Many witnesses saw Halim attack the teacher with a sharp glass and threaten to kill him.

'In legal parlance, it is called Section 326 & 307, voluntarily causing grievous hurt leading to an attempt to murder. It is a very serious charge and comes with severe punishment. The injuries will hamper his professional career and personal life. Any judge would be sympathetic to his case,' Sabina explained.

'He deserved worse. I had every reason to beat him to death.'

'I am glad you beat the life out of him. Men like him deserve no less, but it complicates the matter. We want to tell the judge that this was the impulsive reaction of a dutiful father, not a vindictive parent whose daughter had a flawed dance show.'

'My daughter deserves justice.'

'I have no doubt we can prove him guilty. The truth will eventually prevail, but the journey is going to be rough and long.'

'How long?'

'We are looking at the very least five to seven years of continuous appearances in court; lawyer's fee and media scrutiny are separate. That would cost approximately 40-50 lakh rupees, if not more.'

'Seven years,' Halim said, astounded. 'You've got to be joking.'

'That's how it is. The case will pass through the lower courts; proceed to High Court and in all likelihood move to the Supreme Court. The punishment for rape is seven years in jail which may extend to lifetime imprisonment. That is our best-case scenario.'

'Can we keep Ayla away from this dirty business?' Halim said.

'I can't promise that,' she said. 'They may insinuate that she not only actively participated but initiated this affair. They might even say she led him on. Certain sections of the press will call her a foreigner with loose morals. He will use all his connections to make your life difficult. There is no getting around that.'

'How's that justice? My daughter's reputation will be sullied.'

'I know it is not what you want but letting that man off is worse. He raped your daughter, what will stop him from doing this to some other girl?'

'How can we counter these framed charges?' Halim asked.

'Controlling the narrative is the key to win this case. We will have to fight dirty in order to prevail.

'First, we amplify this case in front of the media. The more heat it generates, the more pressure there will be on public authorities to get to the root of the matter and conduct a fair investigation. Ayla will have to come out in the open and tell the world exactly what happened.

'Second, you have to give a press statement about how he tried to extract every penny out of you for the arangetram. Third, we look into his background. If this has happened now, it must have happened before. We need to search for more of his students and see if there are any victims willing to testify in front of a judge. If we can find another girl with a similar story, then we have him.

'If you are patient, we can make Ranmohan pay for his actions,' Sabina said.

'Will that be enough to heal her wounds?' Dayê intervened.

'It's a start.'

There was an uncomfortable silence in the room. The attention shifted towards me.

'You don't have to rush into a decision. Go home and think over it,' she advised.

~

Dayê and Bavo argued all through the drive back home. We had gone to Sabina in search of an answer. Instead, we came back with many more questions.

Bavo wanted to take Ranmohan on. Dayê, on the other hand, was worried about the cost and repercussions of going after Ranmohan.

I favoured Bavo's stand. My heart burned with vengeance and I wanted to see Ranmohan rot in prison for the rest of his life. At the same time, I was mortified about coming out in the open. Every time I recalled the assault, I felt I was going through the trauma all over again. Just telling my parents had been an ordeal; I couldn't even imagine what cross-examination by lawyers or media scrutiny would be like.

'When all of this is over; after all the negative publicity and sordid reporting, no one will want to marry her. And what will we do if they send you back to Turkey? We can't have that. I beg of you to let this go. You have already broken half his bones. Let's erase this incident from our memory once and for all,' Dayê said.

'Have you forgotten what happened to Bapîr when I left Mardin? Do you know how many bullets were found in his body? Seventeen.

'I still have nightmares about the day he was shot. I ran away from my problems once and it cost my father his life. I will not abandon my daughter.'

'We are not abandoning Gulum. But we need to abandon this case, for her sake. She will relive the horror a hundred times in the court. Ayla refuses to eat properly and just sits in her room, not saying a word. Every time she is stressed out, she gets panic attacks. I have seen her shiver from head to toe. She has recurring nightmares. It scares me. Do you want her to stay like this for the next seven years while this case drags on from court to court? You tell him, Ayla,' Dayê pleaded.

But, I stayed quiet and looked out of the car window. They had no idea what I was going through. No one did.

'Please, please swallow your anger; it is our duty to put Ayla first. Talk to Sabina and ask her to settle the matter anyhow.'

Bavo remained silent. When we reached home, he took the family portrait and threw it against the wall. 'I cannot let this go.'

'This court case will consume our lives, I know it. I feel it in my heart. My only plea is to insulate Ayla from it. The sooner Ayla can put this behind her, the better. Send her back to Turkey. She can start her life afresh,' Dayê said.

'I will pursue it in Ayla's absence. It doesn't matter whether it takes seven years or ten. We will fight for justice,' Bavo spoke with finality.

Once again, my destiny had been determined by a compromise.

14

Practice or Punishment?

Guru Chandrashekhar

I had high hopes from Drishti. She possessed the right blend of talent and persistence to achieve greatness. More importantly, she didn't crib about extra hours of dance practice. She was the only dancer at Pratishtha who had the potential to replace Ayla.

Ayla's departure was the perfect opportunity for her to make a mark. I focused all my energy on training her.

I even secured an invitation for Drishti to perform at the prestigious Khajuraho Dance Festival. Ayla often complained she didn't get a platform under my tutelage; Drishti wasn't going to suffer from a lack of opportunities.

It was one of the biggest and most renowned dance festivals in India held at the mesmerising Khajuraho Temple of Madhya Pradesh.

There was something mystical and other-worldly about full-moon nights at Khajuraho. The moon's glow added a sheen to the atmospherics when the dancers performed, and the music echoed across the temple's ancient walls.

I wanted Drishti to win over the dance world at this event. We had three weeks to come up with a spectacular choreography. We shut everything out and gave ourselves to dance. The practice went on for eight hours every day without fail. After a long time, I felt calm and happy. Ayla's name was buried deep in some dark corner of my mind.

~

'Come on, Drishti. You can do much better,' I said during the class. 'Unless you get this right, we can't move forward. Each and every part of your body has to be at your command. When you reach that level of control, you will perform wonders at Khajuraho. Let's try again.'

I don't know if she even heard me. She was busy wiping sweat from her face and catching her breath. It was a hot May afternoon, without a hint of breeze. She was sweating profusely.

The other students had taken a water break, but I had asked Drishti to continue until she got the steps right. It was important to fix this movement.

'I don't feel good. Can I take a water break?'

'Of course, you don't feel good, Drishti, and you won't until you have mastered this movement. No water breaks till you get the steps right. Focus.'

She tried again and repeated the same mistake. We had been practising for five hours straight and my patience was running thin.

'You are too slow off the block. Tap your feet on the floor faster. You need to shorten the duration of the movements to keep pace with the music. But remember, if you shorten it too much, it will take away from your dance. It's a fine balance. You must feel it.'

'Guruji, I need one sip of water, please.'

'Enough with that already,' I snapped. 'There is no water till you get this right. Ayla never once asked for a water break.'

I immediately regretted the reference. She went quiet. Her face revealed a sense of anger, before she cloaked it. A voice in my head said it was time to pause. I was going to allow her a water break after one more attempt.

Drishti turned left with the beat but didn't pause as expected. There was a frightening noise as her head hit the floor. I ran towards her. Her eyes were half open. She murmured.

'Drishti! Drishti, can you hear me?' I panicked. Her forehead was burning.

'Water. Water.'

'Hold on for a second.'

Another trainee passed a bottle of water to her. I sincerely hoped this accident wasn't serious. We had a performance in less than ten days. I couldn't afford her falling sick. She gulped down the water at one go.

We rushed to the hospital.

~

The nurse put an oxygen mask and put her on IV.

'How is she, doctor?' I asked.

'It's a case of acute dehydration. She will be all right in a few hours.'

'Then, why the oxygen mask?'

'She has difficulty breathing.'

'You shouldn't have pushed her so hard. She often comes home complaining of a headache,' her mother reprimanded.

'I have pushed her harder in practice many times before. She has never collapsed like this in the past.'

'Five hours of dance in this heat is too much. She should take complete rest for a week at least,' the doctor said.

'I am afraid that is not possible,' I said. 'She has a big performance coming up next week. She needs to train for that. Maybe, she can rest for two-three days and get back on her feet.'

'In my professional opinion, you should postpone the performance,' the doctor said.

I laughed at his pompous response. 'I can't shift the Khajuraho Festival because Drishti lost her footing. She is a professional. She will cope, she has to,' I insisted.

'Do as you must then,' the doctor replied and left.

'We should listen to the doctor. She is in no condition to dance right now,' Drishti's mother said.

'I understand your concern but there is no reason to overreact. A few precautions will do the trick,' I said.

'This is a once-in-a-lifetime opportunity for Drishti. She can't give it up at any cost. Don't take the doctor's words too seriously.'

'Look at my daughter. She is on a ventilator. What you do is not practice, it's punishment. There are things more important than dance.'

Like what? I thought to myself.

To my mind, dance took precedence over everything. It was the whole purpose of my existence.

~

Drishti didn't come for training for the rest of the week. Her cell phone went unanswered. I was angry at her mother. This was her doing. Two days before the dance festival, I called the organisers and told them Drishti would not be performing.

They were livid. The invitation cards had been printed, banners designed and the line-up announced. They would have to change the entire schedule to work around her absence. They were disappointed by her, but they were let down by me.

On Thursday, after ten days, I finally got a call from her. It was too late. I wouldn't speak to the organisers to reinstate her spot at the dance festival. However, I was prepared to take her back in the natyalaya if her apology was sincere.

'Namaste, Guruji.'

'Drishti,' I said with a mix of worry and anger, 'where the hell have you been? Do you know I had to cancel the performance? You should have at least taken my phone calls or replied to my texts.'

'Sorry, I wasn't able to respond earlier.'

'When are you coming to Pratishtha?'

'I won't be able to come to Pratishtha anymore.'

'What do you mean? Are you not keeping well?'

'My parents think I should leave Pratishtha. They say, it's too hot in the natyalaya without an air conditioner. They want me to train at Studio Anubhooti.'

'You can't be serious. Ranmohan is a crook. Did you not see what happened to Ayla? Drishti, you need to have faith in me. So what if I pushed you hard once? You won't become a great dancer without me.'

'This is not about Ayla. This is about me and what I want. And I don't want to be in Ayla's shadow anymore.'

'You know, that's not true. I have given you opportunities Ayla never had.'

'No. You have given me opportunities that Ayla should have had. I can't replace her. I don't even want to.'

'Fine. Go to Anubhooti. Ruin all the good work that we have done for the past six years,' I said and threw the phone against the wall.

I had no reason to return to Pratishtha anymore. I swore to myself that I would not return. I had failed my quest; I had failed my family. I had had enough of dance. Frankly, I was sick of it. It didn't make a difference one way or another.

15

Time to Go Home

Ayla

Dayê knocked on the door twice and entered the room. 'Dinner is getting cold. Join us at the table.'

'Not hungry,' Bavo replied.

'There is halva, at least taste it,' she said.

'I don't even like halva, just let me be. How many times do I have to tell you, I am not hungry?' Bavo snapped.

Dayê just kept looking at him as he shut the bedroom door on her face. His outbursts had increased over time, but none was as rude and direct as this. He took offence at anything and erupted frequently. It broke Dayê's heart.

All the joy that she had derived from preparing the halva disappeared. There was helplessness in her eyes as she returned to join me at the table with a forced smile. She sat passively without taking a single bite of the food.

After a few moments, she got up from the dining table and went to the kitchen, stifling her sobs. I thought of going up to comfort her, but no sympathetic words came to my mind. My presence would only aggravate her pain, so I walked back to my room in despair. All three of us had withdrawn into our own shells. We had closed our eyes and ears to each other's suffering.

~

Three months passed, and Bavo was still in an exasperated state of mind. He spent most of his time with lawyers and at the shop. Sometimes, he preferred to spend the night at the shop, ignoring Dayê's repeated pleas to return. I had never seen him act so aloof and irate before.

Bavo's carpet business had taken a hit. The new budget imposed an additional two per cent tax on all imports. Moreover, the customs officials demanded exorbitant bribes to clear the orders.

Even when he was home, Bavo remained silent, and almost invisible. He locked himself in his room and listened to ghazals.

He couldn't let the incident go; none of us could. It cast a dark shadow on our lives. No amount of halva that Dayê cooked or words she used helped change that.

All communication channels broke down in my family. We were three desolate individuals living under the same roof. Only Dayê spoke to me, sometimes, and even those conversations seemed forced.

'I should never have listened to that vile fortune-teller. He is the reason behind our suffering,' she said disconsolately.

Bavo squarely blamed himself for not being able to protect me.

The fault was entirely mine. I was cursed. It was my presence that brought misfortune to my family.

There were so many things I could have done differently, but I always chose the worst option. I could have gone to

Turkey for higher education, but I was too stubborn. Had I taken the autorickshaw back to Pratishtha, instead of Anubhooti that day, things would have been different. Fate had urged me to return to Pratishtha and I had overruled it.

~

'Bavo?' I said, and pushed open the door to his bedroom. He was resting with his eyes shut.

'I have a headache, Gulum. We will talk at breakfast tomorrow.'

'Okay,' I said.

I knew I wouldn't see him in the morning. He would leave home before I woke up.

'Wait a second,' he said, changing his mind. 'Come and sit here. Are you all right?'

'Please don't abandon me. I am sorry for not listening to you earlier. From now on, I will do everything exactly as you say,' I said.

'I am not angry at all and I will never abandon you. How can I? You are my only child.' He hugged me and patted my back.

'But you never speak to me. You don't even talk to Dayê.'

'I have been fighting many battles, and sometimes, they get the better of me. I don't want to bog you down with my troubles. That is why I keep to myself. I dread the mornings because I am afraid the obstacles will prove too much. I am just tired.'

'I am sorry you have to go through so much for my sake. Is there anything I can do to make things better?'

'There is indeed something I want from you.'

'I will do anything, Bavo. Just name it.'

'I want you to return to Mardin. A friend of mine knows the Dean of Mardin Artuklu University. He has assured you a seat at the College of Law. He will also help you with your visa. The Turkish State is looking to become a part of the European Union. They are taking several political reforms including greater civic rights for minorities. It is an opportunity to get out of here and start a new life. It is time for you to go home.'

Bavo said this in the most casual way, but I could sense the plea in his voice. He wanted, more than anything, that I leave Delhi behind me. He wanted me to give up dance.

For one brief moment, I hated him for asking me to leave, but I also knew I had no other option. I couldn't deny his wish.

'What about dance?' I asked.

'Your dance days are over. There is no going back to Bharatanatyam.'

'Mardin is our home. I want you to go there and put all your effort in studying law. You can make our voice heard at international forums, so the dream of Kurdistan can finally come true. I hope to see you become a great lawyer and, one day, the first woman judge of Kurdistan.'

'I promise to make your wish come true.'

'I knew you wouldn't let me down,' he said and kissed my forehead.

I was about to leave his room when I turned and said, 'When does the session begin?'

'In two weeks' time.'

~

Amca, my uncle Mustafa Boran, *Teyzi,* Aunt Saglam and their twenty-year-old daughter, Irina, were settled in Mardin. They offered to let me stay in their house. Bavo readily agreed. When he told Dayê about the arrangement, many of her fears about sending me away were assuaged. She did not hesitate to give her consent.

Perhaps, it was for the best. I would be far away from the world of dance and its sordidness. Mardin would give me the peace I never found in Delhi.

Before I knew it, Bavo was driving me to the Indira Gandhi International Airport. It was a cold and gloomy November night. The streets were deserted. Even the moon was sulking behind a cover of dark grey clouds. I had a sense of foreboding—I was going away, forever. I would never see India again.

~

A young couple walked hand-in-hand towards the boarding gate at the Ataturk airport in Istanbul. Love blossomed on their faces like white lilies in spring. They couldn't stop smiling. The woman's cheeks, she must have been in her early twenties, were full of colour. I put my hand on my face, it was dry and withered.

We fall in love with people who share our beliefs and values. We look at them and our heart leaps with joy. Their presence brings a smile on our faces, their words bring warmth to our souls. They are, for the lack of a better word, special. No one had ever made me feel that way.

I wasn't even sure if I craved that feeling anymore. I couldn't take men at their word. Their presence caused discomfiture.

~

Mustafa, Saglam and their daughter Irina were waiting to welcome me at the airport. Looking at the three of them together, I felt a pang of jealousy.

Teyzi Saglam was a real beauty. She had a fair complexion and cheeks as red as a rose. Her wide smile accentuated her features. The rich colours of her clothes were striking. She wore a beautiful yellow Kurdish gown which had flower motifs all over. Visible underneath them were layers of more colours—magenta, brown and red. There was no attempt to coordinate or match them, only a yellow belt around her waist kept them in order. Her head was covered with a long scarf.

The vivacious colours of Kurdish attire struck me after so many years of being away from this community. Dayê didn't wear it in Delhi because people mocked her, but Aunt Saglam had no such compunctions in Mardin. It made me realise I was away from home and yet I was home. It was confusing, but it didn't matter anymore. I was here to stay.

'The last time I saw you, you could barely stand on your feet. Every time you fell, you created such a ruckus that Vahide and I would have to sing for an hour,' she said, and held me in a warm embrace.

'*Merheba*,' I greeted Uncle.

'*Merheba*. How was your journey, Ayla?'

'Comfortable. I slept through the flight,' I replied.

'Hi, Ayla,' Irina greeted me with a smile. I replied courteously and shook her hand. She was two years younger to me and thin as a stick. She had long, black hair that reached till her waist and her kohled eyes were beautiful. She was twenty-three years old but looked no older than a teenager. We were going to the same university together.

Uncle Mustafa wore a short black-coloured vest teamed with a long cream-coloured shirt. I caught a glimpse of his infamous red skull cap visible beneath a small turban. Dayê had told me many stories about how young women in Istanbul were besotted with his skull cap and beard. Back in the day, his smile and the dimple on his left cheek caused many young women to go weak in their knees.

Young Kurdish men grew a beard and moustache as a proof of their manhood and Uncle Boran had the thickest beard in the city. He was particularly picky about his scarves and wore different colours every day.

His reputation as a womaniser caused many elders in the community to disregard him as a worthy suitor for their daughters. The long list of women admirers depleted over time. He found himself single at the age of thirty-five.

He saw my aunt at one of the famous bazaars of Istanbul. It took him one glance to fall in love with her. It didn't matter that she was ten years younger than him. When he asked her name, she ran away without looking back. He followed her all the way to her house and didn't leave until she agreed to see him again. Six days later, they got married.

~

I was almost knocked down by a strong gust of wind. Snowflakes were swirling and dancing out of the sky. The city was enveloped in white mist.

My aunt mentioned that this was the coldest winter in a decade. The sky was dark with no sign of the sun. People wore multiple layers of woollens and preferred staying indoors. There was a forecast of a blizzard. I suddenly felt tired and weighed down. I wanted a cup of hot tea and a warm bed, but I had to make a stop on the way.

Irina's house was an hour's drive from the airport. I kept looking out of the car window, soaking in the sights of this strange new city that had once been my home. It was very different from Delhi. There were no marble or glass buildings. Everything was made of yellow stone, even the modern cafés and hotels.

There was construction work going on everywhere.

'What are they building?' I asked Amca.

'The Governor, Turhan Avyaz, wants to return Mardin to its historical roots. They have refurbished 760 original buildings by tearing down the concrete ones—returned each structure to its beginnings.'

'When the project is completed by 2015,' he said, 'all the power and phone lines will be placed underground and the city will make it to the exclusive list of UNESCO World Heritage sites. It will be a promising new venture ensuring more tourism and a thriving economy.'

'I don't think so,' Teyzi said. 'First, they decided to modernise the city and dug up half the places. Then it occurred to them that the traditional look would bring in the revenue from tourists, so they destroyed the newly constructed structures. Mardin is neither traditional nor modern. It is just broken and noisy.'

After a bumpy drive, we reached the Old City. Everything was the colour of yellow—sand, walls, houses and even the hills. The yellow sand influenced everything and everyone without exception. The streets were narrow. Amca's deft driving skills ensured the car negotiated the tight corners.

I looked out of the car window in search of one special and familiar monument: the Great Mosque of Mardin—Ulu Camii. It was part of my family's DNA and no matter how far we were, our connection to the mosque was intact. Dayê had instructed me to first pay my respects at the mosque before going anywhere else.

'Can we stop by to pray at the Great Mosque for a few minutes, Amca?' I requested.

'Don't you want to freshen up first?' he asked.

'Umm. I would like to go to the Great Mosque first, if it is all right.'

'No problem,' he said, and took the left turn towards the mosque.

I was awed by the first glimpse of the façade. The minaret soared high above the city almost touching the clouds. A flock of birds rested on its tip. Next to the minaret was a beautiful ribbed dome. All of Mardin and the vast expanse of mountains and fields were visible from this mosque.

Everything was the same as before. The grand stone entrance with intricate carvings looked stunning. I took off my slippers at the entrance and covered my head in reverence.

It was as plush from inside as it was rustic on the outside. The floor was covered in a green and red rug. Chandeliers hung from the mosque's high ceiling.

The quaint ambience comforted me. I climbed the stairs and walked towards the base of the minaret. The Mesopotamian plains opened up in front of me. Strong winds blew, but they didn't bother me now. The walls of the mosque acted as a shield.

I could almost hear the echo of Bapîr's voice. The minaret

reached out to the stars; I had to strain my neck all the way up to see its tip. Amca reminded me of its history.

'Many people have forgotten that there were originally two minarets, but one collapsed many centuries ago.'

'You will be happy here, Ayla,' Teyzi said. She continued, 'There is a mystic air about this city. It is blessed by Allah.'

~

The Boran's house was located in the Babussor District. It was an exquisite limestone building, a hallmark of this region. I knew they were well off but this place was no less than a medieval castle. Our house in Delhi paled in comparison to its beauty and splendour.

The whole structure was designed around an inner courtyard—a blend of modern embellishments on Arcadian architecture. Every part of the house was polished and shinning. It was tastefully designed and kept in immaculate condition by Teyzi.

The entrance to the house was through a grey door made of stone. It looked more ancient than the house. There were scratches, carvings and gashes on the entrance door. It seemed like the door had been through a lot of struggles, but it stood firm and silent.

'We thought you would like the view,' Teyzi said, as she ushered me to my room on the second floor.

There were two sets of windows. The smaller rectangular one had a wooden slab attached to it and a chair kept behind. It was a perfect study with a gorgeous view. Meanwhile, the other square-shaped window was much bigger. The whole city and the plains beyond were visible from my room.

Darkness had engulfed the city and quieted down the chatter. The golden yellow lights radiated a wondrous glow. I sat staring at the moon from my room's window. The dark clouds covered its glow, but not for too long. Every few minutes, the moon emerged brighter from their shadow.

At one level, it was a relief to leave Delhi and its dark memories behind. Maybe, I could start a new life here.

~

After a wholesome dinner comprising kebabs, and a spicy gazpacho-like tomato soup, I went to bed and instantly fell asleep from exhaustion. I woke up drenched in sweat. His hands were all over me, I was screaming for help.

'What happened?' Teyzi said.

'Nothing. Just a bad dream,' I replied.

'Take it easy today. I will make an omelette for you.'

'Thank you, Teyzi. Can I help you?'

'I will manage. If you like, you can join Irina and me for grocery shopping after breakfast.'

'Sure.'

We walked across two blocks to buy meat, spices and vegetables. A tall woman passed us by holding her baby in one hand. The baby girl had round cheeks and big eyes. She turned her head from left to right refusing to miss anything on the way.

The mother used her free hand to cover her head with a dupatta, conscious of the young men who were eyeing her.

A noisy bunch of young boys were playing football on the street. The ball rolled down to the feet of a young girl standing behind the makeshift goal post.

'Pass.'

'Pass.'

'Pass.'

They shouted all at once.

She was so flustered by the badgering that she hit it in the opposite direction. The ball rolled down the stairway and the boys went chasing after it.

One donkey and a herd of goats stood in a corner of the street, eating grass. They were the only spectators of the football game. The goats made a sound every now and then, perhaps to encourage the boys or maybe they just wanted more food.

Old men sat on stools and played chess to pass time. Rounds of tea and hookah followed. They were in no rush.

Churches and mosques stood face to face but not in the confrontational manner of rivals. They looked peaceful and secure in each other's presence. People wearing skull caps greeted those adorned with a cross, with a smile and a warm embrace. The tension and violence that had forced my parents to leave Mardin was nowhere to be seen.

How so many people lived together in such a small and uneven space was a miracle. There were ancient-looking doors and old walkways everywhere. The streets were so narrow that I could hear the arguments between people in their homes, and the blaring music and news from television sets was audible.

'What about privacy?' I asked Teyzi.

'There are no secrets in Mardin,' she said with a laugh. 'Everyone here knows everything.'

~

'How do you like Mardin?' Irina asked.

'It is cold,' I said, and we both laughed.

'You don't have to be polite with me.'

'I am sorry; I have too much on my mind. I am just tired.'

'I have a cure for that.'

'What?'

'Have you had a Turkish hamam before?'

'I have heard about it, but never tried one.'

'Then that's where we are going first.'

'Shouldn't we take Teyzi's permission?'

She gave a mischievous laugh, 'Dayê doesn't need to know everything. Don't you keep secrets from your mother?' My face went red. I did have a dark secret. I was hiding it from Irina and her family. Dayê forbade me from saying anything. It would have changed the way they looked at me or treated me. I didn't want to be judged. This was my secret, my burden for the rest of my life. I was terribly afraid that people would discover it. The thought of it gave me goosebumps. Before I could speak, Irina had turned in the direction of the Turkish hamam.

'You don't know the joys of bathing until you have experienced a bath here,' Irina said.

The site of the bath, Emir Hamam, dated back to 1290 CE. We were asked to deposit our clothes and belongings at the entrance. I wrapped myself in a pink towel wondering how this was going to turn out.

An attendant led us to a marble steam-room. The hall looked regal, adorned by marble walls and pillars with intricate designs. There was an elevated stone platform (*goebektas*) at the centre of the room where women lay resting.

It was surrounded by bathing alcoves with basins around to wash with cold water.

Some of them were getting a massage or were being scrubbed by young men.

'Irina, I don't want any man touching me,' I said.

'What are you saying? I prefer the rough hands of a man,' she said with a smirk. 'Firoz is a wonderful masseur. You will enjoy him more than the massage.'

Irina was oblivious to the panic and discomfort her words caused me.

'I have changed my mind. I will wait outside.'

'Wait. Wait. I am just joking. I will request for a lady masseuse for you.'

I took a deep breath.

'Lie down on the marble slab for ten minutes. It helps open the pores of the body,' Irina instructed.

I poured water on my body and lay down on the slab. The other women were comfortable being half-naked around one other, including some boys. I was shy and embarrassed. Back in Delhi, the idea of communal baths and spas hadn't gained currency.

Ten minutes later, a well-built and dangerous-looking woman came towards me. Her assistant was carrying a bucket of hot water. I could even see the steam rising from it.

'Lie down on your stomach,' she said.

She soaked my body in warm water and began to scrub the life out of me. My skin turned red like a tomato. She scrubbed me from head to toe like she had some personal vendetta against me. She was wasting her time as a cleaner. She could easily have made a stonehearted killer with those massive hands and ruthless strokes.

The harder she scrubbed, the more she smiled. I was about to scream when she, almost intuitively, eased the pressure. Meanwhile, there were layers of dead skin piling on the floor.

After half an hour, she finally relented. Irina was in another room, probably getting a more delicate massage from Firoz. Maybe, he wasn't such a bad idea.

The lady returned with a sponge, dipped it in the bucket, and squeezed all the lather on my back and legs. Soon, my entire body was covered and then she gave a much gentler massage. I was in heaven for the next forty minutes. I joined Irina in the relaxation room where a different set of women prepared aromatic oils to give us an oil massage.

The masseuse circled her hands around my neck and shoulder, and massaged them. My bones made clicking sounds. All the knots and soreness were dissipating, one stroke at a time.

'How was Firoz?' I asked Irina.

'He was busy with another client. His loss, not mine,' she said, dismissively.

~

Mardin is a quaint town. How else does one describe a city that swears by its donkeys—the most bizarre thing about this bizarre city.

Donkeys' braying disturbed my sleep every morning. The noise was unbearable. I would wake up at 5 am, get out of bed and look out of the window.

Twenty donkeys loaded with jute sacks, marched across the neighbourhood every morning. Men leading the herd collected the waste and put them into these sacks.

'Why not use dust-carts or trucks or something else for garbage collection?' I asked Teyzi during breakfast, one morning.

She looked at Amca with a confused expression. Irina covered her face with her hands. 'She is not from here. She doesn't know,' Irina said in my defence. I wondered if I had said anything wrong.

'What do you have against donkeys?' Teyzi asked.

'People here are more attached to their donkeys than their children,' Irina said, passing me a cheese toast.

'Our streets are narrow and congested. Trucks wouldn't be a viable option to collect garbage. It wasn't impossible for humans to get much garbage collection done either. Waste remained uncollected for weeks and months leaving a foul stench in the city. The streets became a breeding ground for mosquitoes. There was an alarming spread of malaria and dengue,' Amca said.

'Omer Aydin, a local farmer, came up with a solution. He was tired of looking after his donkeys, so he volunteered them for garbage collection. Donkeys, it turned out, could carry heavy loads of up to fifty kilos. Unlike horses, they didn't require maintenance and were far more docile.

'Overnight, they became hot property. Omer became a millionaire within three years. His stock of donkeys grew from twenty-three to 800 in a short span of time. His family now owns the biggest donkey care centre in Mardin. Donkeys are a symbol of pride for the local community. There is a popular idiom in Mardin, 'Always send a donkey to do a man's work.'

16

In Search of Hope

Guru Chandrashekhar

I vowed to myself never to step inside the natyalaya again. Sudha could do whatever she wanted done with the place. I had had my share of ungrateful and selfish students for one lifetime. Every dancer reminded me of Ayla and Drishti, and their memory left me bitter and disappointed.

Months passed but I did not return to Pratishtha. I spent countless hours lying on the bed, staring at the roof, lost in the haze of the recent events—wondering how it all went so terribly wrong. No matter how hard I tried, no matter which way I analysed, I couldn't make sense of my present situation. I felt cheated. I blamed the dancers, parents and the city. Some days, there was no one to blame. Those were the hardest. They reminded me that I had lost.

I read innumerable books on all eight classical dance forms—Bharatanatyam, Kathak, Sattriya, Mohiniyattam, Odissi, Kuchipudi, Manipuri, and Kathakali. I read during the day and I read all night, cut off from the rest of the world.

When I finished the old set of books and that didn't take

too long, I ordered more and then I finished those as well. I spent one year reading anything and everything that came my way until I couldn't read anymore.

When I looked at my reflection in the mirror, I saw a man with a thick beard. There was no purpose in my life. I hated my appearance. Sleep didn't come easy. My savings eventually ran out. What now? I thought to myself. I stayed up many nights and watched random television shows. They were hopelessly boring and predictable. I still watched and criticised them. It made me feel sane. That the problem was with the world, not me.

~

My savings had dwindled to almost nothing. I didn't hear a single human voice for days on end. I was complete in my loneliness and it was biting into my spirit. I longed for answers or at least an explanation.

There was no reason to stay in Delhi anymore; I decided to take the train back home to Thanjavur. I looked out of the compartment window with a mix of pain and relief. The buildings faded away into farmlands. Time had passed me by; more than that, it had left me behind.

I wasn't different from the conquerors who had come here with grand ambitions. This city took them in for a moment of time and spat them out. They had to bend their knee to its will, just like me.

Amma was in the kitchen when I entered the house. She set the bowl of milk aside and came forward to hug me. Her gait was slow and she was limping, but there was a big smile on her face. It was nice to be welcomed for a change. It didn't take long for her to get teary-eyed. I hadn't felt such warmth and love in a while.

'Why didn't you tell me?'

'I wanted to surprise you.'

'I wish your father was here. He would have been so happy.'

I wasn't so sure about that. It was because of his pride that I hadn't come home. Anyhow, he was gone. There was no point ruminating.

I touched her feet, 'How are you?' I asked.

'Good.'

'Why are you walking with a limp?'

'I am fine; the knee gets sore early in the morning.'

Her hair had turned completely white and the wrinkles on her face were a grim reminder that time had passed. I felt a certain panic in my heart. She was the only real family I had left. I wished we could have turned back to when she was young.

'What brings you back, brother?' Vijay, my elder cousin, asked.

Father always thought of him as a son more than me. He took the reins of the dance centre from my father. There was a strong self-righteousness about him. Our differences and distance grew with age. We avoided each other the best we could, but now there was no way to avoid him. Mother had called him for dinner.

'I wanted to spend time with Amma.'

'Good of you to remember her occasionally. Will your dance school survive your absence?'

'I have left it with an able colleague and returned for good.'

I didn't want to tell him, but there was no point lying. Amma looked at me in surprise. I would have to tell her everything later.

'You were overreaching with the shift to Delhi. I had warned you earlier as well. You should have stayed here.'

'I am glad I left when I did. I wouldn't have had it any other way.'

'Why do you look down on Thanjavur? I am living here and I am doing fine for myself.'

'I don't look down on anyone. I found it suffocating here.'

'Yes, well, your father told me what a name you had made after the Habitat performance. He was upset for days. What a fine job you have done teaching that foreigner girl who fell on the dance floor during her arangetram.'

The last thing I wanted to discuss was Ayla. 'Her new teacher is a pathetic excuse for a human being. He didn't prepare her for the arangetram.'

'The media doesn't think so.'

'He has them in his pocket, but what would you know. You haven't stepped out of Thanjavur.'

'You think that makes you so much better. I was the one who carried your father's corpse to the pyre, because you were absent,' Vijay said.

Mother kept quiet throughout the conversation. I felt betrayed by her silence and I didn't want to spend another minute with him. I left for Delhi that very night. I realised something. Thanjavur wasn't my home anymore.

~

There were two bottles of Jim Beam in the kitchen. They were just lying there, unattended. The father of one of my trainees had presented these bottles to me after a successful dance performance.

I fell hook, line and sinker for their shine. Just as I had once fallen for the charms of a young woman. She had wrecked me. I should have learnt my lesson, but I am a fool.

I took one bottle out of the cupboard, admired its simple design and poured myself a drink, in her memory. The television blared nonsense and the bottle of whiskey was good company. She had left me long ago, but the memory of her soft voice and softer skin tormented me. I rarely remembered her, but those rare moments shared with her brought a lifetime worth of pleasure and pain.

I had never touched alcohol in my life, but tonight, I didn't feel the slightest inhibition in gulping down the poison. It set my throat burning. It was bitter and disgusting, but not as bitter and hopeless as my life had turned out.

I poured another glass to feel the same throbbing pain in my throat. I wished to ease my unsettled heart. I wanted to continue for as long as I could. I wanted to know how much alcohol I could consume before it consumed me. They said, it had the power to ruin people, but I was already ruined.

The second drink was slightly more bearable. I laughed at the bottle contemptuously. I had won. One shot after another followed. Two-thirds of the bottle was finished and my eyes were filled with tears.

A violent nausea started in the pit of my stomach. I puked everything out. The floor and the rug were covered with a disgusting, foul-smelling red-and-orange liquid. Blood came out along with the food I had eaten in the afternoon. My breath stank. I felt repulsed.

I dragged myself to the bathroom and was barely able to stand up to the level of the washbasin. I felt dizzy and light. The thought of Ayla, Drishti and Pratishtha didn't trouble me in the least. I smiled through my pain.

I tried to get water from the refrigerator. I tried to walk straight, but I couldn't keep my balance. My head spun and I collapsed.

I kept apologising to her. I promised never to misbehave. But my words were meaningless; she was already gone.

I had lost everything I cared about; I lost her and now I didn't care anymore. The bottle of whiskey was still by my side. It was waiting. That was all that mattered. I opened the second bottle of Jim Beam. Cash was worthless; alcohol was priceless.

I took a long swig from the bottle. A few minutes or may be a few hours passed. The alcohol in my body revolted in one instant. It had the last laugh.

~

When I opened my eyes, I wasn't at home. I didn't have any stains of vomit on my clothes. I was dressed in a perfectly starched kurta pyjama.

I was sitting on the steps of Brihadeshwara Temple in Thanjavur. I shut my eyes and opened them again.

I was not alone. Thousands of people were gathered there just like on the day of the anniversary celebration. They looked at me with expectation and hope. Their piercing gaze was unbearable. My father and mother emerged from the crowd.

They walked towards me. I lowered my gaze in shame only to discover that I was surrounded by bottles of whiskey and vodka. Father took a glass in his hand, poured a drink and offered it to me. I declined. He looked at my mother. She shook her head and went back into the crowd.

'Didn't I ask you to stay in Thanjavur?' he said. 'But you were stubborn. You should have listened to your old man.'

'I wanted to make a name for myself,' I said, timidly.

'Drinking your way to death is a fine example of that,' he said with a typical shrug of his head.

'Am I alive?'

'Only just.'

'I am done with Delhi,' I announced.

'But your work here is not finished yet,' he said. 'Find what you have been missing.'

Before I could say anything, he had disappeared along with the milling crowd at the temple. I was coughing my lungs out. Someone sprinkled water on my face. I woke up with a start.

I was lying on the floor of my house surrounded by dancers from Pratishtha. My throat hurt and my head spun. They looked at me as if I were dead. Sudha stood next to me with a bottle of water in her hand. She helped me get up and sit on a chair.

'Are you all right? Can you breathe?'

'I am...*ouch*...I am fine,' I said. My voice was hoarse.

I was trying to remember the conversation I had with my father a while ago. It felt so real.

'What are you doing here?'

'It is 4th April,' Sudha said.

'So?'

'It is your birthday,' she said. 'We knocked and rang the

doorbell repeatedly, but there was no response. One of the students peeped in through the window and saw you lying on the floor, choking in your vomit. You were mumbling something.'

'My God! But, how did you get in?'

'A student climbed through the kitchen window and unlocked the main door.'

~

I went to the bathroom and washed my face. My eyes were red. My hair had turned white and I had no idea today was my fifty-second birthday. I was a total mess.

I drank a glass of water, while Sudha made tea. She had opened the windows of the hall to get rid of the stench of alcohol. Meanwhile, the students unpacked my birthday cake. They sang me a birthday song, much to my embarrassment. Then they pounced on the chocolate cake.

'We just finished a dance session. They are hungry,' Sudha explained.

They made a whole lot of noise. I don't remember the last time I celebrated my birthday. I was embarrassed, uncomfortable, happy and emotional, all at the same time.

'Was this your idea?' I asked Sudha.

She pointed at the dancers and said, 'It was them all through. I just showed the way.'

That was a version of the incomplete truth. Sudha and I had known each other for almost three decades and this was only the second or third time she had visited my house.

'You seem lost,' she said.

'I had a strange dream. You know, one of those moments when you can't separate the dream from reality.'

Father's advice, *Find what you have been missing,* kept ringing in my ear.

'You have had too much to drink. We will leave you alone. Get some rest,' she advised.

'Please stay for a while,' I said, afraid to be alone. 'It is nice to have company for a change. I am sorry for leaving the dance school; it was unbecoming of me.'

'It's all right. It was a long time ago. I will forgive you if you return to Pratishtha.'

'How are things at Pratishtha?' I asked.

'Pratishtha is falling apart. Some students have left. Many more are on their way out. We need you.'

'I am sorry to hear that but I wasn't doing anything useful at Pratishtha. Drishti and Ayla are a case in point.'

'So what? Do we shut shop because two of our trainees couldn't cope with the pressure?'

'Is that you trying to make me feel better, Sudha?'

'I am not here to make you feel better. Stop seeing the world through the lens of defeat and desolation. For God's sake, Chandrashekhar!'

She didn't mince words.

'You remember how Ayla was when she came to Pratishtha. She couldn't even tie a saree without making a fool of herself. You took her under your wing, disciplined her, scolded her, and most of all, inspired her. You helped her become a great dancer. That's something to be proud of.'

It was difficult to breathe now. Tears prevented me from speaking. I gritted my teeth.

'My two best shishyas left without so much as a "thank you" note. What does that say about me? I have failed myself and my family.'

'Fifteen young dancers remembered your birthday and brought you a cake. No one forced them to make a card for you. Children don't fake love like adults. Their emotions are real. When you pass this judgement on your life's work, I want you to remember that.'

She continued, 'Before I came to Pratishtha, I taught in three different dance and music studios. I saw how teachers exploited dancers and their families. Parents were willing to give any amount of money to see their children succeed and the teachers took advantage of their vulnerability. I couldn't look ten-year-old girls in the eye and lie to them. That is why I joined Pratishtha.'

'We haven't compromised on our ways, even in the face of insurmountable adversities. How many dance studios can say that with honesty?'

'I don't know where to go from here.'

'There are many young dancers eager to learn Bharatanatyam. Let's teach them like we taught Ayla and Drishti. Give them the best chance at experiencing greatness. Let's fight the *good* fight. If you don't want to do it for yourself, then do it to honour your father's memory. He would be unhappy if Pratishtha closed down.'

Sudha was right. I couldn't let Pratishtha fall.

The party was over. The students were getting restless. It was time for them to leave. She stopped at the door and said before departing, 'I hope to see you at the dance school tomorrow.'

I nodded my head.

'One more thing.'

'Tell me?'

'Please shave.'

17

Words that Heal

Ayla

Amca drove us to the Mardin Artuklu University. I was quiet throughout the thirty-minute drive. For some strange reason that I didn't quite understand, I felt as nervous going to college in Mardin as I had going to school back in Delhi. I reminded myself that this is my home. I was born here and these are my people, but it didn't soothe my nerves.

We reached at nine o' clock in the morning and there were about 100-120 students already making their way inside. The university was buzzing with energy and chatter unlike the rest of the city which was laid-back and slow to rise. They seemed like two completely different bodies joined together by a surgeon in a last-ditch effort.

The university had an imposing two-storey edifice with Mardin Artuklu Universitesi written in bold red letters. Everything about the university gave the impression that it was built to impress. The bare open surroundings and fields made it even more noticeable. No one that passed the building or the vicinity would miss or fail to notice the name of the university engraved on a big block in black-and-white calligraphy, and placed diagonally at the left corner of the entrance. It gave the illusion that it was suspended in mid-air. Only one corner of the block touched the ground.

Ahead of the entrance was a fifteen-metre pole with the red-coloured Turkish flag fluttering in the wind. The bigger and more impressive the university looked, the smaller I felt in its shadow.

I walked nervously, holding Irina's hand tightly.

She looked at me and said, 'Ayla, I love you, but don't crush my hand.'

'I am so sorry,' I said, letting go.

A group of girls and boys called out to Irina. They were her batchmates. All the students entering the university seemed to know each other from school, business or some shared family connection. They greeted each other with a familiar smile or gesture. I received curious glances from everyone. I was the odd one out. Irina introduced me as her sister from India and they looked at me with many questions. She told them all about the ragging stories that she made up to scare me. They had a good laugh at my expense. Ragging, it turned out, was strictly prohibited in college. I breathed a sigh of relief.

I tried to get away to my class, but they insisted I stay. I stood there listening to their stories and gossip. They gave me a tour of the university. The campus was chic and luxurious. All the classrooms were air-conditioned. It boasted of a huge library—with a special collection of Rumi's poetry—a state-of-the-art auditorium and a basketball court. The ground floor was reserved for Liberal Arts classes. Meanwhile, my law classes took place in a small room on the first floor. Behind the building was a football field where students enjoyed the sun during lunch hours.

I wore a pair of black denim jeans, brown knee-length boots and a plain blue windcheater. Many girls, especially the Arabs, wore a hijab to cover their heads and faces. In total contrast, there were others who dressed in stylish overcoats and expensive gloves.

I walked to the class on the second floor and took the vacant seat on the left-hand corner, next to the window.

About twenty students were already present, all of them boys. Soon, the number increased to thirty. Their shifty eyes scouted the room for Allah knows what, rested on me for a moment and then hurriedly changed direction. *Where are the girls*, I thought.

The professor entered five minutes later (still no sign of girls) and kept a pile of thick books on the table. The lecture had just begun when a boy wandered into the classroom. He was so immersed in his book that he bumped right into the professor. I let out a chuckle.

'Sorry,' the boy said, not bothering to look at the professor's disapproving expression.

'Take a seat,' the professor replied.

The boy continued to read his book. Strands of his hair fell over his eyes every time he leaned forward. He brushed them back with a flick of his fingers.

He looked like a prince in a green kurta and cream pyjamas. He was light-complexioned and had a thick black beard. He dragged his slippers across the floor, but it didn't annoy me in the least. There was something comforting about his presence.

He was oblivious to the world around him. It seemed as if envy, anger, greed, bitterness and failure wouldn't register with him. They were beneath him. I felt a strange pull towards him.

The professor wore his glasses and asked us to introduce ourselves. Every student rose up from their seat, stated their full name and talked about their interest in law. Some wanted to study so they could practice at the Supreme Court, some wanted to empower the poor, some came from families with a background in law and others aspired to work at the International Court of Justice in Hague. There were as many ambitions as there were students in the room.

'Umair,' the professor called out once, twice, and then thrice but he didn't respond, still immersed in his book. I knew it was him and tried to get his attention. He looked at me with a typical blank expression of innocence.

'Ayla. Ayla Erol,' the professor called out. 'Are you present?'

'Yes, Sir...*Assalamu Alaikum*,' I said and stood up immediately.

'Please introduce yourself to the class.'

'My name is Ayla Erol. I am from Mardin.'

'Your accent is different. Have you spent time in the West?' the professor asked.

'No. I actually lived in India since I was nine years old. I moved back recently,' I said.

'Interesting. Why did you move to India?'

'Because of my father's business,' I said, without elaborating.

~

Subjects such as Public Freedom and Constitutional Law demanded time and attention. The professors gave more homework and assignments than one student could manage. I was asked to memorise hundreds of articles and directives, word for word. Many of my classmates barely slept for three-four hours. All their time was spent in the library.

Law was infinite, and terribly boring. It lacked the colour and cadence of dance. I was used to moving around and working with people. To sit in one place was a struggle. I couldn't spend even a minute by myself without recalling my traumatic past. I had become afraid of my own company. I had to believe in what I was doing and I couldn't learn by rote. No matter how hard I tried, I couldn't convince myself otherwise. If I finished one book, another fat volume awaited. There was no end to this.

I understood the sections and their usage and even used them correctly at home while practising in front of a mirror. However, when the professors asked the same questions in class, I went blank. I mixed one directive with another. My self-worth reduced with every question that I failed to answer. I wasn't a good enough dancer in India and I wasn't a good enough law student in Turkey. I was a failure.

There was something wrong with me, I thought. Perhaps, I was dyslexic or suffered from some other unknown disease of the mind which prevented me from memorising the lessons. I surfed the Internet and found that I had symptoms of many chronic psychological disorders.

I was afraid to talk about it to anyone. What if they shut me in a mental asylum? My classmates didn't like me either. They thought I was snooty because I spoke in English not Turkish.

I thought Mardin was my home, but it didn't feel like home. I was too Turkish in India, and too Indian in Turkey.

The only other misfit in class was Umair. He suffered the wrath of the professors, regularly. It was amply clear he wasn't the least bit interested in law and never finished his assignments. He would often be scolded, and sometimes humiliated too. He put forth a deadpan expression and stomached the insults without being affected in the least.

~

Waking up every morning was another challenge. I had to get through terrible loneliness during the day only to find the silence of the night gnawing at me.

I tried to distract myself with household chores but cooking and cleaning were boring. I wanted to scream out loud and I couldn't even do that. I couldn't express myself. Not at home, not in the university; nowhere in the city could I be alone for ten minutes and give voice to all the rage that had bottled up inside me.

'I don't want to live here, Dayê. Please let me return to India,' I said over the phone, one evening.

'Are the Borans not treating you well?'

'It is not like that. They take good care of me, but I don't like Mardin. I don't have any friends. I am the only girl in my class. Everyone here speaks Turkish or Kurmanji. I don't understand anything. What if I fail? Bavo will never talk to me again.'

'Don't say that. He has such high hopes from you.'

'I don't know what to do.'

'Don't let negative thoughts enter your mind. Go to Ulu

Camii mosque every day. Pray to Allah and all your problems will be solved. I am coming to Mardin this summer. I will be with you in a few months.'

'How is Bavo?'

'He works too hard. He goes to the District Court to attend all the sessions and comes home frustrated and angry. The defence lawyer keeps taking deferments on health grounds. The judge is only too happy to grant them. Sabina suspects the judge is biased. I am worried about your father. He is obsessed with this case. Never listens to me. Doesn't take care of his health and smokes like a chimney.'

~

I started going to the mosque daily. I sat there by myself for hours and prayed to Allah that this difficult time would come to an end.

One morning, the mullah walked up to me. He was an old man who wore a starched *jalabayah,* a long gown, and a white *kufi* or cap.

'What are you searching for?' he said.

'Peace of mind,' I replied.

'The answers you are looking for can only be found in the Holy Quran. *Alhamdulillah* (praise to Allah)!'

I sat at the mosque for three hours every day and read the Holy Quran. As per the teachings of the Prophet, I began to fast every Thursday and Friday.

I forgot my worries in the sea of worshippers, and the sound of the evening prayer. However, the moment I stepped out of the mosque, the troubles took hold of me again. My thoughts inevitably returned to my family faraway in Delhi. I felt overwhelmed by the demands of law.

I waited for a miracle. Every morning, I went to the mosque, pleading to Allah to relieve me of my troubles.

A year passed. Four years of coursework still remained. Dayê's summer trip got cancelled. Bavo fell sick so she had to stay back and look after him. She was constantly worried about his health and complained about his smoking and eating habits.

~

There were dark grey clouds in the sky. By the time I reached the university, there was a heavy downpour. I had to clutch my blue umbrella tight.

I was late. The class had already begun and the professor looked at me, displeased. There was silence. He was in a foul mood.

'Please put your assignment on the desk,' he said without looking up.

I quickly put the umbrella aside, and opened my bag to take out the assignment. When I turned around, I caught Umair looking at me. He shifted his gaze back to his notebook and started scribbling.

He was odd. He looked at people for that extra second as if he was thinking deeply about them. He always carried a pencil in his hand and wrote his assignments using a pencil. When the professors asked him to use a pen, he refused.

The professor walked up to his desk and snatched the paper he was scribbling on.

'You were supposed to finish this assignment at home,' he said.

'I didn't have enough time,' Umair said. 'I will submit it by tomorrow. Please return my paper.'

'Let me also see what important things you are working on in my class.'

'Please don't, Sir. This is personal,' he said with a flush of panic in his voice.

The professor read the note out loud. Umair covered his face with his hands.

'She walked with consummate ease unaffected by the torrential rain. The stream of tears in her heart had run dry. Her pink tunic and knee-length boots revealed a slim figure devoid of love, hope, joy; everything, but bare bones. She was aware of the many eyes which followed her steps. It should have bothered her, but it didn't. She didn't look left or right. Took her seat in the world. There was a silent surrender in her dark brown eyes. The girl with a blue umbrella.'

I looked at my knee-length boots, pink tunic and understood. Everyone was now looking at me and I felt embarrassed and elated at the same time.

'If you pay less attention to Ms Ayla's clothes, perhaps you will find time to finish my assignments. Keep this, Ayla, this was intended for you,' the professor said, and threw the paper in my direction.

When the class finished, I picked up the paper and went to Umair's desk.

'It was so sad,' I said.

'Please don't take this the wrong way. I write about things that make an impression on me. When you walked into the class, your eyes conveyed a sense of surrender. I wanted to put it in words.'

'Are you a writer?'

'A struggling poet.'

~

Umair didn't submit the assignment in the next class either. The professor was so angry that he didn't know what to say to Umair. He simply continued with his lecture.

When the class ended, Umair hurried towards me.

'Ayla, this is for you,' he said, and handed me a crumpled piece of paper and started to walk away. It was a long passage written in his jagged handwriting:

He looked at her with love-starved eyes. If only she saw him once, half a glance, it would have broken down her stubborn resistance. The strength of his conviction scared her, as it scared him. Their paths were destined to cross, but never to meet; she was convinced...They failed each other. When the moment came to choose, they let their fears overwhelm their beliefs. They still liked the rain though, and the memories it brought: bittersweet.

'I hate sad endings,' I said.

He turned around and came towards me. 'I only know sad endings. The start of any love story is anxious and the end is often heartbreaking. It is the middle where everything seems beautiful, doesn't it?'

He smiled. It wasn't the conscious smile of an adult. It was the smile of a child who had just received a kiss on his cheek.

'How do you come up with these passages?'

'I wish I knew. There are days when I keep thinking and nothing comes to mind, and then suddenly there comes a moment when there is absolute clarity. I can see beyond a person's appearance, as if I can look inside their soul.'

'That reminds me of dance. There were moments when I stopped thinking about steps and movements, everything became clear. I miss that feeling.'

'You are a dancer?'

'Well, I used to be.'

'How did you end up in law?'

'It's another sad story.'

'Can't you change it?'

'Change what?'

'Your story.'

'You can't change your story; you can't even escape. Sometimes, I feel like going far away from this noise and clutter. Someplace where I can shut my eyes and just breathe. You know what I mean?'

'Allow me to take you to such a place.'

'Take me,' I said. He was joking. No such place could possibly exist in a town like Mardin.

'Follow me,' he said, and started moving before I could even think.

He led me past the bazaar, down a dingy alley. An hour later, we reached a small mountain at the edge of the city. It was a steep climb on a narrow trail. The sun was about to set. Umair put on the torch-light in his phone.

'Be careful. The rocks are slippery from the rain.'

'How often do you come here?'

'Every day. Mostly in the evenings after the classes.'

We reached the summit after an hour's hike. There were massive rocks scattered all over the place.

We sat together, looking at the moon, lost in our respective thoughts.

'How did you start writing?'

'I guess it had something to do with my mother. She was a lawyer and a real fighter for freedom of speech. At the height of the Kurdish-PKK conflict, she formed a political party for Kurds.

'People rallied behind her. She showed that violence was not the only way to be heard. We could change the system from within and she was gaining support. Her party swept the elections in Diyarbakır,' he said.

'Let me guess, the State came down on her?'

'No, it was our own people. In the annual party meet, PKK supporters sneaked in, removed the Turkish flag and raised the PKK flag which was outlawed by the army. Word got out and she was arrested by the authorities.

'The report says that she killed herself in the prison two days later. It's a sham. Everybody knew that she was murdered.'

'Oh no!'

'I wasn't angry at them; I was sad for them. She was good and she was the kind of person who could make a difference. Her death was everyone's loss. I held both the Turkish State and PKK equally responsible. It left me disillusioned.

'I began to write so that my words could give solace, a moment of peace to someone, anyone who had lost their loved ones to this senseless conflict. I believe that words can change the world, for better or worse. I took up law in honour of her memory.

'Every time I come here, I think of her,' Umair continued.

'I too am reminded of my mother,' I said. 'She constantly has this worried expression on her face. The protective gaze with which she always looks at me. Bavo holding me in his arms and throwing me up in the air when I was a little girl. I miss them.'

Umair believed in Allah. He had faith despite everything he had gone through. I was a cynic. Perhaps, we could learn something from each other.

He moved closer to me. His lips touched mine and I instinctively retreated. I wanted to kiss him, but I couldn't. Something inside me didn't allow it.

'I wanted to share this moment with you. I knew it would mean something to you. This is the first time I have brought anyone here.'

'Why me?'

'There is something very sad about you, and I am drawn to sadness.'

18

Defying Traditions

Guru Chandrashekhar

I woke up before sunrise. The city was absolutely quiet, only the leaves fluttered in the early morning breeze. I took deep breaths and closed my eyes. It was time to break my promise. It was time to return to Pratishtha.

I unlocked the gates and walked inside. I went straight to the statue of Lord Shiva and sought blessings. Next, I put on my favourite Carnatic music.

I danced like there was no tomorrow. Didn't follow any rules or order or traditions. My heart led me into the movements of its own choice. Every step was a new discovery. Every minute filled my heart with delight. Pratishtha welcomed me back with open arms.

My body had become rusty and stiff from the hiatus. What came easily earlier, now took effort. Hands on hips, shoulders slouched—I was panting soon. With every breath, I let go of the exhaustion, the bitterness and the pain. It was my release.

I danced without any expectations. I danced for the sake

of dance and everything else (technique, flow and steps) took care of itself. After an hour, I finally sat against the wall and smiled to myself.

My thoughts inevitably wandered to the past. The initial days of Pratishtha, its growth and the many students who had learnt Bharatanatyam here. What was the point of it all? I had followed every edict of the dance and it brought nothing but misery. Now that I didn't care about tradition, I felt free.

Many of my talented students, their professional dreams and personal ambitions remained unfulfilled. They were unhappy. Conversely, many terrible dancers were content. Why?

Everyone couldn't be a good dancer, but everyone deserved happiness from dance. I had emphasised too much on the former and too little on the latter. My priorities were all wrong. I needed to change. It felt so obvious in that moment.

Dance, at the very least, had to give them joy before it brought them anything else. Somewhere in this mad world, someone had reversed the formula. Dancers needed to be taught values that would serve them beyond the dance floor. I think that is what my father wanted to tell me in that dream. I left Pratishtha pondering over this riddle before anyone else arrived for the classes. I needed more time and clarity before I faced them.

I was done being commandeering and ruthless with my students. That didn't work. I wanted them to feel proud about their attempts and not just their accomplishments. Perhaps, cooperation could take them further ahead than competition.

I didn't know how to begin but I knew that if all of us put our minds together, we would figure it out. Pratishtha could no longer remain just a dance school, it had to transform into an institution of learning. We had to get better at getting better.

~

The next morning, I went to Pratishtha with a purpose. I was ready to act on my hunch. Sudha was in the middle of a dance session.

'I heard you came for an early morning session, yesterday,' she said.

'How did you know?'

'The guard on duty saw you enter.'

'I have something important to discuss with you and the students.'

'Can't it wait till the class finishes?' she said.

'Actually, it can't,' I said.

The change needed to come from the very top. It had to begin with me. I asked the students to gather around. I had been absent for a long time; I had a lot to answer for. They sat in a semi-circle, facing me. Sudha stood behind them.

'Some of you might be wondering where I have been for the past one year and why I am back now. Others might not even know who I am. I am here to answer all these questions.

'Sudha and I started this dance school and we have run it together for many years. However, I have been absent from Pratishtha for over a year.'

'But why?' one student asked whom I didn't recognise.

'Well...umm...The truth is I had begun to hate dance. I wanted nothing to do with it. In fact, I swore I would never enter the gates of Pratishtha again.'

There was pindrop silence in the room. Many trainees looked at each other.

'Why did you start hating dance, Guruji?'

'It had a lot to do with the unexpected and sudden departure of Ayla and Drishti. Some of you might know them. They left Pratishtha for other dance schools. I felt cheated, embarrassed and humiliated. I hated them and I blamed everyone for their exit but myself. I threw away my phone, cut off from the world and almost died. I was on the brink of losing myself.

'Everything changed last week when all of you came to my house. You and the memory of my father helped me realise how much I missed dance and how I had been wasting my life away. Dance has always given a meaning to my life. Without it, my existence is useless. This is why I have returned.

'You may grow up to be lawyers, politicians, engineers and doctors. There will be honorific titles before your names. But these moments that we share are special by themselves. Your co-dancers will always call you by the same absurd nicknames that you now keep for each other. They will always have stories to tell. Isn't that amazing?

'The certificates will go inside lockers and you will forget all about them; but you will always remember the applause. Build friendships, learn humility and help one another grow. That is what I want to teach you.

'My mother once told me, never besmirch the pride of my family. You are the only family I have now, and my pride is in your hands.'

There was no applause to follow my long-winded speech. Just a silent understanding between us worked like magic. My students had always feared me, but now, I saw a tinge of respect in their eyes.

~

We developed a balanced routine of dance, running, and strength training to keep the students engaged and physically fit. These changes were scary. They were a departure from the tradition and everything I had learned. The new model of training was premised on the needs of the dancers. Their movements, their expressions were more personal now. They smiled more genuinely. They gave everything on the dance floor. Initially, I was reluctant, but gradually, I allowed them to express themselves. It made them happy and that was important now. I didn't know where that would lead us. Many in the dance community would dismiss our initiatives.

Many of the new trainees were passionate. They came to the natyalaya an hour prior to the dance session and practised all by themselves. They reminded me of the dedication Ayla had shown at the beginning of her dance career. As a Guru, I craved that kind of commitment. I was proud of each and every one of them.

Soon, news of our training model spread far and wide. More and more people were interested in finding out about it.

Fifty-five students applied for the summer batch. Three of the students, who had left Pratishtha, wanted to return. We welcomed everyone with open arms, no questions asked. After all, it was a fresh start.

This arrival of dancers posed new challenges. We couldn't possibly manage so many students in one batch without compromising on the quality. Thus, we started three separate batches—in the morning from seven to nine; from two to four in the afternoon, and an evening class from five to seven, with twenty students each.

19

Shimmy

Ayla

Life wasn't so dull anymore. I actually looked forward to the time at the university.

Even the weather turned more benign. Spring arrived in style. Pink-and-white bougainvillea made everything beautiful and colourful.

After the annual exams, the mood in college turned festive and lively. Preparations for the Inter-college Belly Dance Festival were in full swing. No one cared about the lectures anymore. Girls practised shimmy in the corridors and washrooms. Shimmy was this incredibly difficult dance move where dancers sensually moved their bodies. There were more than 100 variations of this move, each more difficult than the other. I came home early from college and saw Irina, too, practising shimmy in her room.

'I don't understand what the fuss is all about,' I asked her.

'It is the only festival in Mardin that anyone gives two hoots about. Three judges, including the legendary actor Beren Kaya, will see the performance and select a winner. Last year, more than 10,000 girls took part in the contest across Turkey. The final round was held in Istanbul, and broadcast on television. The winner received 5,00,000 liras.'

'That's twice my college tuition fee.'

'The competition began only two years ago, but it's growing like crazy. The girl who won it last year became an international celebrity. She was average-looking and even her dance wasn't all that great. By the time they finished grooming her, she had turned into a diva. I was stunned at her transformation!

'She will represent Turkey at the beauty pageant, next year.'

'I get it.'

'You should also take part in the contest,' Irina said, more out of an impulse than anything else.

I panicked at the very thought of dance. 'Are you mad? There is no way I can do this. I don't know a thing about belly dance.'

'So what?'

If Irina had made up her mind, it was impossible to convince her otherwise.

'It is not so difficult, trust me. If you agree to take part, mother will allow me, otherwise she will have problems. Please do this for my sake. Please. Please. Please. Please. Please. Please.'

'Irina, don't do this to me. Dance is not my thing,' I said, firmly.

'Don't be a spoilsport. Umair will fall all over you when you swing your hips left and right,' she said with a smirk and moved her hips.

This was not a line of attack I had expected.

'*Shhh*!' I said.

Teyzi was downstairs preparing dinner. She could have easily overheard us. Irina laughed and sat down on the bed. She liked getting others in trouble as much as she liked getting in trouble herself.

'He is just a friend. That's all,' I said.

'Just a friend, is he?' she said, 'Do you kiss all your friends?'

'How did you know?'

'So, you did kiss him,' she said, triumphantly. 'Your face was glowing when you returned home late at night the previous week. I knew something had happened. Even my mother noticed the change. *Ayla finally seems to be adjusting to this place*, she told me.'

'Please don't tell Teyzi about him.'

'Of course, I won't, if you agree to participate in the dance festival.'

'I have to go somewhere. I am already late,' I said.

'Just say yes and you can leave for your romantic date.'

~

I met Umair at Sakli Bahce Café. He was sitting in the garden, writing on his notepad as usual.

'I hope you haven't been waiting for too long,' I said.

'That's all right,' he smiled and hugged me, and went right back to scribbling. He seemed to revel in isolation and solitude. Sometimes, I felt like an intruder.

But he was always hungry to share his words and I liked to be the first person to hear them. It felt special.

When the food came, he passed the entire plate to me.

Food, clothes, or drinks; none of these made the slightest impression on him.

'Stop reading now,' I said, and snatched the paper he was writing on. He looked at me with a bemused expression. It felt like I had snatched candy from a child.

'Are you going to cry now?'

'Of course not,' he said. 'Just don't spoil it.'

I threw it right back at him and made a face, 'You are so useless.'

'Agreed. Now, tell me what has got you so restless?'

'Do you know about the dance festival in college?'

'The same one that has half the college girls going bananas?'

'Irina asked me to enrol.'

'Do you want to?'

I liked that about him. He never imposed his opinions. Instead, he tried to listen and understand. There was a simplicity in him and he was too innocent to even realise it.

'I have never attempted belly dance before and this will be in front of the whole university. What do you think I should do?'

'You could try it out.'

'But why?'

'My reasons are selfish. Dance was such an important part of your life, but you never talk about it. I don't understand it. I can't imagine why not. I would love to see you dance.'

'Okay. I will do it.'

'Really, Ayla?'

'Yes.'

I would do anything to make him happy.

~

Standees and posters were placed in every corner of the university. A curvaceous woman in a dance pose stood smiling at the centre and the headline stated, *Join the festival, TODAY!*

The classrooms wore a deserted look. All the sound, chatter and murmur came from the auditorium. I spotted my professor roaming around the hall like a ghost. He saw me and asked, 'Aren't you coming for class today?'

'No, Sir. I am auditioning for the dance competition.'

'Oh!' he said, surprised.

He couldn't imagine me as a dancer. How much I must have changed in the past one year.

'You should take it easy today, Sir. Join us at the dance show. Live a little,' Irina chirped.

The professor did not look pleased at her cheekiness, but before he could respond, Irina grabbed my hand and dragged me towards the auditorium. I turned around. He was still looking at us with a bemused expression.

There were easily 100-200 girls in the auditorium. All of them waiting for their turn. I didn't even know there were those many girls in the university. Many of them wore multicoloured double-drape tribal halter tops that accentuated their figures. The shine of their attire matched the glitter of their make-up. In comparison, I felt under-dressed and under-prepared.

I entered the hall and searched for Umair. He had promised to come but he was nowhere to be found.

I felt a pang of jealousy. He must have forgotten about the festival. He only cared for his words.

My throat felt parched. I knew there would be dancers

but competing against so many women was frightening. The contestants kept glancing left and right, measuring one another. Irina whispered funny remarks in my ear.

The three judges sat in the front row and talked among themselves. The announcer asked the participants to register their names and wait for their turn. The event would begin in the next five minutes. A nervous murmur went up in the crowd.

The first dancer, perhaps overwhelmed by the moment and a burst of adrenalin, danced with a little too much flair. She moved her body with unnatural aggression. In the process, she lost control. She seemed sloppy from her over-exuberance.

Umair walked into the auditorium huffing and puffing a few minutes later. He saw my angry face and put his hands on his ears.

'Ayla Erol,' the judge announced my name.

My heartbeat went through the roof. I forgot the last time I had stepped on the stage.

There was pindrop silence. The music began and everyone's gaze was fixed on me. Suddenly, the unsavoury scenes from the arangetram flashed before my eyes. My mind was playing tricks on me. I forgot my steps.

'You wanted this, Ayla,' the voice resounded in my head.

'No, I didn't,' I shouted. Tears began to flow. I froze.

Don't cry in front of everyone. Dare you cry in front of all these people, I said to myself. *You are making a fool of yourself.* I tried reassuring myself, but I was not prepared for this fight.

A group of girls snickered. The judges shifted impatiently. Umair's face was expressionless. I looked at Irina, the dancers and the judges. Irina nodded her head to egg me on but I was too scared and too humiliated to begin. There was nothing I could do. I ran off the stage.

Umair called after me, but that only hastened my steps. I wanted to escape the situation as soon as possible. I was too embarrassed to face him. He finally caught up with me near the university's main exit.

'Will you stop for a second,' he said, and grabbed my hand. I tried to free myself, but he was holding on tight.

'Leave me alone,' I shouted. Everyone's attention turned towards us. I didn't mean to shout at him; I was shouting at the memory of the man who had hurt me, but I couldn't explain all that. If he knew the truth, he would never look at me in the same way again.

Umair stiffened and let go of me.

'You have been hiding something from day one. At some level, it drew me towards you. I thought you needed time. Well, a year has passed; it's time you came clean.'

'I am sorry. I can't share this with you, not right now, may be never.'

'I have shared my writing without a moment's hesitation. Give me one good reason you can't do the same.'

'I am sorry; I can't be with you. It is too difficult.'

Umair looked at me for a painful moment, turned around and left without another word. I will never forget the hurt expression on his face. It was the end of something beautiful.

~

I went straight to the mosque, sat by the pillar and closed my eyes.

The namazis readied themselves for *ezan*, the evening

prayer. When the muezzin gave the second call, the *iqama*, everyone lined up. I recited the *Takbir* (God is Great) and *Shahada* (There is no God but Allah, Muhammad is the messenger of Allah) in my head. The prayer ended fifteen minutes later, but my conversation with Allah continued.

This is not the first time this has happened. Why didn't you protect me? Umair won't come back to me. You know how strongheaded he is. Please help me, I urged Allah.

He couldn't be so merciless as to take Umair away from me. I promised to fast for ten days and feed fifty saints in return for another chance.

How would I ever return to the university? What would Irina think of me? Once again, I had managed to disappoint those closest to me. Umair had never asked me for anything. He just wanted to see me dance and I couldn't even do that for him. I didn't deserve his love. I realised that Allah was punishing me for my shortcomings.

I sat there till sunset, trying to compose myself, but I couldn't remove the dark thoughts from my mind.

~

The door was ajar. I entered the house and walked in as quietly as I could. I heard Teyzi mention my name and I stopped. She was engaged in an argument with Amca. I stood outside and listened.

'We should send her back to Delhi, immediately,' Teyzi said.

'No,' Amca said. 'We have to wait for Vahide's instructions. She asked us not to tell Ayla anything. We can't go against her wishes.'

'But Halim has had a heart attack. We cannot hide this from Ayla. Anything can happen. She will never forgive us,' Teyzi said.

'Vahide is under a lot of pressure. Let her focus on Halim's recovery for the time being. I will call her in a few hours and offer to come to India along with Ayla. She is all alone there. She would need our help.'

~

The winds were furious and unrepentant. The windowpanes of my room rattled. Even the sturdy entrance door seemed to wilt under pressure.

The lights flickered for a minute and then gave way. Total darkness. The sky was illuminated every few seconds from lightning and thunder. I was scared. Very scared.

Such hostile weather, in the middle of spring, was a bad omen.

My past followed me wherever I went. Bavo was humiliated because of me; indeed, his heart had given way. I was a horrible daughter, unworthy of his love. I was responsible for his condition. It was my duty to save him, but *how*?

A dangerously simple solution took hold of me. I was the root cause of all these conflicts. The court case, the humiliation and the troubles—all happened because of me. If I vanished, all these problems would vanish along with me. My parents would at least have their peace of mind. Dayê would stop worrying, and Bavo wouldn't work so hard and stress over my future. They could go on living happily just the way they had before I made a mess of things.

Everything could be fixed with one small act of sacrifice. It was the only way. My family was more important to me than anything else. I feared for Bavo's life. There was no time to waste. I had to do it right *now*. I had to sacrifice myself for their sake. Allah had willed it.

I got up from the bed and looked out of the window; the street was deserted. No one would know. But, where could I go without being found? Teyzi and Amca would search for me. Dayê would only end up worrying more. Another bolt of lightning illuminated the sky and left me in panic.

There was only one way. I had to go to Allah with my appeal. Maybe then, he would spare Bavo's life. All I had to do was take a leap of faith. The voice inside my head said, 'Do it for the well-being of Bavo.'

I had never felt so scared and vulnerable. This was madness. I wasn't going to kill myself; I wasn't going to run away. That wouldn't solve anything.

My hands trembled as I tried to drink water. The glass felt heavy. It slipped from my hand and crashed. The broken shards splattered all over the floor. I tried to step aside. A sharp piece pierced my right ankle and went inside my foot.

There was blood on the floor. I somehow managed to remove the shard. It would take time to heal, but some scars never go away. My hands were covered in blood. It was a sign. I wasn't going to let Bavo's blood be spilled. I wiped away my tears.

I couldn't bother Teyzi; she was already worried about Bavo's condition. This was my punishment. It brought me pain; it was my penance.

I accepted Allah's verdict. I got up, looked out of the window and let my body go. I jumped.

My body was still for a moment. What a feeling. There was complete freedom and detachment. My worries dissipated into nothing. Fear and horror took over soon. I was sucked down by the force of gravity.

I hit the ground hard. The impact was painful beyond words. My bones cracked. It took me a second to realise what I had done. But it was too late.

No one heard my cry over the sound of thunder. My body went numb within minutes. I couldn't feel a thing. That is what I had wanted all along.

'Forgive me, Dayê,' I uttered before darkness engulfed me.

IV

20

A Prayer for the Departed

Ayla

By the time I was taken to the hospital, I had lost forty per cent of my blood. I was given an injection and put on IV. I couldn't move an inch, but I was wide awake. They wheeled me to the MRI room. Every time they moved my body, I screamed in agony.

The surgeon took one look at me and his face went pale. 'There are lacerated wounds on her spine and the back of her head. Her pulse is extremely high and blood pressure is very low. We have to keep her spine straight at all cost. Get an MRI and an ultrasound done immediately,' the surgeon instructed his team.

I had a crushed vertebra, forty-two fractures and a broken rib. The medical team gave me twenty-four hours to live. My only hope of survival was to be treated at a better hospital in Istanbul.

Amca brought heaven and earth together to save my life. He called up his contacts in the local government and acquired all the permissions and paperwork for an emergency airlift within an hour. We were taken inside the charter air ambulance that would drop me straight to a medical facility at the Istanbul Government Hospital. The doctors had been apprised of my situation in advance. They decided to operate on me as soon as I arrived.

The thunderstorm hadn't abated. The visibility was too low for take-off.

My condition was deteriorating with every minute's delay, but despite Amca's insistence, the pilot refused to take off. Amca sat there praying and hoping for the storm to subside.

'My niece's life is on the line,' Amca pleaded.

'Sir, I understand your situation but there is a storm ahead,' the pilot warned. 'If I fly in it, it could be fatal.' Amca thought of taking me to Istanbul by road, but I wouldn't have survived the twelve-hour journey. We had to sit out the storm.

After two hours of waiting, Amca lost his patience. 'If you don't fly right now, my niece is as good as dead. In Allah's name, I will burn this aircraft down and everyone inside it,' he said and grabbed hold of the pilot's collar.

He meant every word of what he said.

'I will talk to the air-controller,' the pilot said, nervously.

It took another half an hour before the storm abated, and the chopper finally took off.

~

I was taken to the operation theatre. The medical team was reluctant to perform a surgery after the initial examination.

Amca was asked to sign a consent form that stated the chances of survival were thirty per cent and that the hospital wouldn't be held responsible for any mishap, such as death on the table. I was told about this much later. I would never really know how my family must have gone through that harrowing time, praying for my life.

~

'We have braved a storm and come all the way from Mardin so that you can treat my niece. Allah will hold you responsible. I will not sign any form that absolves you of your duties,' Amca declared.

The nurse left to discuss the matter with the head surgeon. He was a fifty-six-year-old man named Dr Abdullah. The doctor was nothing less than a demigod at the hospital. He had graduated with the highest honours from Johns Hopkins and had performed more than 1,500 successful spinal surgeries.

'Assalamu Alaikum,' he greeted Amca. 'I will be performing the surgery and I will do everything in my power to save your niece. You have my word.

'I have a twelve-year-old daughter myself. I understand the value of a young life. With Allah's blessings, she will be fine. Please sign this form and allow me to do the surgery at the earliest.'

Amca relented.

The nursing staff dressed me. Two doctors, two nurses and one ward boy hurriedly entered the OT, shut the door and took positions.

~

'She is out of danger. Still, the next twenty-four hours are critical,' the surgeon said.

'Mashallah!' Amca breathed a sigh of relief.

'We will keep her in the Intensive Care Unit for a week and monitor her progress. I am afraid this accident will have long-term consequences on her mobility.'

'What do you mean? She will be able to recover completely, right?'

'I can't say until further tests, but it seems unlikely that she will walk again.'

'We will be able to figure out the extent of the damage only after a few weeks,' the surgeon said.

'But you said she is out of danger. Doctor, our family is going through a terrible time. Ayla's father is in a hospital in India after suffering a heart attack. Ayla's mother wants me to bring her to India immediately. She is adamant. I cannot give this news to them. She is going to fall apart.'

'I did all I could. I strongly suggest she stays in the hospital for the next few weeks at least. We have to run a lot of tests to determine the exact nature of the injuries. Now is not a good time for her to travel anywhere. She needs complete bed rest.'

~

I opened my eyes; I had no idea where I was. My body hurt and my head felt heavy. I had no energy to even move my head from one side to another. The nurse was surprised to find me awake. They had given me a strong drug to sleep, but it wasn't working. Amca sat next to me and kept his hand on my head.

'You gave us a scare.'

'Have you told Dayê?'

'Yes. She is extremely worried. She has been through a lot lately.'

'I don't know what came over me. I was so foolish.'

'How is Bavo's health?' I asked. My memory was slowly returning.

'How do you know?'

'I heard you and Teyzi talk about him that evening. I panicked after hearing the news.'

'He is still in the ICU. The doctors are taking all possible precautions.'

'I want to be with Bavo and Dayê.'

'You can't, Ayla.'

'Why not?

'Your spine suffered extensive damage. They need to conduct more tests.'

I tried to move my legs, but I couldn't. I didn't feel anything.

I began to panic; I howled and screamed. A nurse came rushing in and gave me an injection. I fell asleep within seconds.

The morning after the surgery was agonising. I experienced pain beyond words, painkillers were of little help. Every minute seemed like an eternity. I cried for hours on end. I could see my legs, but not move them. They stayed unresponsive. Everything felt dark. It was scary to imagine life without my legs. I would never be myself again.

I wanted to return to my parents at any cost. They would find a way to help me. The hospital authorities refused to let me go, however, I told Amca that he had to make it happen. If he didn't, I would drag myself out. There was a huge showdown in the hospital. Three days later, Dr Abdullah finally signed my release papers. He strictly advised against

travelling to India, but I couldn't care less. All I knew was
Bavo's health was deteriorating. The nurse put me on a
wheelchair and Amca took me to the airport.

~

We reached Delhi the next afternoon.

I crossed many familiar streets and landmarks. Everything
looked the same on the outside, but so much had changed.
I wished Umair was here. His presence would have given
me strength. I wondered if he knew about my accident and
suicide attempt.

We passed by many hotels in Mahipalpur and waded
through traffic and noise to reach Vasant Kunj. I was almost
home. On one level, I felt relieved. Dayê and Bavo would
take care of me. They would protect me.

At another level, I dreaded their reaction. I was returning
in a wheelchair. They would be horrified. Ask me why. I didn't
have an answer.

There was a big yellow tent outside my house. Men were
gathered in groups. Such makeshift tents were often set up
in our neighbourhoods during weddings. But, where was
the music?

The confectioners weren't preparing delicacies in big black
pans. I realised what this could be and I felt dizzy.

'Take me to Dayê now,' I said to Amca.

The sound of wails became audible as I entered the house.
Our neighbours, Bavo's clients and members from the local
mosque looked at me, sympathy in their eyes. I didn't care. I
felt panic in the gut. It was unbearable. I only wanted to see
Dayê. Her eyes widened with shock when she saw me in the

wheelchair. She touched it as if to confirm it was real. She couldn't believe it or didn't want to. It didn't matter either way. It was real. She looked at me, her eyes were bloodshot. It was as if life had been squeezed out of her. I had never seen her like this before. She hugged me tight and said my name, the despair palpable in her voice. I couldn't respond. I didn't know what to say or feel. It was all too much. It was surreal. I couldn't believe it. How did this happen to us? Who did this? We were a happy family. We cried our hearts out.

'He thought of you till the end,' Dayê said.

I didn't believe it until I heard it from her. I was waiting for Bavo to come out and surprise me. I desperately needed good news. He was the only one who could have helped me recover—my last hope. How could he have gone away like this. That was not fair. I didn't even get to say goodbye. He would never know how much I loved him. It was killing me from inside.

~

Imam Shamil from Massudpur Mosque was called to supervise Bavo's burial, his *janaza*. He was an old man with a thick white beard. He walked into the house, giving a sympathetic nod to everyone present.

'Brothers and sisters,' he stood in the centre of the room and said, 'let's proceed to the task that Allah has set for us. Take me to the body.'

'Call him by his name,' I said, sternly.

A few faces turned towards me.

'Forgive her, Imam Sahib. She is Halim's daughter,' Amca said.

The Imam didn't answer him. He came towards me and bent down. 'I am sorry for your loss, child. He has left this world for a better place. Allah will grant him peace.'

Amca and three other men guided him to Bavo.

'When did Allah call upon Halim Sahib?'

'It was late in the evening. We brought the body home at sunrise,' one of the neighbours informed.

'Seven hours have passed. There is no time to waste. We should start the preparations at once.'

Amca washed Bavo's body with scented water, and dressed Bavo in a white shroud. The Imam came forward and sprinkled oil on the shroud.

Three men from the neighbourhood rolled a holy rug imprinted with the image of the Holy Kaaba at Mecca. They wrapped Bavo's body in it.

'He is ready,' the Imam said, and everyone rose up.

The Imam led the procession to the mosque. Amca and four other men carried the coffin on their shoulders. All the women, including Dayê and myself, followed them at a distance. The coffin was lowered in the prayer room behind the namazis, who were chanting the afternoon prayers.

The women were asked to go to the upper chamber.

Men gathered around the coffin when the prayers finished. They didn't know Bavo. They had never met him, but they chanted a prayer of forgiveness, the *Salat al-Janazah*. I hoped Allah would listen to them.

I was touched by the solemnity of the moment. These people were strangers and yet they were here for us, in this moment of need. I felt proud to be a Muslim; I was fortunate to have been born as one.

The body was then taken to a burial ground in Chhattarpur. The Imam asked Dayê and me to keep distance from the procession.

The caretaker dug a grave under a banyan tree. He greeted the Imam with deference and paid his respects to Bavo's body. Bavo's body was lifted from the coffin and lowered down. He was aligned perpendicular to *Qibla*, Mecca. With every passing moment, Bavo was going further and further away from us. I longed to take a closer look at him. I asked them to wheel me closer to Bavo. I wanted to take one final look.

They refused.

The body was covered with wooden planks to prevent dirt from going inside. Each man threw three handfuls of soil into the grave, while the Imam recited Quranic verses. As per Kurdish tradition, his grave would be covered with bright fabric till flowers grew inside the grave to provide solace to his soul.

'We created you from it, and return you to it, and from it, we will raise you a second time.'

More prayers were chanted seeking forgiveness of the deceased and reminding the dead of their profession of faith. As per Dayê's wish, jasmine flowers were scattered all around the grave. Bavo liked their fragrance.

'I want to thank all the brothers who came for this brother. *Assalamu Alaikum*,' the Imam said.

The spell that had bound everyone together was broken. The crowd began to disperse. Dayê and I went to the grave for one last look. We were allowed to mourn for three days.

21

It's Personal

Guru Chandrashekhar

'I was at the airport this morning and I saw something disturbing,' Sudha said.

'Sounds serious. Tell me,' I said and offered her a glass of water.

'I saw Ayla,' she said, looking at me closely, expecting a reaction.

'Hmm...That's great,' I said, not sure how to react. 'It has been so long since she left, hasn't it? I do miss her.'

'Did you speak to her?'

'I wanted to, but she looked pale and ghastly. I almost didn't believe that it was her until I looked into her eyes. I even smiled at her, but she looked away. It was best to leave her alone.'

'You are over-thinking. Whatever happened was in the past.'

'She was in a wheelchair, Chandrashekhar.'

'What? You must have mistaken her for someone else. How can Ayla be in a wheelchair?'

'I couldn't believe it either. I know Ayla.'

'I have to find out what happened to her. I won't be able to rest until I do,' I said to Sudha after the class.

'That's a bad idea.'

'Why?'

'Because you can't be professional with her.'

'What are you trying to suggest?'

'You are too attached to her. Her departure almost destroyed you and Pratishtha. It has taken a lot of time and effort to rebuild our institution. You will risk everything by venturing into the past, and I won't be able to save Pratishtha again. I don't have it in me anymore.'

'It's not about me and my name anymore. This time, it is about her. Ayla left a long time ago, but I still feel a connection with her. There is something unfinished between us.'

'If you must, then go ahead. But please don't throw it all away on one student.'

'I won't let that happen. How do I find her?'

'I don't know. I only saw her leave in an ambulance.'

~

I called up all my former students who had trained with Ayla, but none of them had any news of her. I then went about calling all the hospitals in the vicinity of her house; I didn't even know if she lived there anymore. Fortunately, the receptionist at the Spinal Injury Centre told me that Ayla was admitted there two days ago. I went straight to the hospital.

Her mother was standing at the reception, filling up a form. I had no idea how she would react to my presence. I hoped she would understand that I came with good intentions, that our differences were a thing of the past. I stood behind her patiently, while she cleared the payments.

She turned around, looked at me and then walked right past me. There was no sign of recognition on her face.

'Mrs Erol,' I called out. 'I am Guru Chandrashekhar from Pratishtha.'

'What are you doing here?'

'I heard that Ayla is not keeping well. I just came to see if she is all right.'

There was a moment of silent hesitation. It seemed like she was struggling for words. Not so much with what she wanted to say but how much she wanted to reveal. Despair was written all over her face. The receptionist handed her the remaining money.

'No, she is not. My husband is dead. Ayla tried to kill herself in Turkey. She jumped out of the second-floor window of her room. Doctors say she will be in a wheelchair for the rest of her life.'

I was prepared for bad news, but not this. She was young and vivacious. How could all this happen to her. I felt a surge of sympathy for her family.

'I am sorry to hear that. May I see her once? I just want to talk to her and be of any help that I can.'

'I don't think anyone can help us, but you are free to go and see her.'

~

I had looked forward to meeting Ayla, but now I felt a sense of dread. Her mother had no interest or time for my apology. I didn't fancy my chances with Ayla either. Would it change anything?

What if she turned her gaze away and refused to speak to me? She was impulsive and headstrong. She could easily shout at the top of her voice and ask me to get the hell out.

Something made me stay. She needed me more than any other student at Pratishtha.

The ICU consisted of six or seven makeshift rooms separated by white curtains. Doctors in white coats and nurses in light blue overalls floated from one room to another. The eerie silence was occasionally broken by the loud beep of the machines or telephone rings. The air conditioner was on full blast. There was no warmth here.

The room smelled of medicines and disinfectants. Everything was white in colour, including the walls and the bed sheets. Morbidity coloured this hospital.

Wrapped in a blanket, Ayla was staring blankly at the ceiling. She looked vulnerable. Both her legs were lifted upwards in a cast, supported by bandages. There was a folded wheelchair kept next to the bed.

'Ayla,' I said.

She turned sideways and looked at me in astonishment.

'Guruji, how come you are here?'

'Sudha saw you at the airport. She told me about your condition. I was worried and came looking for you.'

She had been crying. Her eyes were red. There was nothing worse than to see her in such a sorry condition. I forgave all her mistakes at once. They seemed small and petty.

There was no trace of bitterness or sweetness in her voice. She had exhausted all emotions. The girl sitting next to me was not Ayla. She was mellow and broken. Life had consumed her spirit.

'How did all of this happen?' I said, pointing to the wheelchair.

'I don't want to talk about it, Guruji. How is Sudha?'

'She is well. We often remember you at Pratishtha. Just the other day, the students were learning a difficult dance move. They completely goofed up. I was reminded of how I got angry once and threw the cymbals at you when you missed the right pose,' I joked.

She didn't laugh. She seemed pained by the memory. I was terribly scared for her.

'The doctors say I will never be able to walk again.'

'They are fools. Don't listen to a word.'

'Visiting hours are over,' a nurse announced and left.

'You should go,' Ayla said.

'I will come back tomorrow,' I said.

~

'Ayla is in a bad state. She won't survive like this. Can you do something?'

'I am afraid not. It is unlikely she will ever walk again.'

'Doctor...surely, there is something that you can do. I mean, she is so young. She can't spend the rest of her life in a wheelchair. What if we take her abroad for treatment?'

'I doubt that will help. We have the most advanced medical technology for spinal injuries in this hospital. You won't get any extra care abroad that is not already available here. However, if you want to get a second opinion, then I won't stop you,' the doctor said.

'I don't doubt your expertise, but this is about her life.'

'It was a twenty-five-feet free fall. It could have been fatal.

She survived because her head landed on soft mud. Her back has suffered extensive damage. She has fractured her vertebrae. The lower spinal cord is supported by iron rods.

'My heart bleeds for her. But the truth is, I can't do much. The recovery is going to be slow. She will require a caretaker for the rest of her life.'

A nurse entered the room and told the doctor he was required in the operation theatre. He picked up his coat and left.

I sat there wondering. I wasn't going to take 'No' for an answer from the doctor. I wouldn't take no from God. It wasn't about dance anymore. This was a question of her survival. I was determined to see her walk again and feel whole again. If a miracle was required, then a miracle would have to take place.

22

Darkness

Ayla

When I was twelve, I asked Bavo to buy me an expensive yellow bicycle. He took out his wallet without a word and paid the vendor. When the time came to mount it, I developed cold feet.

'I will fall,' I said.

'Yes, you will,' he replied. 'But once you learn to ride it, imagine the places you can see. The whole world will be within your reach.'

'Can I go to Mardin?'

'Why only Mardin? You can go even further to your Dayê's town, Orzu, all the way to the Black Sea.'

I dreamt of cycling around the world. Those lofty dreams ended abruptly when I lost my balance and fell on the road. My left knee was badly scraped. A mixture of blood and dust settled on the wound. I began to cry. Bavo came running towards me and took me in his lap.

'I will never cycle again,' I said.

He carried me home and bandaged the wound. A week

later, he took me to the park to try again. This time, I didn't fall.

He had always been a pillar of support. I couldn't imagine a world without him.

I had heard somewhere that time heals wounds. But some wounds run so deep they become a part of our existence. We carry them everywhere we go. They become a burden that weighs heavy on the heart.

I wasn't ready to let my father go.

I clung on to Bavo's memories, afraid I would forget him. My time with him was all I had left. I wasn't going to give that up even if it caused me pain. His memories kept him alive in my heart.

~

Dayê and Amca were swamped with responsibilities: managing the house, business, hosting relatives and preparing food for visitors. Amca came to visit whenever he had free time, while Dayê stayed with me at night. Guruji spent the morning hours with me, every day.

My Facebook wall was filled with pictures of my contemporaries' dance performances, friends travelling to exotic destinations, eating out, clicking selfies and so on. Some girls had even got engaged by now. I was the only one stuck in a hospital, miserable and unhappy.

There were ugly scars all over my hands and legs. I looked at them and felt ashamed of my actions. I had lost the smoothness of my skin. I couldn't wear skirts, shorts or anything else I liked. Every morning and evening, I was injected with drugs.

'You have just one small task which is to bring me tasteless, bland food,' I snapped at the nurse when she got hardly five minutes late. 'You can't even do that on time. It is only because of you that I am stuck here.'

I wanted her to get upset and argue with me, call the doctors, raise an alarm—do anything to break the cursed silence. But she didn't react.

'I am sorry,' she said in her distinct South Indian accent. 'The doctor had called me for an emergency operation.'

She left as silently as she had arrived. I was mortified at my behaviour and regretted it. I apologised to her the subsequent morning. She pretended as if she didn't know what I was talking about. She put her hand on my head. I was touched by her affection.

Dayê didn't even have time to weep in dignity. Bavo's medical treatment and my condition left us with a huge financial burden. The shop was in shambles. The accountant was siphoning off money. The workers were lost without Bavo's leadership. Amca tried to help out, but he struggled with the work culture in India.

The workers didn't respect him. They felt threatened by his initiatives which involved running a lean business with the help of technology. He proposed a cut in salary, and an increase in work hours. It only added fuel to the fire. Three workers quit in protest.

~

I woke up in the middle of the night panting from another one of those recurring nightmares. My throat felt dry. I was sweating profusely. It was pitch dark. There were beads of sweat on my forehead. I was terribly afraid.

My whole body shook uncontrollably. I had no control over my hands or legs. 'Nurse. Nurse. Help me, please,' I screamed.

Fortunately, Sister Mariamma was tending to a patient in the next room. She heard my cries and came running. The doctor was informed immediately.

They gave me an injection. Within a few minutes, the trembling stopped. I felt much better. I asked them what was wrong with me. They had no idea.

The doctor checked my pulse, examined my eyes and ears. He couldn't understand much. Maybe it was a new, incurable disease. I was doomed to die in this hospital bed.

'We will run a few tests in the morning,' he said, looking tired and sleepy.

I swallowed three sleeping pills and asked the nurse to stay in my room until I went to sleep. I didn't want to be alone.

'Should we call your mother?' she said out of concern.

'Don't,' I said, immediately. 'She must be exhausted from working all day.'

I woke up eight hours later. Last night's events were hazy. A severe headache welcomed me to reality. The state of my mind was worse than the state of my body.

I was in tears. I didn't know how to stay calm. There was a churning inside that scared me; I heard strange voices in the pit of my stomach.

~

An adult's pulse rate is usually between 60-100 beats per minute. However, mine hovered around 120.

The doctors refused to give me food or water. They feared it would go into my lungs and choke me. Instead, they put me on IV.

A terminally ill patient told me that the hospital staff kept a brown register in the administration room. It had the names of all those patients who were expected to die. He had managed a peek inside while the nurse was away. My name was second on that list, after him. I was expected to sign out any moment.

I had episodes of sudden, ravenous hunger. One morning, I was so famished, I drank five glasses of milk, one after another, along with a whole pack of oatmeal.

'Get me more food, please,' I said to Dayê.

Two days after that, I didn't feel like eating anything. The sight of food made me feel nauseous. I had lost thirteen kilos by the end of two months.

The menstrual period was agonising. It left me in tears. The periods were unpredictable. Sometimes, they started in the middle of the night when I was fast asleep. I would wake up complaining of pain and a minute later, blood would begin to gush out of my system.

A blackish red liquid came out of me with force. My flow was unending and my sanitary pad would be completely soaked in it. I used the last reserve of my energy to stifle my tears. The first time it happened, I wasn't even wearing a sanitary pad. The nurse walked into my room the next morning, and saw patches of blood all over. She looked at me with a mix of embarrassment and pity.

I often puked until there was not a morsel left in my stomach.

~

I grew addicted to the sleeping pills and painkillers. The pain came with such fury that I had to take immediate action. I began taking six tablets every day.

The continuous dosage of drugs and injections ruined my body. My abdomen bloated and my breasts became saggy. I woke up to an awful headache every morning and the spurts of vomit, with blood in them, happened at an alarming frequency.

I was going down a slippery slope and I didn't know how to stop this pain. Just the sight of anyone entering my room made me want to scream.

There were dark circles under my eyes and my skin became loose and wrinkled. I would have revolted at my sight earlier, but now, I looked at my reflection and accepted it without a word of complaint. This was my fate.

Blood tests showed that I was allergic to gluten and mushrooms. I was put on a strict vegetarian diet. Most meals consisted of curd and brown rice.

The muscles on my back and shoulder developed knots. I needed regular massage to prevent them from deteriorating further.

I was asked to see a psychologist.

~

I missed Umair and wondered if he had already forgotten me. The memory of our last meeting was painful. I wished I had hugged him instead of shouting at him. It would have brought me some closure, peace of mind at least.

Maybe, he didn't wish to speak to me any longer.

There was no going back for us. He wouldn't accept me in this condition and even if he did, how happy could he be with a paraplegic? That was my reality. I would only be a burden on him, just like I was on Dayê. I had to cut him out of my life.

They ferried me from one hospital wing to another. I was promised a cure.

'You are lucky,' the head orthopaedician, a distinguished doctor, said. 'If the internal bleeding had not been treated on time in Turkey; it would have proved fatal.'

My thoughts went to the medical staff in Turkey who saved my life and I cursed them to no end. I didn't regret my attempt at suicide; it was my misfortune that I failed.

I was worthless.

I had been on antibiotics for almost 273 days and there had been life-threatening situations on several occasions. My treatment cost five lakh rupees. This was excluding the cost of medicines and frequent tests that were undertaken at the hospital. Everything that Bavo had saved over the past twenty-seven years was going down this black hole.

The doctors decided to release me. There was nothing more they could do. I was advised to be under full-time care and supervision. However, we didn't have the resources to afford a full-time nurse.

I needed help for the most basic tasks like taking a shower, changing my clothes, and defecation. It was embarrassing to take the nurse's help to use the toilet.

I didn't know what to do with myself. The silence was driving me crazy. A day felt like eternity and the nights were endless. The world was a scary place without hope.

The thought of taking my life entered my head on more than one occasion, but I had to put it away. I couldn't leave Dayê alone now.

Amca withdrew my admission from the Law College. I wasn't going anywhere.

23

Of Laughter and Healing

Guru Chandrashekhar

Ayla's mother was scared. She spent countless nights lying awake and alert in the hospital. By the time she got ready to leave the hospital and go for work, I would have finished my classes and joined Ayla. We spent three hours together. When I left, Sister Mariamma kept a close watch on her till late evening.

Hospitals sapped every bit of energy out of a person, even a healthy one. The overpowering smell of disinfectants, patients being wheeled in on stretchers made the air heavy with defeat and gloom. It was as if all joy and happiness had been sucked out.

I could understand the mental state of the patients by observing their gestures. Those waiting for a diagnosis looked most vulnerable and pitiful. They had grave expression and stooping shoulders. They breathed heavily and looked around at others, wondering what fate had in store for them. Post diagnosis, patients turned inwards from either happiness or grief, and sometimes both. They were now too consumed to notice anything else.

We hide our illnesses and refuse medical treatment until we can no longer afford to do so. We delude ourselves into believing we are safe in our carefully crafted world. It is in medical centres, more than anywhere else, that we come to face the truth of our mortality.

The fickleness of life is a sobering realisation.

Ayla's recovery could never take place in the physiotherapy ward, no matter how many exercises and tests she underwent. They could fix her bones, but not her broken spirit.

She needed to seek refuge in a dream, and how could anyone nurture a dream in a hospital? It was a place for nightmares.

~

'Roll up your sleeve,' the nurse said.

She took the syringe close to her eyes and pressed it a little to push out any air. A drop or two fell on the floor.

Ayla looked at me. Her eyes sought my help and sympathy. I couldn't give her the former and didn't know how to offer the latter. She would eventually roll up her sleeve in resignation.

I switched on the television with the hope that it might distract her. I flipped past Cartoon Network, Star Movies and settled on News Today before I realised that the channel was showing highlights from a Bharatanatyam performance. I changed it immediately. The last thing she needed was the ghosts of her past to torment her. I hoped that she didn't notice the dance.

She looked at me and said, 'Let it play.'

I was hesitant, but she kept her gaze on me.

'I want to see,' she repeated.

I flipped back to the same channel.

The nurse took her hand, determined the entry point and slowly released the syringe into her vein. Ayla's attention was diverted by the dance sequence on the television screen. She barely noticed the injection. The nurse took a piece of cotton, dipped it in antiseptic and pressed it firmly at the point of insertion. Ayla flinched for a second and then continued looking at the screen.

The love for dance still flowed in her veins. It wasn't a momentary distraction. Dance could set her free.

~

'It has been more than six months. She is still on bed rest. I wish I could do more for her,' I told Sudha.

'But you already are doing a lot,' she replied. 'Your presence comforts her. Right now, she needs to be surrounded by people who care.'

'That's the problem,' I said. 'She doesn't have any friends or family here except for her mother. And her mother is in so much stress that she is always serious and fretting. She needs the company of a carefree, happy-go-lucky person. If only there was a friend she could talk to.'

'But there is.'

'No, there isn't. The other girls at the natyalaya hated her, remember.'

'Who said anything about a girl?'

'Then who?'

'Have you forgotten Kartik?'

'Please. He was merely an acquaintance.'

Kartik was my least favourite student at Pratishtha. He had a way of getting on my nerves. I couldn't bear the thought of Ayla's friendship with that good-for-nothing boy. Sudha kept looking at me.

'Fine. I will find out where he is.'

I contacted a few former trainees and found Kartik's whereabouts within a day. He was in Delhi and more than willing to help.

I waited for Kartik outside Ayla's room. I wanted to brief him about her condition first, and then share a few dos and don'ts. The boy was prone to foolishness.

He was supposed to reach by 9:30 am. It was ten already and there was still no sign of him. Late again. He would never learn.

Ten minutes before the clock struck eleven, a young officer dressed in a navy-blue uniform approached me. He walked like a thorough gentleman. As he came closer, he removed the white hat and placed it under his left arm with practised ease.

There was a hint of a smile on his face.

'Good afternoon, Guruji.'

I was stumped. The voice was familiar, deeper now, but still contained traces of its original tone.

'How is Ayla?' he asked.

'She is...well, she is okay now...better than she was a few months ago,' I mumbled.

I still couldn't believe it was Kartik. Before I could tell him anything, he had entered Ayla's room.

24

Dance in a Wheelchair

Ayla

A stranger entered my room without knocking or taking permission. It was enough to make me lose my temper on most occasions, but not this time.

He didn't look like he was from the hospital staff. He had a mischievous smile on his face. None of the hospital staff ever smiled. He looked at me eagerly, patiently. I had seen him before. I wondered for a minute and then it hit me. So much about him had changed, but the hollow cheeks were exactly the same as before, and his hair remained dishevelled despite all the gel that he had used to make it fall in line.

'Kartik?' I said. 'Is it really you?'

He stood there and laughed loudly. I joined in. It felt so strange, to laugh with such abandon.

He held my hand, leaned down and kissed me on the cheek. Even his affectionate self hadn't changed a bit. He pulled the chair forward and sat right next to me.

I desperately wanted to avoid the sob story about my injury and Bavo's death. I had repeated it innumerable times in the past few months. I just didn't have the patience. 'Whatever happened to you?' I exclaimed before he could ask me anything.

'That's a long story.'

'As you can see, I have all the time in the world.'

How unpredictable is life! I thought. I was a talented dancer and he was still making his way, only a few years ago. And now, I couldn't even get out of my bed to receive him. I felt a sharp pang of envy at this change of events. But that only lasted a fleeting second. Now I sat on the bed, laughed and relished the company of an old friend.

He was the same silly boy who had taught me how to tie a saree. I would never forget that. No one could take that away from us.

I laughed at his jokes, even when they weren't funny. I had missed him without even realising it.

'Where did you disappear?' I asked.

'I left Pratishtha when I was sixteen. Dance was never my thing, anyway.'

'That was clear,' I said, tongue in cheek, 'but why didn't you stay in touch?'

'Because, I ran away from home.'

'That's crazy! Where did you go?' I asked.

'I forged my father's signature to take the Marine Nautical Exam.'

'Are you serious? He would have been angry.'

'Luckily, I was on a ship to Canada before he found out. By the time I saw him again, a few years later, I had become the Second Officer in an American shipping corporation. He made peace with it.'

'That's good. So, what exactly is it that you do now?'

'I am a sailor, the navigating officer on board. I steer the ship. My job is to keep the bridge watch between 0000-0400 hours and 1200-1600. Something like driving a car, except a ship is the size of a football field.'

'Wow! That sounds exciting. What was it like on your first voyage?'

'It's an experience. The ocean is spread across miles and there is no human in sight. I fell in love with the blue of the ocean. Some people get lonely or tired, but I was happy being away from the land and noise. And of course, I got ragged.'

'Why?'

'It was a long time ago. I don't even remember it so well.'

'Please, tell me. I am not well. This will cheer me up,' I said, wryly. It was possibly the first time I had taken advantage of my illness. There is a silver lining to everything.

'Ragging happens the first time you cross the equator. According to some story, you have to take permission from King Neptune for crossing the equator. Ragging is the price you pay for safe passage.'

'Spare me the lecture, sailor. What did they do?'

'They shaved off all my hair and smeared red-and-green paint on my body.'

I laughed, imagining the scene.

'That's not all,' he said. 'I had to take a full walk around the ship, dancing to the tune of Vengaboys' *Brazil...Ta ra ra ra ra ra.*'

That cracked me up so bad my stomach began to hurt. Three hours passed in a jiffy. It didn't feel like we hadn't spoken for seven long years.

This is the beauty of true friendships. You can pick from wherever you left.

~

After ten months, the doctors released me from the hospital.

Guruji was supposed to pick me at nine in the morning. He had volunteered to drop me home, but it was already past ten and there was no sign of him. His phone too was out of reach.

'Should we just take a taxi?' Dayê asked. 'We inconvenience him enough as it is.'

'He is very particular about time; I wonder what happened.'

He walked in just right then.

'I am so sorry,' he said, breathless, and almost panting. 'I got occupied with some last-minute work at Pratishtha.'

'Please have a glass of water and catch your breath,' Dayê said.

He gulped down the water in one go and said, 'Let's get going. There is no more time to waste.'

It was a pleasant Sunday morning. The sky was clear and it was perfect weather for long family conversations over tea and steaming pakodas. The roads were fairly empty. I was enjoying the drive and looking forward to going home.

I rolled down the window and soaked in the fresh air. Within fifteen minutes, we had crossed a few malls in Vasant Kunj. Guruji was a little fidgety, and kept looking at me from time to time.

Instead of taking the usual left turn leading to my house, he kept driving further ahead.

'You missed the turn,' I pointed out.

'I didn't take it on purpose,' he said, looking ahead. 'We are going someplace else.'

I looked at Dayê and she seemed equally clueless.

'Where?'

'You will see,' Guruji said.

We crossed Vasant Kunj, drove past Ber Sarai, Green Park and I had a faint idea where we were headed. I hoped that I was wrong because it was a bad, *bad* idea. Guruji stopped the car right in front of Pratishtha's entrance.

'Let's go inside for a couple of minutes, then I will drop you home,' he said.

Dayê was speechless.

Guruji had surely lost his mind.

I didn't protest. I didn't know if I was happy or sad, enthusiastic or scared. I just didn't know what to feel. Meanwhile, he stepped out of the car, unlocked the gates of Pratishtha and looked at me.

I requested Guruji to stop my wheelchair in front of the entrance. I leaned forward and touched the floor with my hands. He carefully wheeled me inside and switched on the lights. They flickered for a few seconds before illuminating the dance floor.

All came back to me slowly—the distinct scent of the natyalaya and the creaking noise of the wooden floor where the nails were loose. I looked at every small detail—everything seemed to be the same, except myself. I had changed beyond recognition.

Back in the days, I had my own key to Pratishtha. I could come and go as I pleased. This space was my home. I looked at the mirrors and a smile escaped my lips.

There was a big sticker on the wall with the message that read, 'Welcome home, Ayla'. There were balloons all over and the walls had been decorated with stars. Now I understood why Guruji got late in the morning. Even Dayê allowed herself a brief smile.

'This is beautiful. Thank you, Guruji.'

'You are welcome. Pratishtha is your home, Ayla. You can come here anytime you wish.'

A few dance students trickled in. They all came to Guruji and touched his feet. These girls were much younger than me; another sobering reminder that I had aged. The students looked at me with curiosity and surprise.

I must have been an odd sight—a grown-up woman in a wheelchair at a dance centre.

I remembered the days when I would be drenched in sweat after long hours of dance sessions without any break. I enjoyed that extreme state of exhaustion. It made me feel alive.

I promised myself that no matter what, I would keep coming to the natyalaya, so what if I couldn't dance anymore. This was indeed home.

~

I sat on the bed and flexed my calves, glutes and hips respectively, for as long as I could. On the first day, I could barely manage to flex my lower body for 10-15 seconds.

I would complete my mobility exercises at any random hour that I could spend with Guruji. If he wasn't there, I would simply skip the exercises. It took ten weeks to increase the duration of training to almost half an hour, every day. With practice, my strength and stamina increased bit by bit to the point where I gained some control over my lower body.

It was slow progress, but progress nonetheless. Guruji, however, wasn't satisfied. He kept pushing me to do more. I think it was just his nature. He didn't know when to stop. He took Dayê and me back to Pratishtha one day. He asked me to do something I thought I could never do again. He asked me to dance.

'What do you mean?' I said.

'You have been doing physiotherapy for the past ninety days. It's time for you to up the ante.'

'Is this your idea of a joke?' Dayê intervened. 'Ayla can't walk. The doctors have given their opinion. If she tries to stand and dance, she will hurt herself.'

'So what, she will sit in a wheelchair and dance.'

'But it is impossible, Guruji,' I replied.

'Always remember this, Ayla, life is going from one discomfort zone to another without losing hope.'

He took the nattuvangam in one hand and began to play. I didn't remember how to begin and looked at Guruji, absolutely clueless.

'Start with namaskaram,' he reminded me.

I brought my palms together and made a circle around my body. I tried to touch the floor and seek blessings. But I couldn't reach all the way down. Guruji didn't stop or interfere. Finally, I closed my eyes and touched the floor with my fingers.

Guruji sang slowly and that helped me stay with the rhythm. I was rusty. Many times, I forgot the movements or mixed them up.

'Don't try to remember the technique. Forget everything else and just dance,' he instructed.

I closed my eyes and let go. The body did my bidding. I don't remember what exact movements my hands performed, I wasn't listening to Guruji's beats anymore. There was darkness and only the sound of my breath rang in my ears.

My fingers pointed outwards instinctively. As I began to move my hands, all the old familiar gestures came back to me, my expressions following my hands.

As the session progressed, I felt much better. I was warming up and becoming more receptive to the beats. I felt a trickle of sweat on my body, smelled its odour. Who likes to sweat. It's undesirable. However, I had come to relish it as a dancer. It proved the effort I put in every day to strive for perfection. There was something therapeutic about it back then, and even now. I felt cleansed by it.

Guruji quickened the tempo. He challenged me to keep up. I began panting fifteen minutes into the session. Years of inactive lifestyle, and dosages of antibiotics had weakened my body.

Regret, jealousy, insecurity and anger found a vent through my dance. Through long and tired breaths, I exhaled my worries away.

I felt a faint tingling sensation in my feet, like a current running through my nerves. There was faint movement in my toe. The fingers were moving up and down at their own accord. That hadn't happened since my accident.

It wasn't initiated by me. It was like an accidental discovery, totally unexpected and completely delightful. Now, I consciously tried to move my fingers with all the energy I could muster.

'Keep going, Ayla,' Guruji egged me on.

I flexed my feet. They were no longer stiff and unresponsive. Left, right, up and down; they moved. I tried to stand up from the chair using my hands for support. It was scary.

The beats became faster now. Dayê stood up. Some girls applauded to encourage me.

I was halfway up from the chair when my legs buckled from the pressure. I lost my balance and fell down. Guruji and Dayê came rushing towards me. I had a small bump on my forehead, but I was smiling. I had overcome my paralysis!

25

One Step at a Time

Guru Chandrashekhar

'There was movement in her legs,' I said, entering the orthopaedic surgeon's chamber. He was engrossed in a report and didn't pay attention to my words.

'What do you mean?'

'Ayla. She tried to stand up and then fell to the floor.'

'That's impossible.'

'So they say. But she proved everyone wrong.'

He took off his glasses, kept them on the table and looked at me. 'I don't believe you. After nine months of immobility, just like that...'

'I was right there. It happened when I asked her to dance.'

'You asked her to dance?' he exclaimed, shocked. 'Are you mad?'

'That's not important,' I replied. 'She tried standing up from her wheelchair. If she can do it once; she can do it again, right?'

'She stood all by herself? No support.'

'Doctor,' I said, 'Ayla is no ordinary girl. She can beat the odds; she always has. How are you going to help her?'

'If that is true then it's great news,' he said, slowly. 'Having said that, it's still going to be a long road to recovery.'

He gestured at me to take a seat and asked the clerk to bring two cups of tea.

'You need to consult different experts, especially Dr Sharma, the sport physiotherapist. He is an expert in dry needling, and corrective exercise based on functional movement assessment. He can help expedite her recovery.'

'I will contact him. How do we begin her training?'

He weighed a few options and said, 'Occupational therapy is a good choice, I think. It works on the principle of intense, frequent and increased stress given to the bones. This can help reverse her condition.

'But it's risky. If we push her too hard, the muscles can completely give way. The effects would be disastrous. Going forward, we need to be extra careful.'

~

Following the doctor's advice, I got in touch with the experts—psychologist, sports medicine specialist and the physiotherapist.

Everyone agreed that she needed to strengthen her mind as well as body, but their approach was different. It was rooted in their area of expertise.

I hoped to execute one integrated plan, but their advice only confused me. They dealt in possibilities which were not definitive. They said, she could recover but it would take anything between six months to six years. Medicines would help her, but that wouldn't be enough.

I asked them a simple question, 'When can Ayla dance again?'

The physiotherapist, a young man, looked at me and shook his head vigorously, as if the question was irrelevant. 'You have to train her like a child. If you want her to dance; first she has to crawl, walk, stand, jump, run and then take the final step.'

'The physical exercises will amount to nothing if she doesn't believe in her abilities,' the psychologist added. 'It's imperative she gains mental strength along with physical exercise. When she acts out of strength, she will automatically begin to dance without much difficulty.'

The sports medicine expert talked about using state-of-the-art techniques like kinesiology and anaerobic training to increase muscle strength and expedite her recovery.

'Australia,' he said. 'They have expertise in biomechanics. Why do you think the greatest swimmers and athletes come from Down Under?'

Undoubtedly, there was an element of truth in all of their advice, but none would work in isolation. They were missing the wood for the trees. I took the best from each of their suggestions and made a plan. I had no qualifications for this role except that I cared for Ayla. That was all the qualification I needed.

The immediate challenge was to prevent her lower body from being dormant, and motionless. It had lost all its strength. She was susceptible to muscle atrophy.

I pushed her to stay active, give up the wheelchair and support herself with crutches. It meant that I use all the available means to stop her from giving up on herself. The toughest thing I had to do was to take away her wheelchair and demand that she used crutches. She protested vehemently against it and even cursed me. I could see how much pain she was in, and how much discomfort I was putting her through, but I had no choice. I couldn't betray an expression of sympathy. I couldn't relent. I had to act tough so she remained determined and driven to walk again. It didn't matter if she hated me for it or if I came to her house unwelcomed.

Every morning, she spent fifteen minutes on a treadmill especially designed for those with leg and spine injuries. This exercise was aimed at re-learning how to walk after sustaining an injury. It helped her walk without putting excessive burden on her body. She would be in tears by the end of each session. It didn't mean she could stop; it was just something she had to get used to. It took a year for her to gain the confidence to stand up on her feet without any support. The recovery was painfully slow and it tested both of our will and patience.

~

'A year has passed since the accident, however, she is still struggling to walk with ease. I don't know what to do,' I said to the doctor, helplessly.

Dr Sharma said, 'It will put too much stress on her legs. You should try aqua therapy.

'According to a leading medical journal, patients who practised aquatic therapy experienced a forty-four per cent increase in fitness levels as opposed to the seventy-seven per cent who opted for land-based exercises. She won't face the resistance on water that she will face on the ground.'

'Where do I take her for a swim? What if she is not comfortable in a pool with others. She has become reserved and withdrawn since the injury.'

'Take her to Siri Fort Sports Complex. I will arrange a private session for you.

'Okay, doctor. Let's do it your way.'

~

Next morning, I went to Ayla's house to share the idea.

'I know how to swim, but what if my legs don't work? What if I sink?' she asked me.

'A lifeguard and a physiotherapist will be present at all times. The moment you feel any discomfort, they will help you out. I will be there as well.'

'But...'

'If you are totally against the idea, then I will drop it.'

'I don't know. Okay. Let's give it a try.'

We drove to Siri Fort Sports Complex after breakfast. Tall and lean basketball players were showing tricks on the court. Tennis and badminton players, golfers, and joggers were sweating it out on the field. This was the kind of energetic environment Ayla needed.

The guard at the entrance stood up from his chair. 'The pool is shut right now. Come back in the evening,' he said.

'Dr Sharma asked us to come at this time,' I said.

At the mention of Dr Sharma, he straightened his posture and smiled deferentially. The doctor was a known figure. He had taken special permission so that Ayla could swim alone in the pool, without any interference.

'Sorry, Sir.'

He fumbled for the keys and searched frantically. Finally, he found them in the front pocket of his unbuttoned shirt. He apologised once again and opened the gates.

~

The physiotherapist joined us a few minutes later. 'Don't worry, Sir. We will not do any difficult exercises,' he assured me.

'Don't make it too easy for her. She needs to push herself,' I instructed.

'Okay,' he replied, a little confused.

Ayla's face was full of anxiety.

'You can do this. I will be with you every step of the way.'

'Okay.'

The physiotherapist and I helped her step inside the pool. She gave a sigh when her body went inside water. I tensed up.

Swimming was a different ball game. She would have to use her legs more than she had since the injury.

Was I sure about this?

No.

Her face tightened with resolve. She held on to the physiotherapist's and my hand and ventured into the shallow end of the pool. The physiotherapist started her off with simple forward and backward movements of legs inside the water. 'It's difficult to stand straight,' she said and often lost her balance. 'I want to get out.'

'Give it some more time. You will be fine,' I said.

We stayed in the pool for 20-25 minutes. It was a step in the right direction. She came out of the pool smiling. It felt good.

When I dropped her home, she seemed tired. It was difficult for her, but she wasn't complaining. I was proud of her effort. We started going to the pool three times a week. Gradually, she got comfortable with the idea of walking and floating unaided in the water. Her muscle strength and, more importantly, her confidence returned in due course of time.

26

Cakes, Birthdays and Revelations

Ayla

Dayê and I went to the hospital for further tests. Two years ago, I had to be wheeled in, but now I was standing on my own feet. Yes, I didn't need support to be taken from one department to another.

I went to the general ward to surprise Sister Mariamma. She was bandaging a young boy who had bruised his knee while playing in the garden. He was crying inconsolably, scared of the injection. She managed to divert his attention with a toy. I was reminded of my days in the hospital.

I stood behind her, silently. When she finished, I tapped her on her shoulder. The other nurses watched the scene with curiosity. Mariamma turned around. She was astonished to see me.

'But, you are standing on your feet,' she said.

I nodded my head in delight and said, 'With crutches, but still!'

'Wow! How did that happen, and in such a short time?'

We hugged.

'What are you doing here?'

'Regular check-up and further tests.'

It felt so good to see her again. She escorted Dayê and me to the test centre and walked me past long queues of patients.

The nurse on duty asked Mariamma who I was.

'She is my daughter,' Mariamma replied.

The test results showed that the swimming and body resistance exercises had opened 'dormant nerve pathways' in my body. The activity-based recovery programme had resulted in functional benefits. Overall, there was significant improvement in my cardiovascular function, muscle strength and bone density.

It verified what I already knew—I was on the road to recovery.

~

'Happy birthday to you. Happy birthday to you, dear Ayla. Happy birthday to you.'

I heard the song and cheering and pulled the quilt down. Dayê, Guruji, Sudha and Kartik were standing next to my bed. It was midnight. Kartik had a blueberry cheesecake in his hand. There was one big candle lit at the centre.

I didn't know how to react. I was just happy.

'Smile, please,' Kartik said.

But, I was in tears. I wished Bavo was here. Dayê came forward and hugged me. It took me forever to gain my composure. It took a lot of time for a smile of gratitude to flash on my face. The people in this room were family. I owed my life to them.

'Happy birthday, Gulum,' Dayê said and kissed me.

'Happy birthday, Ayla,' Guruji said. 'I can't believe you are a twenty-three-year-old woman now.'

'I can't believe it either,' I said, getting out of bed. I touched Guruji's feet and he gave me his blessings, but to be honest, I was more interested in the cheesecake.

I cut a small piece out for Dayê, but instead of accepting it, she asked me to serve Guruji first. He asked me to serve Dayê first and I got fed up and put the piece into my mouth, instead.

'I brought you a present as well. It's right outside,' he said. 'Go, take a look.'

'What is this thing?' It looked like a cycle, except it had two tyres at the back and one in the front like an autorickshaw.

'It is called a Functional Electrical Stimulation bicycle,' he said with a flourish .

'What does it do?'

'It is a customised vehicle that allows you to pedal a stationary leg-cycle called an ergo meter. It will transmit low-level electrical pulses through surface electrodes which will strengthen your leg muscles.'

'What a cool birthday gift,' I said. I liked the idea of this bicycle. I was bored of the usual strength exercises.

~

The following afternoon, Guruji and I went out for brunch. There were more than 15,000 restaurants in Delhi, and innumerable dhabas that served mouthwatering dishes. However, I knew exactly where Guruji would take me.

'Let's go to Nathu Sweets in Bengali Market,' he suggested. Nathu Sweets, which opened in 1939, was a popular sweetmeat shop in Central Delhi's bustling Bengali market that served a variety of sweets and snacks. Guruji was a diehard fan of their legendary aloo chaat. The mix of fried potato fritters, curd, green mint sauce and tamarind was a universal favourite among foodies, and a go-to dish for expectant mothers. Often, many dutiful and some helpless husbands would be seen here, as late as midnight, getting aloo chaat packed for their wives. Some even claimed that Nathu's aloo chaat was auspicious for the foetus.

'It is not what it used to be,' Guruji complained about the present state of Nathu's. He waved at the waiter, who shrugged and went about taking someone else's order.

'Twenty years ago, I knew the waiters by their names and they recognised me too. I didn't even have to order anything, they would simply greet me and bring me my plate of aloo chaat within minutes of my arrival. All of them have left now. The new ones have to be beckoned several times before they take the order.'

'Then, why do you still come here?'

'It brings back fond memories. I visited this joint first time with a friend, aeons ago. She loved golgappas.'

Surely, this friend was more than just that. But the idea of Guruji on a date, even in the distant past, seemed strange. He was always so serious and uptight, I couldn't imagine him chilling with a friend.

'My guess is you were overbearing and she ran away.'

'On the contrary, I indulged her no end. Never said *no* to her, even when she told me she wanted to leave me,' he said, with a smile that camouflaged his pain.

He was a private and reserved man. Those closest to him,

even Sudha, couldn't tell with certainty what was going on in his mind. It was a rarity to see him speak with such candour.

'Tell me more about this mystery woman.'

'Oh no,' he hesitated.

'It is my birthday. You can't say no,' I insisted. I also knew when I could push my luck.

'Please, Guruji.'

'It's not a fun story.'

'Doesn't matter. I still want to hear it.'

27

I Think of Her

Guru Chandrashekhar

'The year was 1990 or maybe, '91. I was practising dance by myself when she walked inside Pratishtha. She was dressed in a white kurta and blue chunni or maybe, a blue kurta and white chunni. Some of the details have faded, but I remember her smile. The way it tried to cover for her awkwardness, but its effect was exactly the opposite. It made her stand out from the crowd. She was beautiful and very uncomfortable with her beauty.

'I lost my voice and stared at her like a fool. I knew she would be someone special in my life,' I recounted.

'My name is Chandra,' I said.

'Imagine that, Ayla. Even my mother had never addressed me as Chandra. We say the most delightfully silly things in love.'

'I want to enrol in the dance class. How is the teacher here? I have heard he is quite stuck up. Is that true?' she asked.

'I just couldn't get angry at her. There was kindness in her voice even when she was critical. She had no idea I was that 'stuck up' teacher. She was expecting, perhaps, an older man.

'He can be tough,' I said. She panicked and made a dash for the exit. 'I think I should leave. Don't tell anyone I had come.'

'Listen, wait.

'You will be fine. At least, try out two or three sessions? See if you feel up to it.'

'But, Guruji,' Ayla interrupted, 'you never allow trial sessions at Pratishtha.'

'Come on, Ayla,' I said with a shrug.

She left without saying yes or no. I was sure she wasn't going to register. 'I couldn't sleep for the rest of the week. I hadn't even asked her name. What if she didn't return?'

'Was she a good dancer?' Ayla asked.

'She was good at many things, but dance was not one of them. She had no hand-eye coordination. The fact that she could stand on her feet without stumbling was no less than a miracle.'

'Weren't you disappointed? Dance means so much to you.'

'I made fun of her dance all the time. Dance helped break the ice between us. I couldn't have asked for more.

'A year passed by in these little games. My feelings for her grew stronger. She was right in front of me, but I couldn't bare my heart to her.

'It was a double-edged sword. I got to see her daily, but I had to maintain distance and decorum. I was her teacher, after all. I had no idea what she thought of me.

'She was nine years younger. My father would have never approved. The dance community would pass caustic remarks about lack of professionalism. It is an unwritten rule: you don't get involved with your students,' I explained.

'What happened then?' Ayla asked.

'I finally got my chance to speak to her. It was an early morning session and she was the only one who came to the class. I wasn't interested in teaching and she didn't seem much interested in dancing either. I ended the session quickly and asked her to join me for a walk to the Hauz Khas Lake. It was a beautiful day, full of possibilities. We had left the world behind, stolen a few precious moments, just for ourselves. I knew I would never find a more intimate moment with her.

'I am very fond of you. I have been since the moment I first saw you,' I told her.

'She looked at me, neither with delight, nor with embarrassment, but helplessness,' I continued with my story.

'Why me? There are many better dancers at Pratishtha,' she said.

'I wish I knew. I wish I could make sense of it, but I can't. I have tried. When I was a child, I watched my father conduct a grand dance performance. I wanted to do the same. It felt right. Something about you, about us feels right,' I told her.

'There was hesitation on her face. It sent a shiver down my spine. I knew her answer would affect me, but I didn't realise my life and death seemed to depend on it. She was going to say no. I couldn't take the thought of that.

'It took all the courage in the world to tell her that it was okay if she didn't feel the same way,' I continued.

'Listen, I...it is complicated with me. I belong to a conservative Jat family from Karora in Haryana. They have fulfilled every wish of mine, even allowed me to pursue an education in Delhi, despite all restrictions and gender prejudices. All they have ever asked in return is that I marry a boy from the same community. They would never approve of us,' she tried to explain.

'I looked into her eyes and saw a struggle in them. I was convinced she wanted to be with me, but the strings of reason were pulling hard at her.

'If it comes to that, then I will go and do everything in my power to convince them. If they still don't agree, then I will walk away knowing I did everything I could. The real tragedy would be if we didn't even try,' I told her.

~

'Her mother found out. She reminded Kanika that they had sent her to Delhi for studies, not to malign the family's reputation. She asked about my caste and profession. The answers made it worse.

'A dance teacher?' her mother asked. 'That's not a *man*'s job. What must we tell the khap panchayat? That your husband wears ankle bells to work every morning?'

'It was only a matter of time before she told Kanika's father. He was livid. He threatened to disown her. In a fit of rage, he withdrew her admission from the college. He had always doted on her, but after hearing about us, he refused to budge.'

'This is a small town. We are part of the community. Our business, our lives, our very survival depend on the cooperation and support of the community. Will they respect me if you marry a South Indian? They will laugh at us,' her father roared with disgust and walked out.

'Her mother cried many tears. She beseeched Kanika to sacrifice her love for the sake of her family. Her decision would have long-term ramifications on her younger sister's marriage prospects.

'She was forced to choose between her family and me. She had immense respect for her family and the sacrifices they had made so she could pursue higher studies. No other girl in her community had had this opportunity. Kanika took pride in the fact that she had never done anything to bring her parents disrepute. And, she did what she had to. In my heart, I knew she would choose her family. It's not that she didn't love me, but she couldn't manage conflicts. It was too big a price to pay.

'Determinedly and decisively, she pushed me away from her life. I never saw her again.

'This tragedy taught me a valuable lesson, Ayla.'

'What's that?' Ayla asked.

'Conflicts are inevitable. True love is simply when you refuse to give up on something or someone, no matter how difficult things become. And we gave up way too easily.'

'I know how difficult it is to lose someone you love. How did you cope?'

'I was angry. Very angry. I wanted to hurt those who had taken her away from me. I was not the same caste or colour, but that didn't matter in the least. I knew I cared for her happiness. Two lives were ruined.

'I decided to prove them wrong. Dance mattered. Dance could change lives. I was going to show them how. I would save children from the prejudices of their overbearing parents. Someday, Kanika's family would realise their mistake.'

'Didn't you meet anyone else?' Ayla interjected.

'I met many wonderful women, but I never felt the same way about anyone again. I had lost my heart to her. I think I searched for her in others. That was unfair to them and to myself.'

'What happened to Kanika?' Ayla asked.

'She died during childbirth three years after her marriage. Her sister came to see me a week after her death. Kanika had left a shawl for me. It still carries her warmth and scent.

'I think of her. Still.'

28

A Deep Breath

Ayla

Yoga sessions took place in one of the corner rooms on the first floor of Tamil Sangam—the de facto cultural centre of the Tamil community in Delhi. Bhanumati Sreedhar, my new yoga teacher, stood in the middle of the room; I wouldn't exactly call that *standing* though. Both her feet were up in the air, hips stacked, while her head and forearms supported her entire weight.

She looked at me and smiled.

'You must be Ayla.'

'Yes, I am.'

I looked at her upside-down body, wondering if I should tilt my face sideways, downwards or just stand upright and speak.

'Why are you upside-down?' I said, unable to hold the thought in my head.

'Who said, standing on one's feet is the only correct way to be? What if we turn our bodies around and change our perspective? Sometimes, the world makes more sense upside down. This posture helps achieve that equanimity.'

My first impulse was to make an excuse and get the hell out but I couldn't think of an excuse, so I sat down on a mat. There were five other girls in the room. They too, were attempting different postures, although with a lot more difficulty, and far less grace than Bhanumati.

They were all dressed in colourful yoga pants. Each of them sat on a yoga mat and twisted their bodies in round, diagonal and straight movements—in all possible and sometimes, impossible permutations and combinations.

I couldn't even dream of attempting those asanas, nor did I wish to. My body was broken as it was. What if a muscle snapped? After chanting *Om* for a few minutes, Bhanumati returned to her normal posture.

She looked quite beautiful when she wasn't practising a gravity-defying move. She had a neat oval face and a dusky complexion. Her cheeks had turned red from all the blood that had been directed towards her brain.

She untied her bun to release her waist-long hair. Everything about her was neat and proper. A small red bindi marked her forehead. Her eyes were lined with kohl.

No one who saw her could guess she was fifty-five years old; she looked not a day older than forty. And there wasn't an extra inch of fat on her body. Her skin was compact and tight.

Sitting right in front of me, within touching distance, her piercing gaze made me feel awkward and out of place. I was unnerved by the proximity. She hardly blinked.

I didn't know whether to say something or look in another direction. I looked down to avoid her direct gaze, but she held my chin up and made eye contact.

'You are so anxious. There are a million thoughts racing across your mind. Calm down. It is all right,' Bhanumati said.

'I am not anxious.'

'You are breathing heavy,' she said, and I realised I was almost panting. 'Sit and relax.'

Half an hour later, when Bhanumati had finished the session, she returned to where I was sitting.

'Recently, I had an accident. I should tell you about it before we begin training.'

'We use first names here. You are Ayla to me and I am Bhanumati to you. Don't worry about your back injury. I could make that out from the way you walked. Your spine is round and posture incorrect. We will have to work on that. Come early morning tomorrow, we will begin with a few asanas to strengthen your spine.'

~

Next morning, I reached Tamil Sangam at 5 am. I took off my shoes and socks before entering the room. She greeted me with a smile and asked me to sit in front of her. *Oh God, the same thing is going to repeat*, I thought.

'It is a lovely morning, isn't it?' she said.

'Yes,' I replied and tried to suppress a yawn. I preferred my bed to a yoga mat this time of the day.

'I want to talk to you before we start. It is important for you to be open. Open to learning, open to ideas and most importantly, open to letting yourself go. Accept your limitations and go easy on yourself, be a kind and gentle soul. That will open the channel for positive energy to flow in. Always remember to breathe and let go.'

'I understand,' I said, but in reality, I didn't get a word.

'Good. Let's begin.'

'Stand up and fold your hands in front. Now, close your eyes and focus on your breath. Take long and deep breaths. Feel the fresh air enter your lungs.'

I followed Bhanumati's instructions, but my mind wandered. I thought of all the work Dayê had to cope with, the payments she owed to creditors.

There were so many thoughts, I could barely stay still. It was torture. My body was shaking and resisting. I needed movement, distraction. Anything to keep myself occupied. Anything but silence.

'There is no perfect pose, no perfect life, no perfect exercise for that matter. If you start living up to ideas of perfection, you'll be in for disappointments and heartbreak. Everybody is different. Every individual is unique. Connect to your mat, connect to your breath and find your own niche.'

I opened my eyes. The room was silent. The place was as calm as it could be.

'Stretch your forearms wide, join them above your head and lift your heels off the ground as high as possible without losing balance, while you are on your toes. See how high you can go. This is called *Tadasana*. It will improve your posture, sense of centre and breathing rhythm.'

I went as high as I could. I couldn't possibly go up another inch.

'Take a deep breath. Let it loosen your body. Now try and stretch even further,' Bhanumati said, once again focusing all her attention on me.

She persuaded me to go higher. I didn't think it was possible, but it was. I did it by myself. All I needed was a push. I lost my balance and almost fell. She just glanced at me with a gentle smile and moved on to the next asana.

None of the other girls who had arrived and taken their place beside me laughed or snickered. They quietly continued with the warm-up. There was no judgement and that allowed me to continue without any fear of ridicule.

After a few more asanas, I was completely exhausted. I hadn't even stepped out of the yoga mat and I was sweating profusely.

'We are going to do the Surya Namaskar today. I want you to pay close attention to the movements,' Bhanumati said.

It wasn't the conventional Surya Namaskar that Guruji taught us at Pratishtha. She added variations to make the exercise tougher. She asked me to hold each posture for a longer duration and taught me to chant slokas. This ensured that the energy was being channelled to certain parts of the body. We did twenty-five namaskars in half an hour.

Bhanumati didn't stick to one formula. Instead, she took inspiration from different dance forms and natural movements to design a more wholesome, strenuous workout.

In one such asana, I had to balance my weight on one leg, while holding the toe of the other leg, raising it to hip-level and then to the side. The pose required immense strength and balance. My legs just refused to move beyond a point. I realised just how weak my back mobility was.

We hadn't run or danced or done anything that seemed laborious, and yet I felt as if my body had been put through a rigorous training session.

Bhanumati wrapped up the session with *Shavasana* (corpse pose). She asked me to lie down on the floor and close my eyes. And then she helped me communicate with different parts of my body one after the other, starting from my toes all the way up to my head. She asked me to focus on each one of them separately and thank them for their effort. It was a way to build mind-muscle connection—my first lesson in body awareness.

After a few minutes, I sat cross-legged, rubbed my hands together and placed them on my eyes. The heat was supposed to revitalise my body.

The first class concluded.

Everything seemed to have slowed down and I felt a sense of calm as I stepped out of the cultural centre.

~

I sat close to her during the class and did exactly what she did. If her fingers were curled for a particular asana, I curled my fingers too. I became her shadow.

There were days when she would push me to the limit, and then there were times when she would go easy on me. She could gauge my mood, as if by telepathy. I came to the centre every morning and let go of my fears and worries. Yoga became my escape.

All the muscles in my body were being activated, some, that I didn't even know existed. Bhanumati taught me the correct way to breathe so the fresh air went all the way to my lungs. Apparently, I had been breathing all wrong. She also explained the importance of visualisation. So, I visualised myself walking and moving without any difficulty.

'Get back to your roots,' she said.

Sometimes, I succeeded and at other times, I failed. Every day, I stretched my body beyond limit, until I realised the limits were only in my head.

Bhanumati introduced me to the idea of mindfulness. She encouraged me to introspect, even though it made me deeply uncomfortable. Whether it was sorrow over my past or my worries about the future; she asked me to acknowledge the facts without being overwhelmed by emotions or creating stories around them. She taught me how to take control of my life.

The workout diversified to include disciplined postures, purification procedures (shatkarmas), gestures (mudras), breathing and meditation. From the basics of body mechanics, I graduated to the subtler aspects of the discipline.

'The real injury is not in your body. It resides in your heart. Once your heart heals, your body will follow,' she said.

I conversed with my feet, fingers, calves and knees. They were impassive at the beginning, almost angry at my ignorance.

I had felt the soreness in certain body parts when I practised meditation. They had been hurt in the past, abused. I tried to direct my breath towards my spine, shoulders and thighs. They were stiff and tense. I relaxed. *I was safe*, I told myself.

Yoga and dance helped me breathe easily. In the past, I would be overwhelmed by challenges. All my troubles would come together and form an impregnable wall but now I brought my focus to my breath and that helped me relax and let go.

My periods became less painful and timelier. My diet was consistent, and I put on weight. Mentally, I felt less hassled. I was able to cope with problems better. I even slept well.

'The source of your *klesas* or inborn afflictions is

the unresolved conflicts of the past. They have attached themselves to you like a tumour. You need to loosen their grip on you,' Bhanumati explained, during breathing exercises.

'I can't forget all that has happened in my life.'

'I am not asking you to forget your unpleasant past,' Bhanumati explained. 'Don't dwell on it, don't let it torment your soul. Accept it and it will no longer disturb your peace.'

~

There were at least a hundred people inside the noisy canteen filled with noisier fans. Bhanumati bought coupons for two veg thalis. We had come out for lunch to celebrate my completion of one year of yoga.

The Andhra Bhavan canteen was teeming with activity. Waiters moved around in haste carrying steel bowls filled to the brim with sambhar. Every few minutes, a young boy carrying a mop would go to an empty table and wipe it clean in one sweep, right before a new customer would take a seat—an endless cycle.

Our food arrived within minutes. It wasn't just another thali, it was the mother of all thalis comprising yoghurt, sweet, aloo-subzi, bhindi, daal, rasam, sambhar, rice, chapati and poppadom.

Each dish was more delicious than the other, or maybe I was too hungry after the session. Rasam, with an abundance of spices, soothed my sore throat. I lost myself in the myriad options. It all looked so appetising that I didn't know what to eat and what to discard. There was no way I could finish it all.

'The quantity of food is incredible,' I said.

'That's true,' Bhanumati replied, 'unfortunately, they waste a lot of food here. Once you pay for the thali, everything is available in unlimited quantity. It makes people lose all sense of proportion. It actually shows the true character of people.'

'How does a thali show the true character of people?' I asked.

'Just look around. They ask for one, two, even three refills. They don't have the hunger or the appetite, but the availability of unlimited options makes them gluttonous.

'It is the same with life. Most people lose perspective when they come in contact with wealth and fame. Their greed overshadows common sense. Only a smart few will resist the temptation and live within their means. Has that ever happened to you?' Bhanumati asked.

'What?'

'Losing perspective.'

'I don't know about perspective but I did lose my way when I earned recognition from the dance community. The pressure was too much. I guess, I wasn't cut out to be a professional dancer,' I said.

'That's a rather harsh judgement.'

'My journey in dance is complicated. You won't understand.'

'I am not a dancer but I know a thing or two about dance and the challenges that come with it. My mother was a Sadir, a traditional solo dance, performer. Talent like hers came once in a century. I saw her struggles with my own eyes.'

'I had no idea. Did she perform anywhere?'

'She wasn't allowed to; she committed suicide,' Bhanumati said, bluntly.

She said it so nonchalantly that I just sat there, looking at her. I couldn't believe it.

'Why?'

'Circumstances. She was forced to marry. Her career was sacrificed; her life as she knew it was over. She couldn't accept that.'

'She could have continued dance after marriage, couldn't she?'

'They forbade her. That was the condition set before her marriage. They forced her to fit the frame of a meek, submissive housewife, who had no ambitions beyond the well-being of her family.

'The sound of her exquisite footwork couldn't be heard beyond the pillars of the house. The joy on her expressive face was dead behind the impassive walls of domesticity. There was no applause, only tears to show for all her brilliance.

'She killed herself when I was ten—tied a rope around her neck and hung herself from the ceiling fan. I opened the door of the room and saw her lifeless body. That image still haunts me.

'She threw her life away. Didn't even think of what would happen to me,' she said.

I was silent for a moment as I tried to digest all she had told me. Then I said, 'I can imagine what your mother must have gone through because I tried to take my life once and almost succeeded. It wasn't because I loved my family any less.'

'Why didn't you tell me before?'

'I am ashamed of my action. My spine injury is not the result of some freak accident. Two years ago, I tried to kill myself. I jumped out of the second-floor window of my house in Mardin.'

'Why?' Bhanumati asked.

'I was tired of fighting; I couldn't take it any longer. The only thing scarier than death was life. Your mother would have suffered deeply. She must have been helpless and hopeless. That is the only reason,' I said.

Bhanumati whispered in my ear, 'She was the finest dancer in all of Pandanallur Village. Her only misfortune was that she was born into the devadasi community and during that time devadasis were persecuted.'

'Who are devadasis?' I asked.

'*Dev* means God and *dasi*, servant. They were a community of women who dedicated their lives to the worship of a deity in a temple. In Pandanallur, Kerala, they were celebrated as "women of pride".'

'My mother never performed for entertainment; her dance served a higher purpose. Her art enlightened people. It was through a devadasi's dance that a common man experienced divinity,' Bhanumati explained.

'I don't understand. Why did they earn a bad reputation?' I enquired.

'With time, the devadasis became a symbol of sensuality and spirituality. In the past, there was no contradiction between the two. She had become an object of desire and she would still be sacred.

'But some people couldn't accept the nuanced role of devadasis. They deemed devadasis to be prostitutes. Soon, rumours about devadasis spreading venereal diseases were rife.'

'Were they like contemporary dancers?'

Bhanumati snickered at the comparison. 'The modern dancers pale in front of devadasis. They dressed in shimmering silk sarees. They looked more sensual and far more elegant than modern girls look in designer clothes.

'Everyone who witnessed their performance felt special. They would live an illusion that the devadasi was looking at them and *only* them. And, the devadasi did indeed look at them and to her right and left. She looked at everyone and no one in particular.'

'Why did your mother marry at all?'

'A few months after India's Independence, the Madras Devadasis (Prevention of Dedication) Act was signed into law on 9 October 1947. Similar laws were passed in all the states and territories of India.

'Women could no longer dedicate their lives to worshipping deities in temples. It had disastrous consequences.

'Soon, my mother migrated to Madras in search of work. A few of her friends married policemen, musicians, businessmen and even politicians. They were still the most desired women in the community, after all, but they had to pay a heavy price to earn society's acceptance,' Bhanumati continued.

'Dance?' I interrupted.

'Exactly.'

'They wanted to make something extraordinary out of their lives. My mother had to give up her dreams and aspirations.

'Her mother-in-law asked her not step out in front of outsiders, particularly men. In essence, her identity was stolen.

'Appa said to her firmly, "You must realise, this is befitting of our position in society."

'Eventually, Appa got bored of her and found a mistress. She was five years younger than my mother. The loss of dance and the indifference of her husband was too much.

'I was not allowed to dance either, but I could practise yoga. It was "socially acceptable". It helped me preserve sanity in the absence of my mother. I couldn't heal her, but I was determined to use yoga to help other dancers. After fifteen years of practice, I founded the Yoga Healing Therapy,' Bhanumati explained.

'You took an unpleasant memory and made something amazing out of it. You have made a difference to many lives, including mine. Your mother's death wasn't in vain,' I said.

'Thank you. That means a lot to me,' she said. 'May I give you some unsolicited advice?'

'Sure.'

'They took dance away from my mother and she let them. Don't let it happen to you, Ayla.'

~

Her advice rang in my ears. I didn't wish to end up like Bhanumati's mother. Twenty years from now, I didn't want to look back with regret.

Just being able to walk and run wasn't good enough. I felt a strong urge to return to dance, but not in the same way as before. I didn't want to please anyone this time. Nor did I want articles, pictures and write-ups—I could do without the attention.

I wanted to dance for the sake of dance. To hell with everything else.

I had to make a choice and I had to do it now. At this very moment.

I left it to a toss, again. The autorickshaw stopped at the red light and I put my hand inside my purse to take out a coin. A beggar in ragged clothes came asking for alms. She held a sleeping child in her hands.

Her eyes lit up at the sight of a five-rupee coin. She thought I had taken it out for her. I held it between my fingers trying to decide what head and tail stood for. She waited. The girl said something but my mind was elsewhere. Then, she nudged me. The signal was about to turn green.

I was going to flip the coin. I looked at her face, again. The answer was clear. I already knew what I was going to do. My destiny would not be determined by the toss of a coin. I was going to take control of my life.

I gave the coin to the girl and asked the autorickshaw driver to take me to Pratishtha.

V

29

The Last Dance

Guru Chandrashekhar

I was in the middle of a class when Ayla entered Pratishtha. Something about her expression was different, even troubled. Her gaze was fixed on mine, and she stood still, but with no intention to wait. She wanted to talk. I turned towards Sudha. She acknowledged my wordless question with a nod and took over the reins of the class.

'I want to discuss something important.'

'Go on,' I said.

'I want to dance.'

'This is your school. Feel free to attend any number of sessions. I would be delighted.'

'You don't understand,' she said, shaking her head vigorously. 'I want to get back on the stage. I want another arangetram.'

'Another arangetram,' I exclaimed. 'Wait a second. What's going on?'

She recounted everything to me—her lunch with Bhanumati, the story of the devadasis.

I didn't have to ask her if she was sure and explain that this was a decision of monumental proportions. She understood all of that. This wasn't a momentary flicker of passion. Ayla wanted this performance. I saw determination in her eyes. What she had really come looking for was the answer to one specific question: whether I would help her or not.

It brought about so many possibilities and challenges. I remembered the time she had her arangetram and fell on the stage. How her ankle bells had fallen and I had picked them up. They were still with me, safe in the locker.

There and then, I decided I was going to help her with this performance, but I didn't want to tell her that, yet. There was only one thing left to do.

I opened the locker and fished out the ankle bells from a dark corner. They were covered with dust. She would make them shine.

'These belong to you,' I said.

She looked at me with surprise.

'Where did you find these?'

'I was at your dance performance that evening. I kept them, hoping one day, you will return and now you have. So here they are.'

She hesitated to take them from me, perhaps the burden of the previous arangetram overwhelmed her.

'So many years have passed. Can I still dance? Am I too old, too slow?' she asked.

'Yes, you are older and much slower. But if there's anyone who can still do it, it's you. There is one last dance in *you*, Ayla.'

30

The Last Stage

Ayla

'We need a stage that inspires confidence,' Guruji said. 'There is only one auditorium in Delhi where you should host this performance.'

'Which one?'

'Indian Culture and Arts Centre.'

I would never get a space at ICAC. Even in my prime, they didn't invite me for a performance. And there was just one way to perform at ICAC—by invitation only.

It was arguably the most prestigious stage in Delhi, and the authorities were particularly picky, to the point of being snobbish, about the kind of artistes who could be allowed to use their platform. Unless you had a few National Awards to your name, ICAC didn't take you seriously.

There is a famous story of a ninety-seven-year-old ICAC member, who came to watch a ghazal recital by the famous musician Fateh Ali Khan. The member was suffering from severe lung infection. His health was deteriorating; he could barely walk. The doctors and his family advised against it, but he dismissed them with a flick of his stick.

The old man saw the entire performance. When the performance ended, he couldn't even get up from his chair. The gentleman sitting next to him had to hold the chair for him. A caretaker held his hand for support. And then he walked out very slowly in a state of happy exhaustion.

The next morning, he passed away. The ICAC management had a plaque carved in his name. It is still there, right next to the entrance.

'Will they permit me?' I asked Guruji.

'It will be a hard sell.'

Guruji took out his cell phone and dialled the director of ICAC, Rajbir Sharma. After exchanging pleasantries, Guruji moved to the crux of the matter. The director seemed hesitant at first, but Guruji became more forceful as the conversation progressed.

Guruji was one of the few artistes ICAC trusted as far as traditional dance recitals were concerned. Guruji shared a decent rapport with the ICAC administration, and of course, his surname was one to reckon with.

The director invited Guruji over for a cup of tea. The final decision would be made there.

'Let's get going. We don't want to be late,' Guruji said.

'Do I really need to come?' I said.

'The director is a good man, but he is a little stuck up about the policies of the institution,' Guruji said. 'Your presence will help him put a face to the name.'

~

Indian Culture and Arts Centre has a unique, sort of laid-back entrance unlike the massive entrances to the embassies dotting the same lane. The gates of ICAC are no higher than ten feet. They open onto a pathway on either side of which lie fountains, flowers and manicured gardens.

A handful of members could be seen trickling in. There were elderly men and women; the women wore the most elegant cotton sarees while the men looked distinguished in bright Nehru jackets and Fabindia kurtas.

They greeted Guruji—he was, after all, a familiar face who enjoyed the respect of the ICAC members.

We headed straight to the director's office on the first floor. The secretary informed him of our presence. After a ten-minute wait, we were invited inside.

Rajbir stood up from his brown leather chair and greeted Guruji with a firm handshake. He was a middle-aged man. He wore thick-rimmed spectacles that made him look older than his actual age. He flashed a bald patch as well.

'So, she is the prodigious dancer you have been talking about?'

'Yes,' Guruji replied.

'What is your name?'

'I am Ayla Erol,' I replied.

'What a beautiful name,' he said. 'Please have a seat. Would you like a cup of coffee or tea?'

'Tea,' Guruji said, and I requested for the same.

'Chandrashekhar, I am forced to decline your request,' the director said without mincing words.

'She is a dancer with immense potential. We must introduce her to the ICAC audience. They will appreciate her talent.'

'You are putting me in a tight spot. ICAC avoids first-time performers. It's not because we don't believe in young artistes or fresh talent. ICAC supports them immensely,' he said with emphasis.

'But the audience here is very selective. The members prefer established artistes who have built a reputation for themselves. And I am responsible for maintaining that standard. Why don't you start her someplace else? I will personally make sure that her subsequent performances take place here.'

It was a politician's promise. His only intention was to stall. I knew it. Guruji knew it. Without questioning my skills or disrespecting Guruji, he had cleverly washed his hands off. At the same time, he had managed to evoke sympathy for himself. No wonder, he held this prestigious post.

I was already thinking of where else we could hold the dance performance, but Guruji hadn't accepted defeat.

'Don't go by her age. I have trained her for fifteen years. She is the finest to come out of Pratishtha. Mark my words, her arangetram is going to be extraordinary. ICAC is the only venue for such a performance,' Guruji said, with just the right mix of flattery and rationale. 'The who's who of Delhi will talk about this performance for months.'

Rajbir tapped his fingers on the table and went quiet for a minute. Guruji was looking straight at the director without blinking. I could feel the pressure his gaze put on the man.

Finally, Rajbir said, 'If you vouch for her, then I will give her a chance, but make sure she is prepared.'

'I have full faith in her. She will make us proud,' Guruji said.

'Okay.'

The director allotted us a Monday slot, one month from now.

'But Sir, one month is too short,' I said.

'It won't be a problem,' Guruji said, firmly.

After the meeting, I took a detour to the auditorium.

I walked to the stage and looked at the empty chairs in front of me. In a month from now, it would be filled with people and I would be wearing my ankle bells.

~

I needed musicians for vocals, along with mridangam and flute. The total expenditure would exceed 50,000 rupees. I didn't have that kind of money and I couldn't take Dayê's help either. She didn't know about my arangetram yet. I decided to keep it from her till the time was right.

Sudha, who was going to be the vocalist, waived her fee. 'You are part of the family,' she said.

The norm was to pay the musicians, individually. They didn't entertain requests for discounts. However, Guruji hired the whole orchestra as a group instead of making separate deals with individual musicians. Through his effort, the cost of the orchestra came to less than 15,000 rupees.

Kartik volunteered to take pictures as well as shoot the performance. All the elements were coming together beautifully. It enabled me to focus on my dance sessions.

The guest of honour had to be decided. Bureaucrats and politicians were considered ideal. Their presence meant that the performer was under their patronage. They also drew the media. But there was also a downside to inviting them. Most politicians had the tendency to back out at the last minute.

They were always dealing with crisis situations. They would land up in their own time and the performance would be stopped midway to kowtow to them. Consequently, the whole rhythm and momentum would suffer.

I wanted the chief guest to bring a sheen to my performance, not take away from it. Guruji offered to call one of his erstwhile students. Kartik suggested his uncle's name who was a well-established businessman and an art connoisseur.

These options didn't appeal to me. This was a personal show. I wanted someone who had made a difference to my life, but who?

31

A Battle for Pride

Guru Chandrashekhar

'Chandrashekhar,' echoed the voice on the other end of the phone.

'Speaking. Who is this?' I replied.

'Just another humble servant of the art of Bharatanatyam like yourself,' he said, most patronisingly.

It was Ranmohan, I had recognised his voice.

'What do you want?'

'I want to help you.'

'I don't need your help.'

'You are making the biggest mistake of your life. Cancel Ayla's arangetram at once. She has no respect for our traditions. She is a white girl; what do you expect? Enjoy her if you wish, but don't waste your time trying to make a Bharatanatyam dancer out of her.'

'You are a bastard. Keep your warnings to yourself, and don't ever call me. If you come near Ayla, I promise to God, I will finish you.'

'That has always been your problem. You never listen to

your well-wishers. At least, think of your family's good name. Do you really want to spoil that over one outsider?'

'She may be an outsider to you, but she is part of my family. Pratishtha is her home.'

'Your father would have disapproved, but it's also true he never found you worthy of the family name, isn't it?'

I was seething in anger.

'There is no need to get upset. We are both professionals. Let's talk business. How much is she offering you for this arangetram? I will pay you double to drop her.'

'I don't need your money. There is no way you can stop her performance. I will see to it.'

'Oh...I can and I will. You force my hand,' he said, and hung up.

~

There was a knock on my door, early next morning. Ayla's mother was standing outside my house.

'Good morning, Mrs Erol. Please come inside,' I said. She didn't reply. She stood her ground. Her face had turned red and she was fuming. I had never seen her so perturbed before.

'How dare you plan a dance performance with Ayla without my knowledge? There are pamphlets all over the city claiming she is disrespecting dance traditions by holding a farcical arangetram. My workers, my neighbours, everyone has seen these and they are calling me. You are responsible for bringing shame to my family. All of you are the same. You only care about money.'

I looked at her, dumbfounded. I did not know what to say or how to calm her down.

'I won't let them destroy Ayla's reputation. You will not hold this or any other dance performance with Ayla ever again.'

'But that is exactly what they want,' I said. 'Don't you see, they are threatened by Ayla. She is the only who can expose their lies.'

'I don't wish my daughter to set an example for anyone. I want my family to be left alone,' she said with fierce determination. 'Why did you hide this performance from me?'

'This arangetram is not about me, it is about her. It will help Ayla regain her confidence and self-respect. She needs this. I am not taking a penny for this performance.'

'Ranmohan had said the same thing to my husband. Look where that got her. I know what is good for my daughter. If she enjoys dance, then she can practise at your school, I won't stop her but please, for Allah's sake, don't give her false hopes of becoming a dance performer again.'

The phone was ringing incessantly.

'Just give me a minute please,' I said, and went inside to answer.

Rajbir, the director of ICAC, was on the line, 'How dare you hide Ayla's background from me?'

'Her background has nothing to do with her dance. The pamphlets are full of lies. Ranmohan has a score to settle against Ayla. He threatened me to cancel her performance. I didn't agree, so he is trying to cast aspersions against her.'

'I am not concerned about your personal rivalries. I am sorry, your show is off,' he said.

'But wait, it is only a few pamphlets. Their word isn't law.'

'It doesn't matter if they are true or false. It is a perception that is now alive and breathing. It's in every home and on the Internet.

'Truth, falsehoods and rumours will all come out

together. Even you won't be able to separate one from the other. My institution cannot afford to be associated in any way with this,' Rajbir was almost yelling.

'She's innocent. You can't abandon her now,' I pleaded.

'I have no choice in this matter.'

'If you abandon her, you abandon me. I will never perform at ICAC again.'

'It will be an unfortunate loss to ICAC, but my decision is final.'

The phone line went dead. We had built everything from scratch, brick by brick, and all of it crumbled in a matter of seconds. I went outside to reason with Ayla's mother. She was already gone.

~

Within a day, Ayla's arangetram became a matter of debate and discussion in the dance community. I was bombarded with phone calls from my father's contemporaries and students— some called me a liar, cheat and whatnot. It was the theatre of the absurd. We just wanted to hold a dance performance and the world was against it. I tried to speak the truth, but no one was listening.

They thought we were mocking the sacred tradition of arangetram. I received calls from people who had known and worked closely with my father. They advised me not to mix my name with Ayla's. I refused.

Ranmohan went hammer and tongs against us. He followed up the pamphlets with vengeance. He personally cajoled and coerced the auditorium managers against hosting our performance. They were asked to choose between the arangetram of one tainted foreigner and twenty years of association with Ranmohan.

Supporting Ayla is a 'one-way ticket,' he told them in no uncertain words.

They baulked at the thought of confrontation and the negative publicity it would inevitably garner. Ranmohan came across as the wronged teacher, the champion of Bharatanatyam.

I called Sudha and Kartik for help. Our search for another venue started that very moment. Between the three of us, we would surely be able to find one auditorium.

I jotted down the names of all the auditoriums in Delhi— Shah Auditorium, Meghdoot, Lok Kala Manch, Triveni, Akshara Theatre, Shri Ram Centre, India Habitat Centre, Kamani Auditorium, LTG Auditorium, Siri Fort, Zorba, Alliance Française, etcetera. Their sympathy was readily available, not their space.

~

Another day went by without any breakthrough. We were in a desperate situation. I decided to approach schools and colleges that had an auditorium equipped with adequate lighting and sound system. An average venue was better than no venue at all.

I visited around ten schools, went to a few colleges of Delhi University and took a tour of Jamia Millia Islamia too, for permission. I just needed any one of them to agree.

When I called to check the status of my request the next morning, they asked me to wait for a few hours. The application was still under review. I called back three hours later. My patience was running thin.

The DU colleges and Jamia sent their rejection letters. All the schools said, '*No*' to a private performance.

32

The Last Stand

Ayla

'Dayê,' I woke her up, 'please, have your dinner.'

She struggled to stand straight. Her knees had been giving her a lot of trouble, lately. Now, she walked with a limp and refused to consult a doctor, probably because she was concerned about the expenses.

Her voice had lost its softness and there were strands of grey in her hair.

I massaged her legs, while she ate her food.

'You are a good daughter,' she said. 'Now tell me, what do you want?'

'How do you know I want something?'

'First halva, and then the massage,' Dayê gave a chuckle.

'I want to talk to you about my dance performance.'

She stiffened. 'I cannot allow. Let the thought perish from your head, my child. That time has long passed.'

'Please, don't stop me now. Only a year ago, I couldn't even walk and look at me now. I want to see how far I can go.'

'They are rich and powerful. We stand no chance against

them. Had your Bavo been here, it would have been different,' she said with bitterness and sorrow in her voice.

'So, you will let them walk all over us, again? Haven't you let them get away with enough already?'

She kept her plate aside and spoke, 'I don't understand why you crave for their acceptance? These are not our people; they will never ever accept you. Say you hold a successful arangetram, then what? Do you think they will let you establish a career in dance? Not a chance.'

'Our silence will be misread as our failure. You convinced Bavo that I should leave India even though he wanted to fight Ranmohan in the court. You didn't once bother to ask me what I wanted. I never saw Bavo again; it's all because of you,' I blurted, almost choking.

Dayê slapped me. There was shock and horror in her eyes. It was the first time she had ever raised her hand on me. She hit me repeatedly, didn't stop until my upper lip started to bleed. Then, she snapped out of it. She covered her face with her hands.

'Yah Allah!'

Dayê hugged me. I heard her uneven heartbeat as she pressed me to her bosom. I felt the pain she felt.

We sat on the cold marble floor. I looked one way, she looked the other. Her face was eclipsed by her hair. We had made peace with our surroundings. Our life moved on normally, but there was a void inside. A black hole. We were a shadow—dark and despondent. The spark of life was missing.

I walked back to my room in silence. Tomorrow, I would tell Guruji to cancel the performance.

~

'I am sorry about yesterday,' Dayê said, examining my lip, next morning. 'I shouldn't have hit you.'

'It's all right. I shouldn't have said what I did. I was angry. I didn't mean a word of it. I will do what you think is right.'

'Then go ahead with your arangetram.'

'But...you said something different...How...What made you change your mind?'

'I was up the whole night. I couldn't help thinking about the past. You were right, I was adamant that we drop the court case. Perhaps, things would have been different if you hadn't gone, maybe your Bavo would have been alive.

'All I wanted to do was protect you from hurt and humiliation. I was just looking out for you.'

'I know, Dayê.'

'Your father loved you very much. The last thing he said to me before Allah took him was, "Keep her happy."

'I want to fulfil his last wish. Go ahead with the arangetram. Do it for your Bavo,' she said.

~

'I have tried everything—every school, college and private organisation, even embassies. None of them agreed,' Guruji said, disappointed.

'We haven't found anything either,' Sudha said. 'Kartik and I spoke to more than fifty people, but the discussion always fell through. The deadline is approaching. Maybe, we should postpone this performance, give time for the negative publicity to wane.'

'Thank you for trying so hard,' I said to all three of them. They had put everything aside for my cause and that meant the world to me. 'I know how frustrating this is, but this performance is now or never. It can't be postponed. I am afraid that will be the end of the road.'

'It won't come to that, Ayla,' Guruji said. 'I have been mulling over a possibility. It's the absolute last resort, but we have reached a stage where we must consider this seriously.'

'What is the idea?' Kartik asked.

'We should hold the arangetram in Thanjavur. I can make the arrangements without any difficulty.'

'That makes sense. We should go to Thanjavur,' Sudha agreed.

There were indeed many advantages of performing outside Delhi. We would be able to find a good stage, for starters. Moreover, we would be away from the media glare, and yet something about it didn't feel right.

'I don't want to go anywhere else; I don't want to run away.'

'But we have no other choice. Your arangetram is two days from now. Where are you going to dance?' Guruji said, visibly flustered.

'I can think of a place,' a voice intervened.

It was Bhanumati. I quickly got up to greet her.

'What are you doing here?'

'I read about your arangetram in the newspapers and thought I should help.'

'You can't. We have covered every auditorium in the National Capital Region. There is no space available.'

'Why do you need an auditorium?'

'I don't understand. What do you mean?' Guruji asked.

'Dance was never restricted by space, lights or even sound systems. These are only add-ons of the modern era. You already know of women who dedicated their art to the supreme being. They performed in temples where everyone would be welcomed without pride or prejudice,' Bhanumati said.

'We can't hold an arangetram in a crowded public space,' I said.

There was a moment of silence before Guruji spoke, 'Why not!'

It got all of us thinking. *What if it was possible?* My mind was racing.

'We can do this at Bangla Sahib Gurudwara. It has a big outdoor space with marble flooring and it welcomes people of all religions. They won't have any objections to the performance,' I said.

'It's not the worst idea,' Guruji said. 'But it's not going to be as simple as walking in and dancing. Bangla Sahib is the biggest Sikh shrine in Delhi. We will have to take multiple permissions from the gurudwara authorities, find adequate space and not come in the way of the devotees. No, I don't think we can do this at Bangla Sahib. There is no time.'

'What about Nizamuddin Dargah?' I asked.

'Too crowded,' Guruji said.

'To my mind, there is one temple where we can hold this recital,' Guruji added.

All of us looked at him.

'Where?' I asked.

'Malai Mandir. My father was childhood friends with the current pujari. He could help us,' Guruji said.

Guruji phoned the priest and asked for an urgent appointment. Ten minutes later, he was headed to Malai Mandir. There were less than two days for the performance. This *had* to work.

33

Lord Murugan's Abode

Guru Chandrashekhar

The sign at Malai Mandir's main entrance read, *Yaamirukka Bayamain* (Why fear when I am there).

It was the kind of reassurance I was looking for.

Next to the entrance, flowers, garlands and rose petals were arranged in baskets by the dozens. I purchased a basket. *Never go empty-handed to someone's house*, mother had taught me. The sanctum sanctorum of Lord Murugan stood atop a small hillock.

The temple was taller than any high-rise in the vicinity. The sound of planes that took off from the Indira Gandhi International Airport nearby could cause a problem during Ayla's performance. They would drown out the sound of the music.

Malai Mandir was unlike any other place of worship in the capital. It didn't have the splendour of Bangla Sahib or the vigour of Nizamuddin Dargah, but it possessed a simplicity unknown to other places. I stood in a queue, at the circular pavement surrounding the temple, waiting for an audience.

A young woman, walking with the help of crutches, took a round of the pathway. There was a silent determination in her eyes and courage in her heart. I prayed for her speedy recovery. It gave me a sense of satisfaction to pray for her well-being. Perhaps, our happiness was more dependent on one another than we cared to believe or acknowledge.

~

A long queue of devotees stood at the entrance awaiting the priest's blessings. The priest arrived soon, he didn't smile but his grace was unmistakable in his unhurried demeanour. He expressed himself with a nod of his head and a subtle movement of his eyes.

I vaguely recognised him from my youth in Thanjavur. He would often visit us. Back then, he had a moustache and would dress up in colourful shirts. Time and circumstances change all of us.

In a priest's avatar, he wore a cream-coloured dhoti and left his upper body bare, and his forehead was smeared with vibhuti, sacred ash.

I waited for half an hour, while he listened to each devotee, accepted their gifts, placed them in front of the idol and put a tilak of vibhuti on their foreheads. He didn't assure anyone of good fortune but asked them to find courage to withstand the difficult times.

'Pranam, Sir. My name is Chandrashekhar; I am Dharmesh's son. I had called you in the afternoon for a meeting.'

'You look just like your father,' the priest said. 'He was a good man and a dear friend. I was pained to hear about his passing.'

'Thank you for seeing me on such short notice,' I said.

'This is the house of God. You don't need an appointment here. Besides, your father and I shared a special friendship. I still regret not being able to attend his cremation. The obligations at the temple kept me occupied.'

'How did you two know each other?'

'We went to the same school, played cricket and got into a lot of trouble with the principal, on more than one occasion.

'We lost touch a few years after school. He was immersed in dance and I left Thanjavur to study in Vivekananda Ashram. On my return, I went to see his dance recital. That is when we rekindled our friendship. This time, it was at a much deeper level.'

'How so?'

'Our professions were different, but our roles were quite similar.'

'What similarities can exist between a priest and a dance guru?'

'He offered youngsters guidance through the medium of dance, while I provided solace to old people through faith. Our work, in essence, was to give people hope and strength.'

'Then, I am at the right place,' I said. 'Allow me to be honest with you; this is not exactly a courtesy call. I came here to seek your help.'

His demeanour remained unchanged. Perhaps, this was expected from all those who visited Malai Mandir.

'We will discuss your problems,' he said, 'first take a moment to pay your respects to Lord Murugan.' I complied.

I bowed in front of Lord Murugan and the priest put a tilak of vibhuti on my forehead.

'Now, tell me, how I may help you?'

I explained the whole situation to him. How Ayla had been wronged. 'They were using all possible means to silence her. We need the temple space for her performance day after tomorrow. We didn't want to massage our egos or get back at them, but in our own capacity, this is an offering to God,' I explained in one breath.

'Take a round of the temple and put your mind at ease, while I go over everything that you have said.'

A dance performance in a temple, watched over by the heavens. There would be no superficiality. Just the dancer and her art. Malai Mandir was perfect for the arangetram.

When I returned, the priest was still in deep thought. 'I have to say, this is a very strange request. Frankly, I don't know what to do.'

'Do whatever you can. We need this,' I pleaded.

'You are like family and your cause does seem genuine. I am going to talk to the committee members and see if they are open to the idea. But I can't promise yet.'

'That's all I ask. I can't tell you how much this means to me,' I said.

'One more thing, if they do agree, you cannot charge people to watch this performance, make noise or have any kind of barriers for entry. The temple space is open to all. Everyone is welcome here without inhibitions,' the priest said.

'I understand. Please present a strong case for us. Her dance is divine. It speaks to the Gods.'

'I will do everything in my power. Come back, tomorrow.'

~

'Did they agree?' I enquired, the next evening.

His sullen expression revealed the answer.

'No, they didn't. I am sorry. The committee wasn't comfortable with the idea of hosting a dance performance inside the temple premises.'

'What was their main concern?'

'If she were a South Indian, they could have still considered her, but she has no local linkage. That didn't inspire the committee. Malai Mandir doesn't host dance performances unlike some other temples,' the priest said.

'With all due respect, your committee is full of cowards,' I said.

'I know your intentions are not to stir trouble. But these are realities we cannot ignore.'

'Yesterday, you told me that your duty is to help people find their path, give them hope. You failed to mention they had to be South Indians, else you would ask them to be on their way.'

'Chandrashekhar, this is not my decision.'

'I am the Guru at my natyalaya. Every decision I take is a reflection of my own beliefs. It serves as an example for my students and the world at large.

'You are a Guru too. If God's messenger shuts out the voice of truth, then what hope is there for the rest of us?' I said, and began walking away.

There was nothing more to be said. He was a good man, but good men needed to stand up in this bad world.

I was near the exit when I heard the priest's voice, 'Wait, Chandrashekhar. What would you have me do?' he asked.

'Nothing. Do what you believe is right. Whatever that may be,' I said.

He looked at me in silence.

'I have been a priest for the past so many years. People with broken spirits, terminally ill patients, and those lost in the chaos of life come to my door in search of solace. I haven't found the solution to any of their problems, far from it. But I have sent them back with the will to fight till their last breath.

'All that will be forgotten, if I help you. They will call me the priest who allowed the sacred ground of God to be used for private interests. My contributions will be washed over by the controversy this performance shall invite.'

'You are right. It might happen. I have no idea what the outcome of the performance will be. But the outcome of not having this performance will certainly be horrendous. A young girl will lose her faith.'

'Is your cause so noble and your student so good that we sacrifice not only our careers, but our reputation too?' the priest questioned.

It all came down to this one moment. The words I said next would seal Ayla's fate and the course of our lives. I had no idea what the right answer was. Was there even a right answer?

I looked him in the eye and let the words flow from my heart.

'There is one thing I can say with conviction. I have taught dance to many students, but this arangetram will give meaning to a life.'

'So be it,' he said. 'Let's hold this spectacle with an honest intention and a sincere heart. Leave the rest to Lord Murugan.'

I touched the priest's feet for no words could have expressed my gratitude.

34

Arangetram at Last

Ayla

I woke up to the chirping of birds in the morning. As soon as I stepped into the balcony, the sparrows vanished. A strong breeze blew and all the clothes that were drying on a rope flew hither and thither. The sun had disappeared behind the dark clouds. Would it rain? I prayed to the weather Gods to be a little patient, until my arangetram.

There was a crumbled leaf on the floor. It was so delicate that I was afraid someone would crush it with their feet. I picked it up and preserved it between the pages of my favourite book. Some believe they bring good fortune, others say they are cursed. What would it bring me? Hope, perhaps.

As if on cue, Dayê came to my room and gave me a box.

'What's this?'

'Open it.'

I opened the box and a saree washed in the same colours as the Kurdish flag—red, yellow, green and white—was revealed.

I looked at Dayê, speechless.

'Red symbolises the blood of those sacrificed in our struggle for freedom; green is for the beautiful mountains and rivers of Kurdistan; the white band epitomises peace.'

'And what about the yellow sun in the centre?' I asked.

Dayê smiled, 'It's the most important of them all. It represents the rebirth of the Kurdish nation. Your Bavo wanted you to be the voice of our people. Today is that chance. He will be watching you,' she said, and embraced me.

By the time I got dressed and reached Pratishtha, it was already eleven. Time was flying. I don't remember feeling so nervous about any performance ever. The knot in my stomach was getting tighter.

Guruji was already there. 'Why are your eyes red and swollen?' Guruji asked.

'I didn't get much sleep last night, and I have been unwell since morning. I feel feverish. What if I fail again, Guruji?'

'Then be such a spectacular failure that the world takes notice,' he said in all seriousness. 'I have faith in you, you shall not fail. Come on, let's go through the routine once again.'

'All right.'

When I started to dance, I stopped thinking. That gave me some respite. I knew the sequence well and performed it without any glitches. Guruji reminded me to take deep breaths and maintain my pace. Kartik and Sudha reached the natyalaya an hour later. Kartik helped lighten up the mood with his lame jokes. I felt better in their company.

After the rehearsals, Kartik and Guruji left for the temple, while Sudha and Dayê stayed back to help me get dressed. After all these years, I still needed help tying a saree.

Guru Chandrashekhar

There was a dust storm outside. Everyone was rushing home to avoid its fury while we seemed to be heading straight to its eye. There were only a few visitors at the temple and they were in a hurry to leave as well.

'At least, she won't have to face too many people,' Kartik tried to console us. I was more worried about the rain. People, we could manage, but rain was another matter.

The small section of the temple which we had selected for the performance was covered with a mix of dust and leaves. There were a few loose pebbles on the floor as well. Ayla was going to dance barefoot and the smallest disturbance could lead to a grave injury. We had to make sure the floor was spotless.

Kartik and I started cleaning the area. He got hold of a broom and I picked all the pebbles from the floor. Every time he cleared a portion of the floor, another layer of dirt settled down at the same place. It was a pointless exercise until the dust storm stopped, but we continued to clean and pray.

An hour later, when the storm abated, I bought a basket full of rose petals and placed them on the floor in such a way as to create a separation between the dance area and the space for the audience.

There was no curtain, no backstage and no green room. This floral line was the only separation between the audience and Ayla. I liked the thought. The absence of walls brought the two entities closer. The fragrance of the rose petals elevated one's mood.

There were many inherent challenges in this performance.

Malai Mandir is a confluence of a million sounds—the priest's hymns, ringing bells at the entrance, the sound of the breeze and birds, and general chatter. None of these were in our control.

Soon, the orchestra members arrived. They looked at the sky every now and then, conscious of the dark clouds gathering.

'What if it starts raining?' one of the musicians asked.

'Keep playing,' I said.

I set up a mat for the orchestra members on the right side of the floor. This performance was going to test their skills as well. They would have to support the performance till the end, unplugged. The strength of their instruments would have to overcome every obstacle. We weren't allowed the use of mikes or amplifiers.

The sky was an ominous mix of grey and purple. Every few minutes, an airplane roared past the temple, drowning out all the other voices. Nothing could be done about it.

~

A car stopped in front of the temple's entrance. She stepped out carefully, climbed one step at a time and held the ends of her saree. Sudha and Mrs Erol walked beside her.

Ayla was no longer the timid creature I had encountered earlier that afternoon, nor did her eyes look swollen. She had changed colours with the evening sky.

Her fingers and toes were dyed red with alta.

I led Ayla all the way to the stage and then I released her hand. This is as far as I could go. It was up to her now.

Ayla

'Good evening,' I greeted the people who had come to watch me dance. 'Thank you all for coming this evening. Your presence means the world to me. I still can't believe I am standing here amongst all of you.

'The first act of the evening is *Meenakshi Sloka*. These are hymns of praise dedicated to Meenkashi, the wife of Lord Shiva. When I began to prepare for this arangetram, I gave a lot of thought to the opening sequence and spent days considering different options. Once I read the *Meenakshi Sloka*, I knew I had to begin with it because it reminded me of my mother.

'She introduced me to Bharatanatyam when I was a child. She had to put aside her dreams, comforts, even necessities, for the sake of my dance, but she never complained.

'Fifteen years later, to this day, she continues to stand by me like a rock. Dayê, you have always been in the shadows; with this sloka, I want you to take centre stage.' The vocalist began to chant the sloka and the strength of his voice took hold of the arena.

With the onset of the first verse, all other activities ceased. The only conversation in that moment was between me and Goddess Meenakshi. Through my dance, I praised the Goddess for her wonders and sought her blessings.

I identified with the duality of Goddess Meenakshi. She was the embodiment of courage as well as gentleness. Women like my mother were not weak and defenceless. Nor did they have to choose between tenacity and grace. My dance was an ode to this duality. My expressions and movements conveyed each and every intricate aspect of the Goddess's charisma, whom I pictured as my mother.

Goddess Meenakshi radiated the splendour of a lotus. She was a powerful, beautiful woman with a piercing gaze. I danced like a possessed woman, a Goddess in disguise.

This was the shortest sequence of the performance; it concluded within minutes. It was extremely important for me to focus all my energy, let the music flow within me, and brace myself for the challenges ahead. That evening, I had many obstacles to overcome.

Guru Chandrashekhar

This was when the dance performance truly began. There was no story and no abhinaya in Mallari. It was pure dance, or nritta, and the movements showcased the dancer's prowess.

It asked for the audience's full attention. Everything about this act was invigorating. It was also one of Ayla's favourite sequences, where she could exhibit her free-spiritedness.

A drop of water fell on my face. I looked at the dark clouds in the sky; it had already begun to drizzle. The dance sequence became twice as difficult on a wet floor, not to mention dangerous. *Should the performance be paused*? I debated with myself. We couldn't risk an injury.

I looked at Ayla and was about to step in, but she gestured through a subtle movement of her head that she would manage. I had no choice but to respect her decision.

Ayla went back and forth in measured rhythmic steps. She made extravagant circles with her hands, bent her body from one side to another, effortlessly. She jumped to her left and lost her footing in the water. I almost had my heart in my mouth. She was able to stop just in the nick of time and continued the dance.

The rain was testing her resolve now. The musicians were struggling. Their instruments were giving way. The sounds were subdued by the rains and winds. They looked at me questioningly. I asked them to continue. The audience was getting drenched too, but none moved from their place; they weren't going to abandon her.

She moved her hands forward, diagonally and upwards in a matter of seconds, like flashes of lightning. She paid no heed to the rain or the wet floor. Her hands went all the way up from both sides, her palms met each other in a namaste at the pinnacle of her reach and her body bent forward in a graceful bow. There was divinity in her.

Ayla smiled despite the overwhelming obstacles. She was enjoying herself. Ayla was always a fighter and she was going to fight to the finish. It was the greatest place for a dancer to be—in the moment. She had a childlike innocence in her dance and a bit of reckless daring in her soul. It had gotten lost somewhere in the past. I saw a hint of it that evening.

After completing the second sequence, she moved to a higher pace with clean and crisp movements.

There was an exchange of energy between Ayla and the audience. It was as if they asked her, 'How fast can you go?' And she communicated through her eyes, *Faster than you can imagine.*

Humans are drawn to speed. It makes us feel alive and extraordinary. We need to break barriers because they reassure us of our limitless potential. Ayla was in the fast lane.

She now switched into the final and the fastest gear of the

Mallari. She went as fast as she could, possibly faster. Water splashed all around her. She was in the middle of a cyclone or was she the cyclone herself.

She needed to be most careful. It was easy to lose control and make an embarrassing mistake in the rush of the moment. The head and the heart had to be in sync. There were times when each needed to take the lead and the other had to absorb its ego. Such finesse cannot be taught by a guru; it is the privilege of a dancer.

She was pushing herself to go faster; the musicians too strained themselves. The spectators had to jerk their heads to follow her movements. She was completely drenched.

I was afraid, it was too much. The dancer and the musicians went beyond the levels I had seen them attempt during the practice sessions.

She carried on fearlessly, without a single fault. My hands were trembling. Just as soon as the piece had started, it was over. Those were the longest minutes of my life.

There was thunderous applause. I looked behind and to my surprise, the whole area which was empty only a few minutes ago was now filled to capacity. Even the priest left his duty and came out of the shrine. The rain stopped. It had surrendered to Ayla's will.

People saw her for who she really was—a free spirit.

There were families, youngsters, and elderly people in the audience. Some of them had an understanding of this dance form, but most were clueless.

The atmosphere was surreal. People stayed for the sheer beauty and charisma of her dance. Dance could indeed dissolve boundaries.

Ayla was at the peak of her skill and it was there for everyone to see. Her movements were immaculate. She was swift when the beats picked up and she would effortlessly bring her body to a sudden halt when required. And then take off like a volcanic explosion at the tap of the mridangam. The best was yet to come.

~

She was soaked to her skin. Her hair broke away from its moorings and fell across her face. She brushed it aside with a flick of her hand and looked at the audience. Just this once, I didn't ask her to restrain those locks.

Ayla tried to speak but she could barely catch her breath. A young boy in the audience went up to her and offered a bottle of water. Some people laughed. She smiled and took a sip. Everyone began to clap and egg her on.

'Thank you. Thank you so much,' she said.

'There is one person here whom I want to thank above all others. I would not be standing here if it weren't for him. In fact, I wouldn't be standing at all. I was in a dark place, last year. My dance career was written off and worse, I had given up on life. I wanted to kill myself and end my suffering once and for all. Guruji shook me out of my stupor. He believed in me when I didn't believe in myself.

'When I was a young girl, I thought Guruji had a magic wand that he used to create fantastic choreographies. He made me realise that the magic was within me. This act is my Gurudakshina. I will now be performing the *Chalamela Varnam* in Nattakurinji Ragam. It is in *Adi Talam*.'

Our mutual respect had always been private and

unspoken. We had never felt the need to share our feelings, not even with each other. For the first time in my life, Ayla made me feel worthy of my name and lineage. I was as proud to be Chandrashekhar as I was of being Balasubramaniam. I looked back at the many sacrifices and failures of my life— Ayla made everything worth it.

This performance had long gone past the designs that were made at Pratishtha; it had the elements of surprise and splendour. Everything was heartfelt and real. This was true of the highest traditions of Thanjavur. Her dance was real, not rehearsed. I accepted her Gurudakshina with humility.

Varnam is the most enthralling and challenging sequence of a dance recital. It is the piece every great dancer takes pride in. No traditional solo recital is complete without the Varnam. The forty-minute-long piece is a treat for the spectators. It promises to take them through the troughs and peaks of love.

The Varnam began on a slow note. She approached different corners of the stage with outstretched hands. In a matter of seconds, her movements became fast and pointed, interspersed with subtle expressions.

Even if the earth were to split open and swallow everyone in its bind, people wouldn't have stopped looking at her performance. She spoke to each and every member of the audience without saying a word. She was everywhere, all at once.

No one was untouched by her brilliance and beauty. She came to the very edge of the stage and balanced her body on one leg. People could almost touch her; all they had to do was reach out. Even when she bent down, she did it with utmost ease. Gravity obliged.

And then, her movements slowed down. We were both capable of great feats on the dance stage, but we had let our pride get in the way. It almost destroyed us. We were difficult together, but we were miserable apart. Distance and time are strange. They draw people apart mostly, but sometimes, with a twist of destiny, they bring people closer than ever. We were fortunate.

I was ashamed of myself for abandoning her, but all that was in the past. We were united in this moment.

The dance was unhindered and free but the expressions were intense. She now stood on the tip of her toes. The musical beats egged her on and she created a spectacular scene.

When she finally concluded the Varnam, I breathed a sigh of relief. She had maintained continuity and consistency in her performance. That was no mean feat. Ayla had passed another, possibly the toughest of tests, with flying colours. The audience too felt the elation and applauded her.

At this stage, the dancers usually took a breather. They were spent from the Varnam and recuperated backstage with water and energy drinks. This was the break in the performance where they changed costumes, while the audience absorbed all that they had seen in the previous one hour.

Ayla's was not one such arangetram. We didn't have the luxury of either a green room or intervals. This performance was a non-stop spectacle.

Ayla

'I am now going to perform *Indendu Vachitivira Padam* in Ragam Suruti, and the *Misra Chapu Talam* (seven beats). It showcases the anger and sarcasm and eventually the nonchalance of the nayika, the heroine, when she witnesses the deceit of her lover, the nayak. I want to dedicate this act to every woman who has gone through life-changing challenges and emerged stronger.

'My object of affection is not a man; it is my art. I have shared a complicated relationship with dance. There was a time when I adored it to no end. My life began and ended with Bharatanatyam. Then came a phase where I hated it.

'Both these emotions were extreme and toxic. They consumed me. It took me years to accept dance for what it is. I don't hate or love it anymore; I don't expect anything from it. I accept it as the most beautiful, the truest part of my life,' I said.

Just then, an elderly, balding man made his way into the crowd. '*Band kariye ise. Iske liye* permission *nahin hai*,' he said loudly. I looked at Guruji with dread. They were going to make us stop just when we had found our confidence. All we needed was another twenty minutes to finish the performance. There was no way he was going to grant it. It was the end of the road. I walked towards Dayê, feeling cheated out of yet another performance.

The priest intervened, 'Balasubramaniam Asokan ji, they are about to finish. Give them twenty more minutes. They are not bothering anyone.'

'Pujariji, I had clearly told you that dance cannot be permitted inside Malai Mandir. It's a matter of the temple's reputation. You cannot overrule the committee's decision. Stop this tamasha right now.'

'I request all of you to get moving. Don't crowd this space,' he commanded.

The audience looked at him but none moved and no one spoke.

'I am the head of the temple committee and I am asking you to leave.'

The boy who had offered me water began to clap. More people joined him and they were all looking at me, urging me to continue. I didn't need convincing. I took centre stage.

'I am ordering you to put an end to this, Pujariji. She is an *outsider*,' he asserted.

'No, Sir. She is one of us.'

Guru Chandrashekhar

Like eyes are the window to the soul, the padams, musical compositions based on love, reveal the personality of a dancer. They are the purest form of storytelling. The dance began with Ayla sitting on the floor. Late at night, she hears a knock on the door. It's her lover. She can't understand if she is angry or happy to hear from him. She has every right to feel both. He has come at her doorstep after a long gap just when she had given up on him. Anger takes control over her, and she delays in answering the door to appease her vanity.

Moments pass. She can no longer hold herself back. There is a deadpan expression on her face and her eyes examine him from head to toe. Every cell of her body burns with anger and envy.

The beauty of this piece resides in the movement of Ayla's eyes and the agility of her body. She answers and expresses intense emotions without any extravagant movements. It is no less than a miracle to convey hatred and anger for a lover without any utterance.

She rolls her eyes and makes a sarcastic gesture aimed at shaming the hero for his philandering. She moves both her hands and asks if he has confused her house with some other woman's.

Go back to the woman you deserted me for, she says through a dismissive gesture of her hands and walks further away to increase the distance between them lest he used it to his advantage.

At a deeper and personal level, she is heartbroken and nostalgic about the loss of her youth. Her description of that beautiful woman, somewhere, communicated the memory of her own younger self.

There was anger in Ayla's heart, still. She was bitter at the manner in which the dance community had treated her. She remembered how they had abandoned her when she needed them most.

This rendition was her act of vengeance. She fleshed out all the sarcasm in the world and directed it at the people who had rejected her, who had tormented her and most of all, who had caused ill to her family. Her message was clear—I am still standing, still dancing.

I had learned more from Ayla in this dance sequence than she had from me. She performed it to perfection.

Ayla's maturity blossomed in this sequence. She let go of her past and found purpose in her life. She rediscovered her love for dance and made peace with the demons of her past. She was not only a better dancer, but a better human being.

'The final dance sequence of this arangetram is Tillana. I dedicate this to the most special person in my life, my father.

'Bavo is my hero. The biggest regret of my life is that

I never got a chance to bid him goodbye. Through this dance sequence, I want to let him know that I am honouring his memory by living my life to the fullest. He is always in my thoughts,' she announced.

Ayla was fighting back her tears.

It was through a Tillana that a dancer reflected on her training, from the very first day when she had stepped barefoot on the cold dance floor and warmed the surface with her feet till the present moment. It brought together each and every aspect of the rigorous training. Every sequence that seemed unnecessary, tiresome or difficult would be utilised on that stage, at this grand conclusion of her formal training. It encompassed the journey Ayla had embarked more than a decade ago.

The audience had had its fill; they had been thoroughly entertained and elevated. They needed time to absorb all that they had witnessed for the past two hours and share their experience with others.

Tillana was the last cut of refinement made to a sparkling diamond. It added an extra smile on the faces of the spectators. She tapped the ground with her right foot and then her left, without a pause. The musical beats matched her steps. The orchestra pushed their limits and so did Ayla.

The ground beneath her feet shook. It was the coming together of the dancer and the orchestra.

Ayla made a semi-circle through her footwork. Next, she took a 180-degree turn, the limits of her body once again put to test. It had it all—the rapid movements, followed by stillness and marvellous expressions. Her eyes darted from one side to another, her feet moved back and forth. There was no exertion; everything was smooth and flawless like the movement of the winds and the waves. She carried the power to destroy but chose to lend life and beauty to the world. She was extravagant; she was dynamic.

It had taken her countless hours, sweat, blood and toil to make something so arduous look so disturbingly simple. This was to be the end, but Ayla didn't stop to take a bow.

She stood still for a moment and looked at the heavens, almost like she was seeking permission.

She closed her eyes, extended both her arms sideways and moved uninhibitedly in repeated circles. It didn't have any resemblance to any act in Bharatanatyam; I was confused at this sudden change in tempo and tenor.

Ayla was oblivious to the world. She had stopped dancing for others; this came from her heart. She started to whirl in circles as if she were in a trance.

Her mother had a smile on her face; she knew what was happening.

'The Sema Dance of the Whirling Dervishes,' she answered my quizzical look.

Of course. I was amazed at how she even thought of it. The Sema Dance is part of the spiritual tradition of the Sufi tribe (*Mevlevi*) in Turkey in which dance becomes a medium to connect with the divine. With every whirl, they abandon their ego, move closer to God until they reach a balance. It was Ayla's absolute surrender to God and her Bavo.

My eyes welled up. She put her hands up in the air and did a full turn and another and another and came to a stop.

There were no limits to her dance, it dissolved boundaries and found harmony. She was no longer an *outsider* trying to make her way in. She no longer craved acceptance and had made peace with her differences. Ayla, in her uniqueness, belonged to both the worlds, equally.

Everyone was on their feet. Her mother's tears flowed as freely as her daughter's steps.

Silence descended. Ayla's eyes were moist. She folded her hands and took a bow.

A resounding applause followed. From the pujari to the worshippers, friends to passersby, everyone nodded their head in admiration and amazement. Some people gathered around Ayla but she looked in the distance, beyond the milling crowd. The committee head had returned with three policemen. They were too late.

There was a smile of redemption on her face. She was, for that brief moment, the same young girl who had walked into my dance school full of wonder and hope.

Ayla's last dance was a beginning.

Epilogue

Guru Chandrashekhar

The four of us returned to Pratishtha after the performance. It seemed fitting. It's where this journey had begun. Kartik was elated. He was having an animated discussion with Ayla's mother about the performance. She had a smile on her face; she looked content. It gave me such pleasure to see them in this state. *It was worth it*, I thought to myself. All the pain and sacrifice that it took to make this happen. Sudha entered the studio with coffee and food.

'Where is Ayla?' she asked.

'She is changing,' I replied.

'Kartik,' I said, extending him a cup of coffee.

He was looking at his phone. I vividly remember the expressions on his face: they changed from impassive to anticipation and then to disbelief. Only, he couldn't find words. He was now standing, now pacing, now sitting. Unable to hold ourselves any longer, Sudha and I both broke out into collective questions. He looked at us, darting his eyes from one to the other.

'Guruji, forgive me but I did something without your permission. Or, for that matter, Ayla's.'

'What?'

'I made a live stream of Ayla's arangetram video on the Internet.'

'And?'

'Come and take a look.'

More than 120,000 viewers had already seen her dance on YouTube and Instagram. It had been tagged on Facebook and several online portals, as #thefallendancer #DanceofaRefugee. It was unbelievable. That evening, a star was born.

Ayla

I just sat down on the floor of the changing room in Pratishtha trying to take it all in. My heart beating feverishly. It's over. It's done. *You did it*, I reassured myself. I can't describe what I was feeling at that moment. I was grateful, I was happy, I was sad. I was everything I had ever been. I was complete. I just wanted to hold on to someone. I wished Umair was here. He would have seen that not all stories have sad endings. That there was indeed hope for us.

Acknowledgements

The spark of this story came from a word '*Arangetram*' that was uttered innocently in a casual exchange and forgotten soon afterwards. However, words and stories have a tendency to take a life of their own. Curiosity stoked it into a fire fanned consistently by virtue of guidance, review and encouragement from Abhinaya, Mukaddes, Nimisha, Nidhi, and Preeti among others. It is not possible to mention all those whose support was instrumental to this endeavour, except through the story itself. I hope it speaks to all of you.

Printed in July 2019
by Rotomail Italia S.p.A., Vignate (MI) - Italy